W9-CBG-132

DEATH COMES TO THE SCHOOL

Center Point
Large Print

Also by Catherine Lloyd and available from Center Point Large Print:

Death Comes to London
Death Comes to Kurland Hall
Death Comes to the Fair

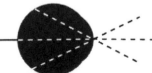

**This Large Print Book carries the
Seal of Approval of N.A.V.H.**

DEATH COMES TO THE SCHOOL

CATHERINE LLOYD

CENTER POINT LARGE PRINT
THORNDIKE, MAINE

This Center Point Large Print edition
is published in the year 2019 by arrangement with
Kensington Publishing Corp.

The text of this Large Print edition is unabridged.
In other aspects, this book may vary
from the original edition.
Printed in the United States of America
on permanent paper.
Set in 16-point Times New Roman type.

ISBN: 978-1-68324-198-9

Library of Congress Cataloging-in-Publication Data

Names: Lloyd, Catherine, 1963- author.
Title: Death comes to the school / Catherine Lloyd.
Description: Center Point Large Print edition. | Thorndike, Maine :
    Center Point Large Print, 2019.
Identifiers: LCCN 2019006610 | ISBN 9781643581989 (hardcover :
    alk. paper)
Subjects: LCSH: Great Britain—History—Regency, 1811-1820—
    Fiction. | Anonymous letters—Fiction. | Married people—Fiction. |
    Villages—Fiction. | Murder—Investigation—Fiction. |
    Large type books.
Classification: LCC PS3616.E246 D429 2019 | DDC 813/.6—dc23
LC record available at https://lccn.loc.gov/2019006610

This book is dedicated to my uncle Colm Harrington, a man of great worth and great kindness who is no longer with us. Rest in peace.

Acknowledgments

I'd like to thank Sandra Marine and Bianca Blythe for stepping up and reading this book super fast for me! I'd also like to thank Kat Cantrell for her Biblical knowledge.

For anyone interested in the history of education in the nineteenth century I suggest *The English Common Reader* by Richard D. Altick, a social history of the mass reading public 1800-1900.

DEATH COMES TO THE SCHOOL

Chapter 1

Kurland Hall, England
December 1820

After three years of marriage, Lucy, Lady Kurland, was used to Sir Robert's rather ill-tempered demeanor at the breakfast table. He hated to chat, which often frustrated her, because there was usually much to discuss about the upcoming day. Unfortunately, her husband had a tendency to hide behind his newspaper and offer only the occasional grunt to any conversational effort she attempted.

Such was the case on this particular winter's morning, but for once, Lucy had little interest in engaging him in conversation. Despite having slept heavily, she was tired and somewhat cantankerous herself. The yuletide season was fast approaching, and although her duties no longer involved managing the rectory, and her father, there was still much to be done.

"The post, my lady."

"Thank you, Foley."

Lucy accepted the silver tray the butler offered her, and sorted through the collection of letters and bills, separating her correspondence from her husband's.

"There's a letter for you from your aunt Rose, Robert. She appears to be in London."

"Hmm?" A hand appeared around the side of the newspaper, and Lucy placed the thick letter in it. "Thank you."

Lucy tapped her fingers against the stack of letters. She didn't want to open any of them. They would be full of sympathy for her health and well-being, and she really didn't want to think about it anymore. Not because she was unappreciative of the concern, but because she didn't need to feel any more miserable than she already did.

She sighed, her gaze shifting outside, to the dark clouds and barren landscape of Kurland Hall home park. The trees were stripped bare of leaves. A slight frost made the spiked grass glint in the occasional strip of sunlight that managed to filter through the greyness. There was also a wind blowing, which made her reconsider her plan of walking into the village. She had promised to visit her father at the rectory and was expecting several of the village ladies to call on her at the hall in the afternoon for tea.

There were plans to be made for the festive season that would require the assistance of everyone in the vicinity. Lucy bit her lip. She had no stomach for marshaling the forces of the local gentry, who sometimes required delicate handling in matters of precedence. She held the highest social rank in their small community, and many looked to her to set the tone. Usually, such battles energized her, but today . . .

She placed her napkin on the table and picked up her letters, pushing her chair back.

"Damned incompetent government," Robert muttered to himself behind the wall of his newspaper. He still had ambitions to become a member of Parliament but had not yet found a viable seat.

Still hovering beside Lucy, Foley cleared his throat. "Are you quite certain you have finished, my lady? You've eaten only half a piece of toast."

"I'm not hungry." She offered him a brief smile as he pulled back her chair. "Can you make sure the fire in my sitting room is alight, and can you ask Mr. Coleman to bring the gig around in half an hour?"

"Certainly, my lady." Foley bowed low. "And maybe a fresh pot of tea? I know Cook has just baked some scones, which would be just the thing with some strawberry jam and cream."

"The tea would be lovely."

She left the breakfast parlor and headed toward her sitting room, where, despite her concerns, the new maid had already lit the fire, warming the frigid space. Sitting at her desk, she sorted the stack of letters, putting the one from her brother, Anthony, who was currently stationed overseas, aside to read later. He at least would have no idea what had befallen her, and was refreshingly concerned only about his prospects of a glittering career in the Prince of Wales 10th Hussars, and how to achieve them on a somewhat limited budget.

She broke the seal on a bill from her dressmaker in Hertford and perused it. She had sufficient funds to pay the amount out of her quarterly pin money, which she managed meticulously to avoid having to ask Robert for additional funds. Not that he wasn't already a generous provider. Unlike a lot of the gentry, he had derived the bulk of his fortune from the industrialized north and that inheritance had only multiplied during the years of conflict and the current political turmoil.

She studied the last letter in the pile. It bore no postmark and had no signature scrawled across the corner to frank it. The paper was cheap, and the handwriting uneven.

Lucy frowned as she opened the single sheet and attempted to read the labored script.

You will die alone and childless. None of your heathenish spells will work. The Turners have cursed you forever.

Lucy blinked and reread the single line. There was no signature. Who would send such a thing, and *why?* She fumbled for her handkerchief, afraid that someone would see her crying, and mortified at her own weakness.

She'd come to consider the local healer, Grace Turner, a friend. Was it possible that behind her affable mask, Grace still blamed Lucy for what had happened in the past? Lucy forced herself to take a deep, steadying breath.

"This ridiculous urge to cry at anything must stop," Lucy told herself out loud. "You are a very lucky woman who lives in a beautiful house, with a man who . . ." She paused. "Who didn't even notice you'd left the breakfast table."

But why should he? She'd done nothing but snap his head off every time he'd attempted to speak to her over the past few months. No wonder he'd retreated behind his newspaper.

"Your tea, my lady."

She hastily straightened and hid the letter under the pile.

"Thank you, Foley."

"And the gig will be ready for you at eleven, if that is convenient."

"That will be perfect."

She kept her bright smile on her face until the butler had left, and consulted her daybook as to the tasks that awaited her. She would speak to Cook and Mrs. Cooper, the new housekeeper, then would trek upstairs to change into warmer outdoor garb. Sitting around moping was not her way, and there was plenty to do. Her twin brothers were due home from school at the end of the week, which was probably why her father was desperate to speak to her. Keeping them occupied and helping others would at least make her feel like a useful member of society.

"Sir Robert."

"What is it, Foley?"

Major Sir Robert Kurland lowered his newspaper and stared at his elderly butler, who was regarding him with a distinct lack of approval.

"Do you wish me to start clearing the table?"

With a sigh, Robert folded his paper and looked around the breakfast room. "Where the devil is Lady Kurland?"

"She left the table about a quarter of an hour ago, sir." Foley's accusing stare intensified. "She barely ate a thing."

"What are you? Her *nurse?* If she isn't hungry, she isn't hungry." Even as Robert said the words, he was aware that he might have erred. The fact that he hadn't noticed what was going on around him was remarkably remiss of him. "Did Lady Kurland ask you to speak to me about anything in particular?"

"No, sir. But I thought she looked a little tired. We're all so worried about her below stairs."

"I'm fairly certain the last thing my wife would

16

want is to cause concern to anyone. She is simply intent on regaining her strength."

"By not eating, sir?"

Robert raised his head. "Foley, I have a great deal of respect for your opinion, but please do not suggest that I am unaware of the state of my wife's health."

"I would never presume to stand between a man and his wife, sir." Foley raised his chin. "But—"

Robert heaved himself upright and grabbed his cane. "Where is her ladyship?"

"She was in her sitting room, but I believe she has gone upstairs to change, Sir Robert."

"Thank you."

Robert made his slow way upstairs. His mended bones were always stiffer in the morning and especially in the cold of winter. The more he walked, the easier it became—until he overexerted himself and had to start all over again. He could at least ride a horse now, even though fear lingered like sourness in the pit of his stomach every time he mounted up.

This winter had been particularly hard on him, leaving his temper as uncertain as his gait. He tapped on the door of their shared bedchamber and went in to find his wife about to put on her bonnet in front of the mirror. She wore a dress in his favorite blue and had styled her hair in a braided coronet on the top of her head.

"I thought Dr. Fletcher told you to rest."

"He told me to rest if I felt tired." She didn't look directly at him, her attention fixed on tying the ribbons under her ear. "I am perfectly well."

"You look tired."

She turned then and allowed him to help her into her pelisse. "I'm going down to the village to speak to my father. I shall return at noon." She picked up her gloves and her basket. "Is there anything else you require of me?"

He scowled at her. "More than a moment of your time?"

"I spent half an hour with you at the breakfast table, and you barely noticed I was there."

"I . . . Damn it, Lucy. I was reading, and I forgot the time, and—"

"And now I have to go out. I'm sure you wouldn't want me to keep the horse standing in this weather?" Her smile didn't reach her eyes. "Sophia is coming to visit Anna at the rectory to talk about the Christmas festivities."

"She and Andrew have returned from London?"

"Yes, and will be celebrating the season with us." She hesitated. "I believe I asked you about this in September."

"And much has happened since then to make me forget," Robert countered. "I look forward to seeing them both."

"As do I." Lucy smoothed down her skirts. "I must go."

"Are you sure you don't wish me to accompany

you?" Robert tried again. "I have a book to return to your father."

"I could take it back for you."

"Or I could meet you at the rectory after I've spoken to Dermot."

She nodded as she pulled on her gloves. "I'm sure my father would be delighted to see you."

He bowed and stood back, then opened the door to allow her to sail past him. As soon as she had disappeared down the stairs, he raised his eyes heavenward.

"You're a bumbling fool, Robert Kurland."

Why had he hidden behind his newspaper? He knew she was unhappy, and yet he couldn't seem to put his concern into words or break through her reserve. Or mayhap it was because she wouldn't even *accept* that he was worried about her. It was like attempting to pet a tightly rolled-up hedgehog in the palms of his bare hands.

He would talk to his friend Dr. Fletcher again and would see if he had any suggestions, although Lucy dutifully took every pill and potion the doctor offered her. But she looked tired and drawn and . . . *sad*. Her indomitable courage and boundless optimism had seen him through some of the worst moments of his life. The least he could do was attempt to help her through her own crisis.

But how?

As he turned to leave, he thrust his hand into

19

his pocket and his fingers brushed against the letter from his aunt. He took it out and studied the neat handwriting. Lucy was very fond of his aunt Rose.

Perhaps there was something he could do, after all. . . .

Lucy sipped her tea and nodded as Anna detailed her plans for the Christmas services. Her sister was in remarkably fine spirits, considering she had to deal with their father on a daily basis. But Anna had always been the rector's favorite child, and despite dropping the odd hint about her inability to find a suitable husband despite the expense of her London Season, he seemed remarkably content to be managed by her.

The notion of her beautiful sister sacrificing her chance of a husband and family simply to keep house for their father bothered Lucy immensely. If it wasn't for the fact that Nicholas Jenkins was a regular and faithful visitor to the rectory, and still unmarried, she might have attempted to persuade Anna to let her chaperone her into local society—such as it was—and mayhap even take her back to London for another Season.

"What do you think, Lucy?" Anna was looking at her expectantly, and Lucy scrambled to collect her thoughts.

"I do apologize. I was woolgathering."

Her sister reached out to pat her hand. "Your

head is in the clouds today. It is so not like you. Are you sure you are feeling quite the thing?"

"I am perfectly fine." Lucy attempted to quell her sister's concern. "What do I think about what?"

"The notion of having the children who attend the village school sing at the evening church service the week leading up to Christmas."

"I think that is a wonderful idea. Have you spoken to Miss Broomfield about the matter?"

Anna grimaced. "I was hoping you might do it for me, Lucy. As you and Sir Robert founded the school, she might be more willing to speak to you. She *is* somewhat intimidating."

"I'm more than happy to ask. I haven't met her yet and was planning on seeking her out. I'll call on my way back to Kurland Hall. How is your new kitchen maid settling in?"

"She is very eager to please and gets on well with Cook and all the other staff. I couldn't ask for anyone better."

"I'm glad to hear it. She's Mr. Coleman's oldest granddaughter."

"I know. She was busy chatting to him in the kitchen when I was just out there. It is nice to finally have a well-settled staff."

A bell sounded in the distance, and Anna rose to her feet. "That might be Sophia arriving. I'll order more tea."

"It might also be my husband," Lucy called

after her. "He thought he would visit Father to return a book he borrowed."

"Then I'll make sure we have plenty of hot water, or perhaps the gentlemen will forgo tea for something stronger."

Despite Lucy's earlier fears, the rectory appeared to be running smoothly under Anna's sunny command. Her father seemed happier, too. He had a curate willing to devote long hours to the spiritual welfare of the parish, which allowed the rector to follow his passions for horseflesh, hunting, and the pursuits of a country gentleman.

"Lucy!"

Sophia Stanford came into the small parlor and rushed over to embrace Lucy. She wore a bonnet with tall pink feathers and a luxurious fur-trimmed pelisse in a dashing shade of green.

"I was so disappointed that you didn't come to visit us in London in September," Sophia scolded as she drew her arm through Lucy's and settled them both on the sofa. "We were all looking forward to it, and then I received Sir Robert's note that you were not well enough to travel. I reminded the children that we would be spending the Christmas season here in Kurland St. Mary, which helped alleviate some of their disappointment."

"Did Mr. Stanford accompany you today?" Lucy asked.

"No. He's at my old home, interviewing my

mother's land agent and keeping an eye on the children." Sophia smiled. "He really does take remarkably good care of me *and* our family."

Anna returned with a tea tray and had barely set it down before there was another arrival.

"Mrs. Fletcher and Miss Chingford," the new maid announced just as Penelope and her sister came in the door behind her.

"There is no need to be so formal, Fiona. We *are* practically part of the family," Penelope said as she curtsied. She took off her bonnet, revealing her blond ringlets and perfect complexion. "Good morning, Mrs. Stanford, Anna, and Lucy. We saw the Stanford carriage and decided to step in and pay our respects."

Anna raised her eyebrows at Lucy behind Penelope's back and then moved forward. "Please join us for some tea. It is always delightful to welcome you both here."

Lucy had always thought it was a pity that Anna had not been born a man. She would've made an excellent diplomat.

Within moments, Dorothea Chingford excused herself to search out the curate on a matter of spiritual guidance, leaving Anna and Lucy to deal with her older and far more outspoken sister.

Penelope took off her gloves and settled into a seat. Despite her limited budget as the village doctor's wife, she always looked like she had just stepped out of a fashion plate. "It seems my sister has set her cap at Mr. Culpepper, the curate. What do we know about his family? Are they wealthy?"

"I believe his father is a vicar in the west of England and has several other children," Lucy offered.

"Then probably not wealthy at all." Penelope wrinkled her nose. "What a shame."

"You realized that marrying for love rather than wealth was an excellent idea, Penelope. Why should your sister not follow your example?" Lucy asked.

"Because she isn't as foolish as I am."

"Are you not happy in your marriage?" Lucy raised her eyebrows.

"I am very content with my choice, although if my dear Dr. Fletcher suddenly inherited a fortune, I certainly wouldn't regret it or turn it down." Penelope turned to Anna. "Has Mr. Culpepper said anything to you or your father to indicate his intentions toward Dorothea?"

"He hasn't said anything to me," Anna said cautiously. "Would you like me to *ask* Father to speak to him?"

"I'll speak to him myself." Penelope folded her hands in her lap. "I cannot have my sister wasting her youth on a man who has no interest in her. As you both know, I wasted far too many years waiting for Major Sir Robert Kurland to marry *me*."

After another wry glance at Lucy, Anna handed Penelope a cup of tea. "I believe you made the right choice in the end. It is quite obvious that Dr. Fletcher adores you."

Penelope patted her golden curls. "As he should, seeing as I condescended to forgo the rank and privilege my beauty deserved to marry a *nonentity*."

Sophia choked on her tea, and Lucy patted her on the back. Within seconds, Penelope was interrogating Sophia about current London fashions, leaving Lucy free to sit in comparative peace.

Dorothea Chingford would make an excellent bride for the curate. They had known each other for three years and always sought each other out at social and church events. Dorothea did not have her sister's ambition and would welcome the opportunity to stay in the village she had grown to love. In the village, there was a small house owned by the church that would suit the young couple to perfection. Lucy made a mental note to remind her father to offer it to George Culpepper if the wedding took place.

"Lucy, are you still expecting us at Kurland Hall this afternoon to discuss the arrangements for the Christmas festivities?" Penelope inquired.

"Yes, indeed." Lucy placed her cup on the side table. "In truth, I should not stay much longer. I have to go and speak to Miss Broomfield at the school."

Sophia pouted. "You are leaving already? I have barely had a chance to speak to you."

"I will gladly avail myself of your company at Kurland Hall this afternoon. In fact, why don't you and Andrew stay for dinner after that?"

"What an excellent idea." Lucy looked up as Robert entered the room with her father. He bowed over Sophia's hand and then kissed it. "I was just coming to extend the same invitation. How are you, my dear Mrs. Stanford?"

"I am very well." Sophia smiled up at him. "Your best friend makes an excellent husband."

"I am glad to hear that."

As Robert spoke to Sophia, a bud of resentment unfurled in Lucy's bosom. Her husband was being remarkably charming for a man who'd barely bothered to manage three sentences to her over the breakfast table.

"May I bring the children with me today?" Sophia asked. "They are looking forward to seeing you both immensely."

Robert cast a wary glance at Lucy. "I'm . . . not sure. Lucy has not been well. She might—"

Lucy cut across him. "I would be *delighted* to see your children, Sophia. How could you think otherwise, sir?"

Sophia looked uncertainly from her to Robert and then back again. "I am glad to hear that, seeing as I am about to add to the brood." She patted her stomach. "Not until next Easter, I believe."

A chorus of congratulations rained down on Sophia's head, while Lucy smiled and smiled. Just to make matters worse, Penelope sighed extravagantly and came to stand beside Sophia.

"I was going to wait until after the festivities to reveal *my* news. But I must confess that I am in an interesting condition, as well," Penelope revealed.

Lucy stumbled through another set of congratulations, and then, while she was unobserved, she left the room and climbed the stairs to what used to be her bedchamber. She fumbled for her handkerchief and couldn't find it as tears dripped down to mark the patterned muslin of her bodice.

When the door opened behind her, she delved inside the top drawer of her old dressing table and pretended to be searching for something.

"Is that you, Anna? I was just looking for a clean handkerchief."

"Lucy."

She stiffened as a warm hand slid around her neck and she was turned into the comfort of her husband's arms. A large handkerchief was pressed into her palm.

"It's all right."

For a long moment, she did nothing but breathe

in his familiar scent and simply allowed herself to be held. Eventually, she used the handkerchief to blow her nose and eased out of his arms.

"Pray excuse me. It's not that I'm not delighted for both Sophia and Penelope. It's just that it should have been *me* announcing *my* news, and—"

"I'm fairly certain that neither of them noticed you were upset." He was watching her carefully, his attention fixed on her face. "Have you told Mrs. Stanford what happened?"

"It wasn't something I was comfortable revealing in a letter. I intended to tell her when she arrived." Lucy dabbed at her eyes "But how can I do that now, when she is so happy?"

A small frown appeared on his forehead. "Surely, she would still want to know."

"That I am incapable of carrying a child?"

"Lucy . . . that's not what Dr. Fletcher said."

His unaccustomed gentleness made her chest hurt. "I do not want to put foolish fears into Sophia's head about her own current condition."

"If she truly is your friend, she will notice you are out of sorts and will ask for an explanation. Do you plan on *lying* to her?"

"I hadn't thought about it." She raised her chin. "What do you suggest?"

"It is hardly my decision to make, my dear. I'll tell Andrew the truth. I would rather not lie to *my* oldest friend."

"Then may I suggest you don't?"

He stepped away from her. "I do *not* want to argue with you about this."

"I wasn't aware that we were arguing."

"But we soon will be, because every time I attempt to discuss what happened, *you* turn it into a battleground."

Tears started in her eyes again, but she ruthlessly held them back. "Are you suggesting that everything is my fault?"

"No! I'm attempting to—"

"Because you would be correct. Everything *is* my fault. Now, would you kindly remove yourself from my presence so that I can compose myself?"

He visibly set his jaw. "I am your husband. Surely, I am entitled to express my feelings for you and discuss what has occurred."

"As far as I am concerned, you have already done everything required of you, sir."

"So I'm supposed to ignore the fact that you are tired and miserable?"

"Yes!" She stamped her foot. "I would feel much better if everyone would stop remarking upon it and let me be!"

"Everyone?" He took a step back. "Ah, I see."

She gathered the last of her pitifully stretched resources. "Can we not discuss this at home? I do not want my father to hear us arguing."

"We are not arguing." He shoved a hand

through his hair. "You are merely angling for a fight, and I am refusing to indulge you."

"Then if you will not leave, can you continue to indulge me and allow me to continue on my way?"

He studied her for a long moment before moving to one side. He flung open the door and bowed low. "My lady."

She went past him and practically ran down the stairs and out the front door, forgetting her bonnet in her haste to leave. She didn't want him to be kind and understanding. She wanted him to . . . What *did* she want?

Mr. Coleman emerged from the kitchens and handed her into the gig. "Major Kurland said you were ready to leave, and to give you this." He placed her bonnet on the seat beside her. "Now, let's get you home."

"I need to visit the schoolhouse first."

"Then I'll take you there, but no loitering around in the cold, now, my lady."

Chapter 2

Kurland St. Mary School occupied a building, owned by the Kurland estate, on the edge of the village, close to the duck pond and open fields. It had once housed one of the village smithies and had fallen into disrepair when the family left to live in Hertford. It was built of sturdy brick and stone. The gutted interior had been restructured to allow for one large classroom and a cloakroom, where the students could hang their outdoor things.

At the rear of the property was a separate door into the teacher's living accommodation, which continued above the schoolroom. As the Kurland family had endowed the school, Lucy had spent many months poring over the designs and interviewing prospective teachers. Miss Broomfield, the current teacher, had only recently taken up the position, after the previous teacher, a woman Lucy had liked tremendously, had left to marry one of the local farmers.

Miss Broomfield had come highly recommended by an acquaintance of her father's; Lucy hadn't formed an opinion of her yet. Because of the nature of a rural village, most of the children who did attend came after they had fulfilled their obligations to their families. Some of them worked on the local farms; others in the villages or alongside their parents at home.

Robert had insisted that all the children who lived on the Kurland estate should have the opportunity to attend school, but there were many parents who resented the time their children spent away from home, and considered the idea of education wasteful. Lucy had insisted that girls be offered the chance to attend, as well, which had scandalized everyone in the county, except perhaps her father and her husband.

In truth, very few of the girls attended, but two of the older ones had been employed to assist the teacher and were paid well enough to stop their families from grumbling. Lucy climbed the steps and pushed open the door that led into the cloakroom of the school. The smell of damp clothes and unwashed bodies engulfed her, and she tried not to breathe too deeply.

The door to the schoolroom proper was ajar. Lucy could hear voices chanting a multiplication table. There were often more children at school during the winter months, when there was less for them to do on the land. The design of the school included a large fireplace, which kept the building warm even during the coldest of days. She suspected some of the children came to school simply to be warm for a few hours, and she could hardly blame them.

"John Thacker!"

Lucy flinched as the teacher's cane smacked on wood.

"Yes, miss?"

"Are you sleeping again?"

"No, miss."

As Lucy opened the door, the sight of the schoolmistress greeted her, cane raised, ready to strike the small boy cowering in front of her.

"Good morning, Miss Broomfield," Lucy called.

The teacher froze in place, the tip of her cane quivering an inch from the boy's ear.

"Who are you, and what are you doing in my schoolhouse?"

Lucy raised her eyebrows. "I'm Lady Kurland."

"Lady *Kurland!*" Miss Broomfield lowered the cane and placed it on her desk. "I was not expecting you."

"Obviously." Lucy gave the teacher her haughtiest smile. "May I speak with you for a moment?"

"If you insist." Miss Broomfield pointed at an older girl sitting quietly at a desk on the side. "Rebecca, take over the lesson. I shall return momentarily."

"Yes, Miss Broomfield."

Lucy patted John's head as she passed him, and followed Miss Broomfield into the more private part of the school. The teacher held the door open for Lucy and closed it behind her before going to stand behind her desk, her black skirts rustling as she walked. She was shorter than Lucy, her features were sharp, and she held herself ramrod straight, like a soldier on parade.

"I would prefer it if you send a note asking if it would be convenient for me to speak to you before you arrive at my school, Lady Kurland."

"In future I will bear that in mind." Lucy declined the offer of a seat. "I came to inquire as to whether the children would be available to sing at one of the Christmas services."

"At Kurland St. Mary Church?"

"Yes. Have you continued Miss Brent's music lessons?"

Miss Broomfield's dark eyes narrowed even further. "I am not in the habit of wasting valuable hours in the schoolroom on such frivolous undertakings, my lady."

"Then perhaps you might reconsider your position." Lucy's smile was pleasant enough, but she didn't intend to be talked down to. "I'm certain it was made clear that we expect the children to receive a *well-rounded* education."

"When most of them barely know their alphabet?" Miss Broomfield snapped. "And arrive at school too tired and lazy to apply themselves?"

"Most of them have already put in a hard day's work before they get here," Lucy reminded her. "I agree that reading and writing must be a priority, but there is always time for music and art."

"Humph." Miss Broomfield's determined expression didn't waver. "I am not convinced that children should be allowed to perform in front of an audience. We do not want to put ideas into their heads."

"Ideas about what?" Lucy asked.

"About other ungodly occupations, such as a career on the *stage,* or thinking they are somehow special because they have performed for their betters."

"As they will be performing in front of their own parents and families, I hardly think it will turn their heads." Lucy reached behind her and rested one hand on the bookcase. Despite all her protestations to the contrary, she sometimes did feel terribly tired.

"But still, Lady Kurland—"

"Thank you for your time." Lucy gathered her resources. "If you do not feel you can help with this matter, I will inform Sir Robert and my father of your decision."

Miss Broomfield frowned. "I didn't say I *wouldn't* help out, Lady Kurland. I merely suggested that it doesn't sit well with my conscience. I am, however, well aware that my position here rests on my ability to appease the whims of my employers."

"Indeed, it does." Lucy inclined her head an

inch. How could her father and Robert have offered this dreadful woman the position? If Lucy had been well enough to interview her, she doubted Miss Broomfield would have won *her* approval. "If you prefer it, I could come in and teach the children the carols myself."

"Oh, no. That won't be necessary, my lady," Miss Broomfield said quickly. "Just send me a note as to what they need to learn, and I will set one of the girls to the task."

"Thank you." Lucy nodded. "While I am here, is there anything else you need to discuss with me, Miss Broomfield?"

"Well, the chimney in my part of the school appears to be partially blocked," Miss Broomfield said begrudgingly. "I dare not set a fire in there."

"I will send someone to deal with that directly."

"Thank you." Miss Broomfield's smile was less pinched this time. "Other than that, the accommodation you have provided is more than adequate."

"I'm glad to hear it." Lucy turned toward the door. "Is John Thacker really falling asleep every day?"

"Indeed, he is. I cannot understand why he even bothers to attend if he can't keep his eyes open!" Miss Broomfield walked around her desk to join Lucy. She smelled of damp wool and strong lye soap. "His sister is almost as bad."

"It is probably because his mother has just had another baby."

The teacher sniffed. "And how many children does that make? Ten now, is it?"

"Surely, the good Lord tells us to accept what is given to us and rejoice in it," Lucy countered and mentally made a note to send poor Mrs. Thacker some extra provisions from the Kurland Hall kitchen. The family lived on one of the outlying farms, and the house must be full to bursting.

"Well, as to that, there is such a thing as *abstinence,* my lady."

"Indeed, but who are we to judge what is right in another couple's marriage?" Lucy said sweetly.

"As I have never *been* married, or wished to indulge in such a union, I can hardly comment, Lady Kurland."

"Exactly."

Lucy returned to the schoolroom, Miss Broomfield behind her. John Thacker was already asleep, his head cradled in his arms on the desktop. He wasn't the only child who had taken advantage of the teacher's absence to take a nap. Lucy cleared her throat quite loudly, and several heads shot up. She nodded at Josephine Blake, who was helping one of the little ones read from the Bible.

"Thank you for taking such good care of the children while I talked to Miss Broomfield, Rebecca and Josephine."

"You are most welcome, my lady." Rebecca Hall cast an apprehensive glance at the teacher. "I did my best, but—"

"That's enough, Rebecca. You can resume marking the spelling tests." Miss Broomfield reclaimed her cane and took up her position in front of the suddenly attentive and silent children. "We shall continue with our recitation. Good *day,* Lady Kurland."

Having been summarily dismissed, Lucy returned to the carriage and allowed Mr. Coleman to hand her into her seat. She would have to talk to Robert about Miss Broomfield. She didn't believe the woman had the right characteristics to be in charge of young, impressionable minds. Her obvious sneering at those less well educated or fortunate than herself had not won Lucy's approval. As her husband held far more outlandish notions about educating the masses than Lucy did, she assumed he might want to reconsider his decision.

Lucy sank back against the cushions of the carriage and contemplated the leaden skies. There was definitely a hint of frost in the air and a breath of winter rolling in across the barren fields. She acknowledged the curtsies and pulled forelocks of the villagers as she drove down the main street, but didn't stop to talk to anyone, which was unlike her. In truth, she was exhausted, and if she wished to be a competent hostess to her afternoon guests, she would need to resort to a restorative nap.

Both Grace Turner and Dr. Fletcher had insisted that she needed to eat more, but her appetite had deserted her. She shivered as the carriage turned out of the village street and onto the road that led to the gates of Kurland Hall. Perhaps it was time to abandon the gig and ask Mr. Coleman to bring out the older, more comfortable closed carriage.

"Almost home, my lady," Coleman called out as they turned into the elm-lined drive up to the hall.

"Thank you."

She caught glimpses of the back of the hall, which still displayed its timber-framed Elizabethan origins, through the bare trees before the carriage came around to the front entrance, which had been modified and modernized by Robert's father. Due to five hundred years of familial meddling, the interior of the hall was somewhat confusing. Occasionally, guests ended up in the wrong wing of the house or had to be rescued by the staff.

Robert loved his family home and refused to admit it could be improved upon. Despite the fact that her father had knocked down the medieval rectory and had rebuilt it in modern, Adam-style square stone, Lucy secretly preferred the hall. If Robert did not have an heir, five hundred years of continual occupation of the hall by the Kurland family would come to an end, and his cousin, Paul, a despicable rake who had been banished from the country, stood to inherit everything.

Lucy shuddered at the thought as she stepped out of the carriage to find Foley already opening the front door. It was her duty to provide her husband with an heir, and so far, she had failed him.

"Welcome back, my lady."

"Thank you." Lucy removed her gloves as she stepped inside. "I'm going to speak to Mrs. Cooper, and then I'll be going up to my bedchamber. Ask Betty to attend me there."

"Yes, my lady." Foley took her gloves. "I shall find her immediately."

By three o'clock, Lucy was sitting in her drawing room, pouring tea for her guests, who included her sister, Anna; Penelope Fletcher; and Sophia.

Foley appeared at the door and announced new arrivals with all the formality of a county ball.

"Mr. Nicholas Jenkins and Mrs. Jenkins, my lady."

Lucy rose to greet her elderly guest and led her toward the chair closest to the fire. "Thank you so much for coming, Mrs. Jenkins. Would you care for some tea?"

"I'd prefer something stronger." Mrs. Jenkins winked at Lucy. "Hot whiskey and ginger would certainly help my sore throat."

"I'll tell Foley to bring you a glass immediately."

Lucy spoke to Foley and then paused by Nicholas Jenkins, who had stopped to talk to Anna. "Thank you for bringing your grandmother, Nicholas."

"My pleasure, my lady." He bowed over her hand. "I am always her willing servant."

Anna touched his sleeve. "I will escort your grandmother home today and save you another trip."

Nicholas smiled down at Lucy's sister. He was a tall young man with a pleasant face and dark brown eyes. "You are all that is considerate, Miss Anna. I will look forward to your arrival." He winked at her. "And mayhap persuade you to stay awhile and enjoy our company at dinner."

Anna smiled back. "Thank you, Nicholas, but I have to be home this evening. My father is anxious to discuss the arrangements for the Christmas church services."

"Another time, then."

Anna moved away to speak to Mrs. Jenkins, leaving Lucy the only one to see the frustration on Nicholas's face. Impulsively, Lucy lowered her voice.

"Don't give up on her quite yet, Mr. Jenkins."

"I won't." He sighed. "But I must confess that sometimes I wish your father to the devil."

"I quite understand the sentiment," Lucy said.

"She won't leave him," Nicholas continued, his gaze fixed on Anna. "And I am at a loss of how to persuade her otherwise."

"We will think of something." Lucy patted his sleeve. "Do not despair."

She accompanied him to the door and met Foley, who was returning with more guests.

"Mrs. Greenwell, Miss Greenwell, and Miss Amanda Greenwell, my lady," Foley puffed.

Nicholas bowed to the new arrivals. "Good afternoon."

The older daughter, Margaret, held out her gloved hand and pouted. "You are leaving? But *I* have just arrived."

Lucy glanced at Miss Greenwell, aware of her coquettish tone and fluttering eyelashes. Was it possible that Anna had competition for the village's most eligible bachelor?

"Alas, I must depart." Nicholas kissed Miss Greenwell's hand and stepped back. "I do apologize. I have some errands to run for my grandmother."

He nodded at Lucy and set off down the hallway. He had certainly matured during his years in London and was far more formidable than Lucy remembered. If there was a way to extricate Anna from the rectory, Lucy was certain he would find it.

"What a shame Mr. Jenkins couldn't stay," Mrs. Greenwell commented as Lucy led her into the drawing room. "He is such a pleasant gentleman, and so attentive to his grandmother."

"Indeed." Lucy settled the ladies on the couch,

next to Sophia. "His parents died when he was quite young, and Mrs. Jenkins brought him up when he wasn't at boarding school."

"I know it was a delightful surprise to find such an eligible gentleman in such a rural location." Mrs. Greenwell smiled at her daughters. "I believe Margaret finds herself to have much in common with him."

Lucy looked around the room to ascertain exactly where Anna was, and then leaned closer to Mrs. Greenwell. "I have a suspicion that Mr. Jenkins has set his sights on my sister, Anna."

"She is quite beautiful," Mrs. Greenwell agreed with a sigh. "But he has not made a formal application for her hand yet, has he?"

"I don't believe he has."

Mrs. Greenwell visibly brightened. "Then perhaps when he is given the opportunity to spend more time with my Margaret, he might change his mind."

Lucy couldn't blame her for her optimism. Marrying off one's daughters was a primary concern of any loving mother. She doubted the Greenwells had the resources to afford a London Season for either of their daughters, so they had to be content with attending county balls and meeting young men at their neighbors' houses.

While she might *sympathize* with their plight, she had no intention of allowing Margaret Greenwell to monopolize Nicholas Jenkins.

Anna deserved to marry a man who not only had loved her for years but was also the heir to a viscount.

"Good afternoon, Lady Kurland."

Lucy turned to find one more guest slipping unobtrusively into the drawing room.

"Josephine, how nice to see you. Did you accompany the Greenwells?"

"Yes, my lady." She curtsied.

The girl still wore the drab blue muslin dress and pinafore she had worn earlier at the school. Lucy wasn't quite certain of the relationship between the Greenwells and Josephine Blake, who acted as a part-time companion to their daughters, as well as carried out her duties at the school.

It was Lucy who had persuaded Robert to offer the paid position to Josephine. She knew how hard it was to live on the charity of others and hoped the money Josephine received gave her at least a small measure of independence. Not that the Greenwells appeared to mistreat her. They just made if obvious that Josephine was not to be considered a young lady at home or as part of their immediate family.

Rebecca Hall, the other girl who worked at the school, was from the large family who operated the remaining smithy in the village. She had marched up to Kurland Hall and had stated that she didn't want to go into service and wanted to keep learning. Impressed by her desire to improve herself, Robert had not hesitated in offering Rebecca employment, as well.

"Come and sit down, Josephine. You must be worn out after working at the school."

"Worn out?" Mrs. Greenwell looked up. "She only has to assist Miss Broomfield, Lady Kurland. It is hardly an onerous task."

Lucy smiled at her guest. "Just the mere thought of dealing with a dozen children makes me tired. I was at the schoolhouse this morning. I have nothing but admiration for anyone who undertakes such a task."

Margaret shuddered. "I would not step foot in there. Those children smell quite dreadful, and I suspect some of them have *fleas*."

Anna spoke up before Lucy could open her mouth. "That's because they often do not have access to those things you take for granted, Miss Greenwell, such as hot water to wash in, spare clothes and boots, and sometimes even enough to eat," she said. "Come and sit with me, Josephine, and I'll pour you some tea."

"Don't encourage her to sit, Miss Harrington!" Mrs. Greenwell's laugh was patently false. "She'll fall asleep, and then where will we all be? I thought she could take notes about the meeting and be helpful, otherwise I wouldn't have brought her with us."

Josephine stepped back so fast, she collided with Lucy. "I'm quite happy to offer my services."

45

"I accept your offer with gratitude, but first sit down and have some tea while I gather my thoughts." Lucy said.

Lucy took hold of Josephine's elbow and steered her over to where Anna was sitting. Anna patted the spot on the couch next to her, and Josephine sat down, casting a wary glance over at Mrs. Greenwell, who was still smiling, if a little rigidly. Knowing that Josephine was in safe hands, Lucy turned her attention to the rest of her guests and made sure they were all supplied with sufficient tea, coffee, and the delightful little cakes Cook had sent up from the kitchen.

When everyone was settled, she cleared her throat. "Shall we begin our meeting?"

Josephine went to sit at Lucy's desk and took up her pen expectantly.

"Thank you all so much for joining me." Lucy smiled at her assembled guests. "Firstly, Sir Robert and I have decided to hold a ball on Christmas Eve."

Mrs. Jenkins spoke up. "How lovely! And how very kind of you both."

"I am looking forward to it already!" Margaret exclaimed to her sister.

"We have also decided to hold a dance for our estate workers and the villagers, with games and presents for all the children."

"A very worthy cause." Anna clapped her hands. "How can we help?"

Lucy unrolled her list. "I have jotted down a few suggestions, and I would certainly value everyone's assistance. Perhaps we might start with the more practical arrangements and move on from there?"

An hour later, after all the women had spoken up and agreed to provide what Lucy asked of them, she folded up her list.

"Thank you." Lucy straightened her shoulders. "Now all that is required is for me to write out one hundred and fifty invitations and have them delivered in time."

"I can help you with that," Anna and Sophia both said at once.

"And I will send Dorothea to aid you, as well," Penelope added. "She needs an occupation other than staring soulfully at the curate."

"Speaking of letters . . ." Mrs. Jenkins opened her reticule. "I received one this morning that quite sent me into a flutter."

"An invitation?" Lucy asked.

"No, a letter addressed to me, with no return address. It was most impertinent!" Mrs. Jenkins held it out to Lucy. "Please read it to everyone and save my eyes."

Lucy put on her spectacles, unfolded the single sheet of paper, and read aloud. "Your grandson is a libertine and a thief. Beware this snake in your bosom!"

Lucy lowered the paper to stare at her elderly

guest. The tone of the letter reminded her of the note *she'd* received that morning. "What a ridiculous and hurtful thing to say! I do hope you paid no heed to such nonsense."

Mrs. Jenkins patted her ample bosom. "I must say it did give me something of a turn. Why would anyone say such a nasty thing? Nicholas is neither a thief nor a libertine."

"He is a most upstanding gentleman," Anna spoke up. "No one would believe anything other than that." She went to sit in the chair beside Mrs. Jenkins. "Please, my dear, ma'am, do not concern yourself with such nonsense. Someone was clearly attempting a horrible joke at your expense. I have no idea why."

Mrs. Jenkins dabbed at her eyes with her handkerchief. "But there were rumors that he misbehaved when he was in London. You know that yourself, Miss Anna. In truth, you—"

Anna quickly interrupted the old lady. "I did nothing of any import. Nicholas was young and learned from his mistakes. I have complete confidence in his integrity."

Margaret sniffed and whispered rather loudly to her sister, "As if *she* would be privy to Mr. Jenkins's innermost thoughts."

Lucy glanced at the sisters, but as Anna didn't seem to have heard the unkind comment, she decided not to say anything. Margaret reminded Lucy of Penelope at her most waspish.

"I would take no heed of that letter, Mrs. Jenkins," Lucy said firmly. "Did you mention it to your grandson?"

"No. I received it only this morning."

"Then I wouldn't bother him with it. The sooner such nonsense is ignored, the sooner it will go away." It was good advice. Now she needed only to apply it to herself. "Of course, if you receive any more correspondence in the same hand and in the same mean-spirited manner, then please do share it with us, and I will confer with Sir Robert. He takes a very dim view of such matters, I assure you."

"Thank you, my dear." Mrs. Jenkins put her handkerchief away. "I must confess it did give me rather a start, but I cannot believe ill of my dearest grandson."

Lucy looked at Anna. "Perhaps you might escort Mrs. Jenkins home and stay with her until Mr. Jenkins returns?"

"I would be delighted to do that, ma'am." Anna stood and reached down to clasp the older woman's hand and help her to her feet. "Foley has already arranged for the carriage to be brought around to the front door, so we can leave at your convenience."

"Then we'll be off immediately. It looks like it might rain." Mrs. Jenkins said her good-byes to the ladies, gathered her reticule, cloak, and walking cane, and was escorted tenderly down the stairs by Foley and Anna.

The Greenwell ladies also rose and approached Lucy.

"Thank you for your hospitality, Lady Kurland," Mrs. Greenwell said. "I am certain that Mr. Greenwell will be delighted to help out with the servants' party. He holds some rather advanced views about the equality of man."

"As does Sir Robert," Lucy countered. "It sounds as if they will deal extremely well together."

"I do hope Mr. Jenkins will attend the ball," Margaret Greenwell said.

"I am fairly certain he will," Lucy agreed. "He is most particular in his attentions to his grandmother and to those he considers friends."

"So I understand." Margaret sighed. "I wish *I* had thought to escort Mrs. Jenkins home. It was a remarkably clever move."

Lucy stiffened. "Anna and Mrs. Jenkins are old friends. They deal extremely well together."

"According to local gossip, Miss Harrington is all goodness, *apparently*." Margaret's smile disappeared.

"As she is my sister, I can confirm that she is indeed the kindest person I have ever met. It was *my* suggestion that she should accompany Mrs. Jenkins, not hers. She is not the kind of person to put herself *forward*." Lucy held the younger woman's gaze until Margaret blushed and looked away.

Mrs. Greenwell cleared her throat. "We should be going. My husband does not like to keep the horses out in such chilly weather."

"Then I shall escort you to your carriage." Lucy opened the door into the hallway.

She waited until the Greenwells' carriage pulled away before she slowly returned to the drawing room, where Sophia awaited her. Would it be possible to speak to her dearest friend without mentioning what had happened to prevent her much longed-for visit to London the previous summer?

Lucy hesitated in the doorway, but Sophia was already closing the distance between them, her expression concerned and her eyes full of tears. Sophia held out both her hands and took hold of Lucy's.

"Oh, my *dear* Lucy, Penelope told me your news. I am so sorry, my friend. Why did you not write and *tell* me?"

"I thought it would be better to tell you in person, although I see that Penelope has been busy gossiping instead."

Lucy allowed herself to be maneuvered over to the couch and sat stiffly beside Sophia.

"It is hardly gossip." Sophia squeezed her fingers. "You know she is jealous of our friendship and simply wished to display her superior knowledge of your condition." She hesitated. "I still wish you'd written to me."

"I wasn't well enough to write. I had to stay in bed for almost a week—much to my displeasure. Sir Robert threatened to tie me to the bed if I didn't do what Dr. Fletcher suggested, but I had little disinclination to disobey him when I was as weak as a kitten." Lucy tried to smile. "It was the second time I miscarried in a year."

"Oh, Lucy." Sophia handed Lucy her handkerchief. "There are not enough words in the world to express my sympathy."

"Dr. Fletcher says I must regain my strength, but there is so much to do, and—"

"You will allow me and others to help you," Sophia said firmly. "Anna has already confided in me that she is worried you are attempting too much, what with the ball and the village party and—"

"I prefer to be busy. If I sit around simply sewing endless seams, I feel a lot worse."

"But you will allow us to aid you." Sophia held Lucy's gaze. "I refuse to take no for an answer, my dear friend, so accustom yourself to the notion *immediately*."

Lucy smiled for the first time in ages. "Thank you. I will try. As long as you don't overtire *yourself*."

"I am feeling remarkably well now that I've gotten over the first few months of biliousness. In truth, I have energy to spare, and I'm more than happy to deal with whichever of your neighbors proves the most annoying." Sophia paused. "I cannot say I took to the Greenwell sisters. I've already heard the eldest daughter has set her cap at Nicholas Jenkins."

"I believe she has, but as she cannot hold a candle to Anna, I doubt she will succeed." Lucy sighed. "That is, if I can persuade Anna to listen to Nicholas. She seems determined to remain at the rectory with my father."

"Your father does make it very difficult for his daughters to leave, doesn't he?"

"He needs a wife," Lucy said. "Perhaps when we consider whom to invite to the ball, we should research some likely candidates."

"What an excellent idea," Sophia responded. "Then Anna will be free to leave the rectory, and the twins will have a new mother to fuss over them."

Lucy rose to her feet. Simply being in Sophia's company was having a remarkable effect on her spirits. "Let's go down to my study and start on that list immediately."

"Robert, did you interview Miss Broomfield when she applied for the vacancy at our school?"

"Miss Broomfield?" Robert looked up from the book he was reading, stuck his finger in the page, and attended to his wife. "What about her?" They were sitting in his study after an excellent dinner. After his inconsiderate display at breakfast, he was determined to pay Lucy the attention she deserved. "Your father interviewed her. I was rather preoccupied with other matters at the time."

In truth, in the summer, he'd been more worried about Lucy, who had miscarried in the third month of her pregnancy and had been recovering in bed. He had been in the heart of many a battle and had seen sights that would make most men quail, but his wife's quiet suffering was somehow far worse. Attending to the vacancy at the school was a minor issue he had left to his father-in-law.

Despite their earlier altercation at the rectory, Lucy was in better spirits, which he attributed to the happy influence of Sophia Stanford. But she was still rather quiet. Sometimes he almost yearned for Lucy to resume her managing ways, but provoking her into a fight was an uncertain game to play when particular subjects needed to be avoided.

"I went to speak to Miss Broomfield about the children appearing at one of the Christmas services." His wife continued, "She displayed a complete lack of understanding as to the character of the children in her care."

"In what way?"

"She considers them lazy and indifferent students. She scoffed when I attempted to point out that most of her charges work for a living, as well as attend school."

"Miss Broomfield *scoffed* at you?" Robert raised an eyebrow. "Brave woman."

"She obviously considers me to be one of those patrons who have no idea how a school should be run."

"More fool her. Did you attempt to educate her about that matter?"

"I tried, but she was impervious to my suggestions. The only reason she acquiesced to my demands that she teach the music to the children was that I threatened to express my displeasure to you and my father." She put down her sewing. "I even offered to teach the carols to the children *myself,* but even that idea offended her."

Robert frowned. "For once, I am in agreement with Miss Broomfield. You are not well enough to spend your days in that drafty schoolroom, surrounded by children with perpetually runny noses."

She raised her chin, a flash of her old determination glinting in her brown eyes. "I thought you *wanted* me to take up some new interests?"

"I pay that woman a large salary to teach at our school, and I do not expect my wife to be doing the teaching for her." Robert hesitated. "There are many other matters around the estate where you could better use your skills."

"Better than the welfare of the local children?"

"Yes, and far healthier options for you at this moment in time."

"But Miss Broomfield is incompetent! In fact, Robert, you should terminate her employment and look for a replacement over the holiday season."

"Because she disagreed with you about something? That is not like you, my dear. Perhaps we should wait until after Christmas. I will certainly speak to Miss Broomfield then and decide whether she is competent enough to complete her task."

"She is not." Lucy's eyes flashed.

"You are being remarkably judgmental."

"Only because there was something so . . . cold about her."

"What do you mean?" Robert frowned. Over the course of their relationship, he had learned to take note of her feelings.

"I suspect she is one of those women who became a schoolteacher for all the wrong reasons. Do you have her references to hand?"

"I believe Dermot has them somewhere, but—"

"Then I will ask him to find them for me. I'll wager my father did not check them before he hired her."

"We *were* left in a bit of a quandary when Miss Brent suddenly decided to get married and leave her post. In the middle of a school year, you can hardly expect to get the pick of the crop of good teachers," Robert objected.

Lucy sat forward. "We spent many hours discussing the kind of school we wished to endow, and even more finding the perfect teacher to run it. I cannot understand why such things were ignored when you hired Miss Broomfield."

Robert set his jaw. "I appreciate your concerns, my dear, and I intend to speak to Miss Broomfield at the earliest opportunity. In the meantime, you will refrain from involving yourself in the matter until you are feeling better." He raised his eyebrows. "Are we quite clear on that?"

"As you wish." Lucy clasped her hands in her lap and looked down at them.

After three years of marriage and many years of knowing his companion, Robert wasn't fooled by her wifely submission. "I'll have your word on the matter, if you please."

"That I won't go and teach the children?"

"That you will not involve yourself in the daily running of the school at *all*."

She sighed. "In truth, I haven't the energy to deal with a dozen children every day."

"Then why are you insisting that we hold this damn ball and villagers' party?" Robert demanded.

"Because I need *something* to do. If you prohibit me from everything, I swear I will die of boredom and waste away." She reached out a hand to him. "Anna and Sophia have offered to help with all the arrangements, and Mr. Greenwell wishes to speak to you about organizing the activities for the villagers' dance. I will hardly be attempting everything on my own."

Robert hesitated, and she squeezed his fingers. "Please, Robert. Do not deny me this."

"I will not do so, but I will be speaking to Anna and to Sophia to make certain that they are truly helping you and not allowing themselves to be bullied into letting you do everything in your own fashion."

"Hardly bullying, Robert!"

"Managing them, then. You are very good at that."

"Someone has to be, and you can hardly want to assume responsibility for all those tasks yourself," Lucy countered.

"As I've already mentioned, I'd rather not have a ball in the first place," Robert muttered as he kissed his wife's fingers. "But if you will refrain from taking over the schoolroom, *I* am prepared to admit the entire county into my home and endure their presence just for one evening a year."

Lucy smiled at him. "I knew you would come around to my way of thinking."

"After three years of marriage, my love, you have me as well tamed as a lapdog."

"Hardly that, sir. A surly mongrel perhaps?"

He met her smile with one of his own. It was good to see her smiling again, even if it was at his expense. And if he could persuade her not to meddle in the schoolroom, he was more than willing to compromise on a ball that benefited the entire county, rich and poor alike.

Chapter 3

Lucy sorted through the pile of letters Foley had offered her, wondering if there would be another unfranked letter full of insinuations and insults, but there was nothing unusual, and there hadn't been for almost a week. But on the previous day she had spoken to two families in the village who had also received unpleasant letters, and she had reluctantly decided to mention the matter to Robert at the first opportunity.

For once, she was alone at the breakfast table. Robert had muttered something about visiting the stables, which was most unlike him, and had left rather quickly.

Foley cleared his throat. "Would you like some more tea, my lady?"

"Yes, please, and maybe some fresh toast?"

"That would be my pleasure, my lady." His smile beamed out. "Cook's marmalade is remarkably good this year, isn't it?"

"Indeed."

A voice sounded in the hall. "Are you there, Lady Kurland?"

The door opened to reveal an unexpected visitor.

"Good morning, Grace," Lucy said. "And how are you today?"

"I am very well." Grace Turner smiled at her

60

and Foley. "I was out walking and decided to cut across the park, to see how you are faring."

"I'll set a new place, my lady," Foley murmured before pulling out the chair next to Lucy's and leaving the room.

Grace Turner sat down with a thump. Her dark hair was coming free from her untidy bun, and her cheeks were flushed pink with the combination of exercise and cold. Her boots had tracked mud all over the carpet, but Lucy didn't care.

"I found some mushrooms behind the lower wall. I hope you don't mind that I helped myself."

"You are more than welcome to them." Lucy searched her guest's face for any hint of animosity and found none. Grace was nothing if not transparent and had proved her honesty to Lucy in the past. If she still harbored a grievance, as the anonymous letter had stated, surely she would have aired it by now.

"Are you going to use the mushrooms in one of your noxious concoctions?"

"No. They will go in the pot with my stew." Grace placed her bulging bag on the carpet. "I did bring you some more elixir to drink."

Lucy shuddered. "It tastes horrible."

"And it will do you the world of good."

"If you say so." Lucy observed with distrust the small glass bottle Grace placed on the table. Foley brought in more tea and toast, and Lucy shared it with Grace.

"Your blood is too thin. You need to strengthen it," Grace reminded her. "Then you won't feel so tired."

"That would be nice, especially at this time of year, when one is required to participate in so many festive events."

"Like what?" Grace frowned.

"Church services, visiting our neighbors, and organizing the ball, for a start."

"I'm not considered a lady, so I don't have to do any of those things," Grace smirked. "What would happen if you refused to do anything?"

"I would be setting a bad example." Lucy considered that outlandish idea for all of one second and dismissed it. "I could not do it. I am the lady of the manor, and Sir Robert relies on me to help manage his tenants and staff. I would not want to let him down."

"Ha! Sir Robert would be the first one to do away with such nonsense," Grace insisted. "He is the most unconventional member of the landed gentry I have ever met."

"True," Lucy acknowledged. "It comes from his mother's industrial lineage. He does have some rather peculiar ideas about society and how a nation should be run, but he also has a very strong sense of duty."

"I know that to my cost." Grace patted Lucy's hand. "At least promise me you will take the tonic. And if there is anything you wish to ask me about how and when it is best to conceive another child, then—"

"I will certainly do that." Lucy rushed to interrupt her companion before the conversation became far too personal. "There *is* something I wanted to ask you. Have you heard of anyone in the village receiving anonymous letters?"

"No. Why?"

"Mrs. Jenkins received one earlier this week concerning her grandson's lack of moral character."

"Which is ridiculous. Who wastes valuable paper on sending an elderly lady such a horrible thing?" Grace scoffed.

"I hadn't thought of that," Lucy said slowly. "Paper *is* expensive."

"I must go." Grace stood and finished off her tea in one long swallow. "Oh, I almost forgot. Jon Hopewell has collie puppies. He was asking if Sir Robert might like one."

"What an excellent idea," Lucy said. "I'll drive out and see him later today. It might be the perfect yuletide gift for my husband. He is always lamenting his lack of dogs."

Grace left after reminding Lucy to take the tonic twice a day. Lucy dutifully poured herself a draft. It smelled like rusting nails and cabbage. She swallowed it down very fast, followed by copious amounts of tea. In truth, unlike Dr. Fletcher's potions, it did seem to help. She hadn't asked Grace what was in it, deciding it was probably better not to know.

The door opened again and, assuming it was Foley, Lucy barely bothered to look up.

"Oh good. You're still here."

She swung around to see Robert in the doorway. "Goodness, you startled me!"

"I apologize." Robert pushed the door wide open. "I do hope you appreciate your early Christmas present. I just picked it up from the inn."

"I'm hardly an 'it,' my dear Robert." The voice came from the hallway. "You make me sound like a forgotten parcel!"

Lucy rose from her chair in one swift motion and hurried toward Robert's aunt Rose, who was beaming fondly at her. She still wore her traveling cloak, bonnet, and thick pelisse.

"Lucy, my *dear* girl. It is so good to see you again. Robert tells me you haven't been well."

"That is correct. I—" Lucy swallowed hard and fought the rush of tears. A second later, she was drawn into a fierce embrace as aunt Rose patted her hair and murmured soothingly in her ear.

"It's all right, my dear. I'm here to help now."

Eventually, Lucy managed to look up at Robert, who was leaning against the wall, smiling at them both.

"Thank you for inviting your aunt to our home. I hadn't realized how much I missed her until this moment."

Robert shrugged. "I am delighted that you approve of my sudden decision. Aunt Rose intends to make an extended stay with us while her children behave appallingly in London."

"Robert . . . ," Lucy scolded, but Rose chuckled.

"He is quite correct. Between my two daughters, who believe they are too high and mighty to associate with their own mother, and my only son, who is intent on gambling away his inheritance, I am quite disgusted with them. I would much rather spend my Christmas here with people who *appreciate* me."

"We certainly do appreciate you." Lucy linked arms with aunt Rose and walked her out into the hallway. "I suspect Foley has already had our new housekeeper air your room and make it habitable, so I will take you up."

As they climbed the stairs, Lucy leaned down to whisper in Rose's ear. "If you aren't too tired this afternoon, perhaps you might enjoy a trip to one of our outlying farms? I'm trying to procure a puppy for Robert."

"I'm sure that after a short nap I'll be fully restored," Rose said. "And I'd love to join you on your secret expedition."

"I think that's enough for today, Dermot." Robert signed the last letter his land agent had placed in front of him, and put his pen back in the inkpot. "We have made a lot of progress this year, and the accounts are looking very healthy. I'm considering giving everyone who works on the estate an increased bonus on Boxing Day."

"That would certainly be appreciated, sir." Dermot Fletcher carefully blotted the letter and added it to the pile on his side of the desk. "And the estate can certainly bear the cost."

"I'll take another look at the books tomorrow and determine exactly what the percentage increase will be." Robert leaned back in his chair and stretched out his cramped fingers. "I do hope you intend to share the Christmas festivities with us at the hall as usual, Dermot."

His land agent grinned. "Seeing as I'm helping you organize them, Sir Robert, I'll definitely be on hand, and probably underfoot. You and Lady Kurland will be sick of the sight of me."

"I doubt that." Robert looked out of the window. The rain had stopped, and it was already getting dark. "Did you locate Miss Broomfield's references for me?"

"Yes, sir, I did." Dermot hesitated. "I apologize for not scrutinizing them more thoroughly, but at the time when I queried her appointment, Mr. Harrington assured me that her reputation was above reproach."

"And you didn't care to argue with the rector? I can quite understand that." Robert paused. "What did you dislike about her?"

"She offered up only one reference, and it

was from an old friend of Mr. Harrington's and concerned a position she had held three years previously. Unfortunately, I don't have the original letter, because Mr. Harrington kept it. At the time, Miss Broomfield insisted that the reference from her last employer had been mislaid during her relocation. She promised she would hand it over when she found it."

"That's quite unusual." Robert frowned.

"When there was no sign of a new reference being added to the file, I took the liberty of writing directly to the school mentioned in the letter. I received a reply from them this morning." Dermot offered Robert a sheet of paper.

Dear Mr. Fletcher,
Thank you for your inquiry as to the disposition and character of Miss Martha Broomfield. We regret to inform you that she was discharged from her employment at this prestigious school after an investigation uncovered evidence of unnecessarily cruel discipline toward certain students in her care. If you seek to employ a teacher, we would certainly not recommend this person.
Yours sincerely,
Agatha Pemberton
Headmistress, Pengaron School, Cornwall

"Good Lord." Robert looked up. "Lady Kurland was right."

"She quite often is, sir." Dermot took the letter back.

Robert heaved a sigh and stood up. "Then I suppose I should go down to the school and have a chat with Miss Broomfield."

Dermot rose, as well. "I am driving into the village to see my brother. Would you like me to take you to the school?"

"That would be much appreciated. In fact, I need to speak to the good doctor myself. Mayhap you could come to the school with me first?"

"To act as your witness?"

Robert winced. "I hope it does not come to that, but from all accounts, Miss Broomfield might not take her dismissal very well."

"She certainly has something of a temper," Dermot, always the diplomat, said. "I am more than willing to accompany you to ensure you don't get an inkpot lobbed at your head."

Robert consulted his pocket watch. "The children should have left by now. I'm sure they at least will be delighted if the school closes early for the year."

Dermot nodded and headed for the door. "I'll get my hat, and I'll meet you at the front door with the gig, sir."

Within a quarter of an hour, they were on their way. Robert was more than happy to let Dermot drive as it gave him time to view his estate as he passed down the elm-lined drive. It was bitterly cold, and the sun had disappeared behind a wall of thick, sullen clouds. There was almost no one out in the village as they drove along the High Street.

He hoped Lucy and his aunt were already on their way back from their afternoon calls. He would hate for either of them to catch a chill. At least Lucy had responded with great enthusiasm to the arrival of his beloved aunt. He suspected Rose would be a great asset during the yuletide festivities.

Dr. Fletcher's house stood on the opposite side of the duck pond to the schoolhouse. Both front windows at the Fletchers' were already lit up, but the schoolhouse was in darkness. Robert glanced up at the teacher's accommodation, but there was no light there, either.

"Shall we try the main school first, sir?" Dermot asked.

"Yes, I suppose we should start there."

Dermot secured the horse and followed Robert up the path to the entrance of the school. Just as Robert opened the exterior door, someone came out and ran right into him. He fought to retain his balance.

"Let me go! Please! Let go!"

Robert stared down into the terrified face of one of Miss Broomfield's students and gently set her to rights.

"It's all right. I won't hurt you. What's wrong?" he asked.

The girl was shaking so hard, she could barely form words. "Miss Broomfield. I forgot my scarf and went back to get it, and she—"

"Sir Robert . . ."

Robert looked over the girl's head at Dermot, who had gone ahead and now had returned, looking shaken.

"What is it?" Robert touched the girl's shoulder. There was something familiar about her face, but he couldn't remember her name. "Go to Dr. Fletcher's house. Tell him I sent you, and stay there until I come."

"Yes, sir."

Robert went through the second door, which Dermot held open. It led into the large classroom. There wasn't much light apart from that of the dying embers of the fire in the hearth and a single tallow candle burning on the teacher's desk. Miss Broomfield was sitting upright in her chair at her desk and was facing the door, with all the rigidity of a formal portrait painting. Having seen death in all its macabre glory during his career in the cavalry, Robert already knew she wasn't alive.

"Here's some more light, sir."

Dermot walked with him to the front of the room, their booted footsteps loud on the stone-flagged floor.

"Dear Lord . . . ," Dermot breathed as he placed the second candle on the desk. Trickles of dried blood mixed with tracks of ink from the quill pen someone had driven into Miss Broomfield's eye marred the left side of her face. "May God have mercy on her soul."

Even as Dermot crossed himself and prayed, Robert studied the body with an impartial air gained from years of battlefield experience. He gently touched one of her hands, which lay palm down on the desk, and found it already growing cold.

"The quill pen is disturbing to see, but I doubt it killed her," Robert said. "Will you fetch Dr. Fletcher? I'll wait here for your return."

Dermot immediately started for the door and then hesitated. "Are you sure, Sir Robert?"

"Go. You'll be back with him before I manage to limp as far as the duck pond."

Robert waited until the door slammed, and then set about finding more candles to light the macabre scene. It was still too dark to see whether there was any more blood on Miss Broomfield's black clothing, but he couldn't smell the familiar coppery tang on her.

If it weren't for the quill pen stuck in her eye, she would've looked perfectly unaffected by her own death. Robert leaned closer to study the papers under her hands, which appeared to have writing on them.

He is guilty.
She deserves to kno—

The second sentence was unfinished, and a line of ink fell off the side of the page, marring the whiteness of the paper. Robert frowned. Was it some kind of bizarre confession? Had Miss Broomfield killed herself?

"And then stuck the pen in her own eye?" Robert asked the question aloud. "I doubt she had the ability *or* the desire to do that."

"Sir Robert?"

He turned to see his old army friend Dr. Fletcher coming into the room, with Dermot behind him.

"Ah, thank you for coming so swiftly, Patrick. Miss Broomfield seems to have met with some kind of accident."

"So I see." Dr. Fletcher set a large lamp on the corner of the desk, his expression interested as he peered at the body. After his tenure as a surgeon in the army, it was remarkably hard to shock him. "I doubt the pen killed her outright, but you never know." He continued his brief examination. "No sign that she was shot, and no evidence of a struggle. I suppose she could have died of natural causes and then accidentally stabbed herself in the eye in a fit of hysteria."

"Unlikely," Robert said.

"Agreed."

"Then how do you wish to proceed?"

"Shall we take her over to my house?" Dr. Fletcher looked up. "Then I can examine the body more carefully."

"I'll carry her." Dermot stepped forward and took off his cloak. "I doubt anyone will be out and about in this weather to wonder what I am doing."

"We'll vouch for your character if anyone inquires." Dr. Fletcher slapped his brother on the shoulder. "I asked Penelope to unlock the side door so you can bring the body through there."

After the Fletcher brothers left, Robert remained in the schoolroom. He gathered up the scattered papers on the desk and placed them in his coat pocket to reexamine at a later date. He'd already decided that he would have to tell Lucy *some* version of what had happened before she heard it from someone else and was displeased with him for keeping it from her.

He made his way to the back of the school-house, where there was a study, a kitchen, and a narrow staircase up to Miss Broomfield's private quarters. There was no sign of the back-door lock being forced. Robert had to assume that whoever killed the teacher walked in without fear and probably was known by Miss Broomfield.

He glanced up the staircase and laboriously ascended into a landscape of black-and-white shadows thrown by the settling dusk. The oak floorboards creaked as he gained the top landing and struck a light for a candle. From his brief perusal, he found no sign of any disturbance on the upper floor. Everything looked to be perfectly in order: the bed was made, the sitting room was tidy, and the curtains were open. He doubted Miss Broomfield had even returned to her living quarters that afternoon.

He made his way carefully down the stairs and retrieved his cane from where he'd propped it up against the back door. He'd make sure that word was sent out to all the families not to send their children to school on the following day, which would give him time to assess the situation and decide as the local magistrate what action should be taken.

It was completely dark outside the schoolhouse as he locked the exterior door and pocketed the key he'd taken from Miss Broomfield's desk. The warm glow of light from the Fletchers' house beckoned to him, and he set off, trying hard not to lose his footing as ice settled and crackled underfoot. He was glad to see that the horse had been taken to the stable behind the house. Despite his disinclination to ride, his instincts as an ex-cavalry man ran deep.

As he approached the front garden, the door was flung open, and Penelope Fletcher appeared and beckoned to him.

"Do hurry up and come in, Sir Robert."

"Thank you." He stomped his boots on the mat and removed his hat and gloves as he entered the warm hallway. "I do apologize for disrupting your evening in this unpleasant fashion."

"It's hardly your fault, is it?" She set off down the corridor toward the parlor, her blond head held high. "But typical of that irritating woman to create havoc."

"You didn't like Miss Broomfield?"

"She was an unpleasant individual who considered herself my social equal. I frequently had to put her in her place."

"But she was hardly deserving of being killed just for that, was she?" Robert murmured.

"As I didn't kill her, I can hardly answer the question, can I, sir?"

For the umpteenth time, Robert reminded himself how grateful he was that the former Miss Penelope Chingford had broken off their engagement and had married his friend instead. She had very little sense of humor, and a huge sense of her own importance.

"Where's the girl?"

"Josephine? She's here in the parlor. Dermot will take her back home to the Greenwells' after he has taken you to Kurland Hall."

"May I speak with her?"

"Of course. Dr. Fletcher is in his surgery, attending to the deceased." Penelope visibly shuddered. She had yet to come to terms with the fact that her husband was the local physician and not a member of the aristocracy. "I'm sure he will come and find you when he is ready."

Robert waited for Penelope to precede him into the parlor and closed the door behind them. Josephine sat on the couch, wrapped in a large shawl, her feet tucked under her skirts. Her lip trembled when she saw Robert, and Penelope rushed over to her.

"Good Lord. Don't start crying again, dear! Where is your moral fiber? Sir Robert just wishes to ascertain that you are unhurt."

Robert sat on the other end of the couch and rested his cane against the table as Josephine attempted to ease away from him. He rarely spoke to young females and was aware that his somewhat ferocious reputation might have preceded him.

"Sit up straight, young lady!" Penelope admonished the girl. "And answer Sir Robert's questions."

Inwardly Robert sighed. He was unlikely to get anything out of the girl with Penelope standing guard over her. "Perhaps I might impose on you for a cup of tea, Mrs. Fletcher?"

"Of course, Sir Robert." Penelope turned toward him. "With your ill health, standing around in the cold would not be good for you. I shall fetch you one right now."

"Thank you."

With a firm nod, Penelope left the room, and Robert returned his attention to Josephine.

"Would you mind telling me what happened this afternoon?"

She gazed at him, her blue eyes brimming with tears. "I forgot my scarf, and it was so cold on the way home that I turned back to get it. I came into the cloakroom and noticed the door into the schoolroom was open, which was unusual, seeing as we normally try to keep the heat in. I called out to Miss Broomfield, begging her pardon for interrupting her, but she didn't answer, so I found my scarf on the peg and was just turning to go when I thought she said something."

Josephine took a huge shaky breath and dabbed at her eyes. Robert silently offered her his handkerchief.

"And?" he gently prompted her.

"I popped my head into the schoolroom and saw her sitting at her desk, and I *knew* something was wrong, but I kept walking up to her, and . . ." She shuddered and used the handkerchief to wipe away her tears and blow her nose. "And then I saw her *eye,* and I turned and ran."

"Straight into me," Robert added.

"Yes, but I didn't know that, sir. I thought you were the man who'd done *that* to Miss Broomfield."

"Perfectly understandable." Robert tried to sound reassuring. "Did you notice anyone else hanging around the schoolhouse when you came back to retrieve your scarf?"

Josephine wrinkled her nose. "There *might* have been someone. . . . I thought I saw a man at the rear of the building, but I can't be certain."

"You wouldn't recognize this person if you saw him again?"

Josephine shook her head. "To be honest, sir, I was so cold and so intent on getting my scarf that I wasn't really paying attention." She blew her nose again. "I'm sorry, sir."

"There's nothing to be sorry about. You have had a terrible shock. In truth, if you had not returned to the school, we might not have known what had befallen Miss Broomfield until tomorrow."

"When all the little children were arriving at school." Josephine shuddered. "That would have been *horrible*."

"Indeed." Robert contemplated his next question. "Do you have any idea *why* someone might have wanted to kill Miss Broomfield?"

Her tears started again and this time became an unstoppable flood.

Penelope reentered the room with a tray and gave Robert an irritated glare. "Perhaps you might consider leaving all other questions to a more suitable date, Sir Robert. Josephine seems a little overwrought."

"It was certainly not my intention to upset

her." Robert declined to reclaim the handkerchief Josephine offered him. "As the local magistrate, I do have to get to the bottom of cases such as this."

"I'm sure Josephine understands that, but perhaps you have said enough for one night?"

There was a lot more that Robert wished to say, but he sensed his opportunity had ended, and was not foolish enough either to offend his hostess or upset the child. He frantically searched his memory as to Josephine's family but had only a vague sense that they lived in the hamlet of Lower Kurland, which was almost two miles away. He could quite understand why she'd gone back for her scarf if she was walking home.

"Do you live in Lower Kurland, Josephine?"

He received a nod in reply and looked inquiringly up at Penelope.

"She resides with the Greenwell family in the old manor house."

"Ah, that's why she looks familiar. I'll take her home after I've spoken to Dr. Fletcher."

"There's no need for *you* to do that, Sir Robert. Dermot can take her."

"But her family will be worried, and she is technically in my employ at the school, so I am responsible for her well-being," Robert said firmly. "It is no hardship."

He sipped his tea and allowed the warmth of the fire to seep into his aching bones. There was a lot to accomplish. He needed to send a note to Lucy that would inform her of his whereabouts but not encourage her to venture out into the night to find him.

In truth, knowing his wife and her curiosity, he thought it might be better to address the message to aunt Rose. . . .

The parlor door opened, and Dr. Fletcher looked in. "Sir Robert? Perhaps you might care to come with me."

Chapter 4

I think Robert will be delighted by his gift."
Aunt Rose took off her bonnet and walked over
to the fire to warm her hands. "Mr. Hopewell will
deliver the puppies to the stables on Christmas
Eve, and Mr. Coleman will take care of them
until you can present them to Robert."

"I couldn't decide which puppy was the nicest."
Lucy sighed as she unbuttoned her winter coat
and unwound her long knitted scarf from around
her throat. She sank down into one of the large
wing chairs and held her hands out to the fire.
The drawing room was well lit, and the thick
red curtains were closed against the whistling
draughts. "I do hope Robert won't mind having
two dogs to train."

"They'll keep each other company. What
could be better? And let's be honest, Lucy. Like
most men, especially ex-military ones, my dear
nephew is in his element when ordering things
around. He'll positively revel in it." Rose patted
down her hair. "What time is dinner this evening,
my dear?"

Lucy checked the clock on the mantelpiece.
"We keep country hours and usually dine at six.
Will that suit you? I know you have already
endured a very long day."

Aunt Rose sighed. "I must confess that I am rather tired. Would you mind very much if I had my supper on a tray in my room?"

"Not at all," Lucy hastened to reassure her. "I'll let Foley know what is required." She pulled the bell rope. "Why don't you take yourself upstairs to rest?"

Foley came into the drawing room and bowed as low as he could manage considering his rheumatism and advanced years. It was probably time to pension him off, but neither Lucy nor Robert had the heart to insist upon it.

"Good evening, my lady, ma'am."

"Foley, can you ask Cook to send a tray up to Mrs. Armitage? She will not be dining with us tonight."

"Of course, my lady." Foley bowed and turned to aunt Rose. "Before you go upstairs, ma'am, I have a note for you from Sir Robert."

Rose blinked. "For me?" She glanced at Lucy and took the folded sheet of paper from the butler. After searching for her spectacles in her reticule, she donned them and read the note.

"Robert sends his regrets and says he has been detained at the doctor's house and is not sure whether he will return in time to dine with us." Rose looked over her spectacles at Lucy. "I wonder why he told *me* that and not you."

"Perhaps he didn't want you to feel slighted at

him not being present on your first evening with us."

Even as Lucy made the suggestion, her mind was filling with a hundred possibilities for his decision. Why was he at Dr. Fletcher's house? Was something wrong with him or with Penelope?

She half rose from her seat. "I wonder if I should take the carriage down and—"

"He did add a postscript, which, I suspect, was meant for my eyes only." Rose cleared her throat. " 'Do not allow Lucy to chase after me. I do not wish her to take cold.' "

"*Chase* after him?" Lucy raised her chin. "I am not the kind of wife who insists on hanging on her husband's sleeve. I was merely apprehensive for his well-being, but obviously, my concern is not required." She turned to Foley, who had remained by the door. "I will eat at six, or whenever Cook is ready to serve dinner. Sir Robert may or may not be joining me."

Robert took a deep breath and followed Dr. Fletcher into the back room of his practice where he laid out the dead and performed minor medical procedures. Miss Broomfield lay on the marble slab the doctor had bought cheap from an old butcher's shop.

"I found something interesting when I attempted to undress her," Dr. Fletcher said.

"What was that?"

Robert advanced farther into the room, reluctantly inhaling the stinging odor of lye soap and the infinitesimal hint of death that always permeated the enclosed space. It reminded him all too forcibly of his own experience of narrowly avoiding being butchered by an incompetent surgeon on the battlefield at Waterloo. He had Patrick Fletcher's intervention to thank for saving his leg.

"This." Dr. Fletcher held something up.

"It looks like a hat pin."

"That's exactly what it is. I attempted to remove Miss Broomfield's gown, and this pin had been pushed through the fabric."

"Whereabouts?"

Dr. Fletcher moved to the body and pointed at the back of the neck, where there was a small puncture wound. "Here. I cannot be sure, but I suspect that from this angle, the pin was long enough to penetrate the heart and cause internal bleeding. I'd have to open her up to confirm that, but as that is still frowned upon, you'll have to take my word for it."

Having worked as a military surgeon and having trained in Edinburgh, Dr. Fletcher had seen more of the innards of bodies than most physicians. It was a pity that the medical community in England did not universally agree on the concept of further scientific examination, deeming the human body a sacred and untouchable vessel.

"May I?"

Robert took the hat pin and examined it carefully. There were no obvious markings on the head of the pin, which could've been made by any local blacksmith or even manufactured by one of the new factories in the north. He estimated it was almost twelve inches long and saw it had a sharp point. He gauged the length against Miss Broomfield's upper body and slowly nodded.

"It looks long enough and sharp enough to do some damage. Can we assume that someone came up behind her and stabbed her? She might not have known much about it."

"Yes. As I said earlier, there is no sign that she struggled, and so far I've not seen any evidence of bruising to suggest she was held down in any way." Dr. Fletcher took the pin back and placed it on a tray on the side table. "She also wore a gold cross, which I've set aside with her other clothing. Do we know whom to contact to assume responsibility for the body?"

"I don't, but my wife probably will," Robert said absently. His mind was already busy trying to imagine the scene and what had provoked it. "I wonder who would want to kill Miss Broomfield."

"She was not well liked, Sir Robert, I can tell

you that." Dr. Fletcher covered up the body with a white sheet.

"So I understand, but not liking someone is hardly a motive for murder."

"Miss Broomfield and I had more than one heated discussion about her refusal to understand that the children in her care were not lazy and stupid, but merely tired and sometimes hungry. I disliked her intensely, but I never had the urge to kill her for her heartless opinions."

Robert frowned. "You never mentioned this to me, Patrick."

The doctor shrugged as he washed his hands. "I assumed you had your reasons for employing her, and I didn't wish to add to your problems."

"I wish you had." Robert held the door open for his friend. "I feel as if I've neglected my responsibilities."

"As I said, you have had a lot to deal with recently. If I had really believed she was a danger to any of the children, I would have marched up your drive to make my opinion heard."

"I'm too used to my wife being my eyes and ears in the village." Robert continued down the narrow hallway, through the kitchen, and into the more formal part of the house. "I didn't realize how much I'd come to rely on her."

"Well, Lady Kurland is as formidable as you are in her own way," Dr. Fletcher said diplomatically. "How is she feeling today?"

"She still tires easily and is somewhat low in spirits."

"Which is to be expected, considering the events of last summer." The doctor studied him carefully. "Is there anything in particular you are worrying about?"

Robert paused outside the parlor door and lowered his voice. "I *was* intending to come and speak to you before I was waylaid at the schoolhouse."

"About what?"

"Do you think I should dissuade Lady Kurland from organizing all these yuletide activities?"

His companion smiled. "I'd like to see you try. If Lady Kurland wants to be involved in such events, I would encourage her to do so. It will certainly keep her busy and less likely to dwell on the past."

"I met old Dr. Baker in the village yesterday," Robert said. "He suggested I should forbid all activity, order Lady Kurland to stay in her bedchamber for the next six months, and not let her venture out for any reason at all."

Dr. Fletcher's smile faded. "Firstly, did you ask for his advice?"

"Of *course* not, but—"

"Secondly, can you really imagine *ordering* Lady Kurland to remain secluded for six months?"

Robert considered that. "No."

"With all respect to a fellow practitioner, Dr. Baker is of a generation that believes ladies are delicate hothouse flowers who should be protected and cosseted from every incoming breeze. You and I marched with an army and know that women are far hardier than most men realize."

"Women perhaps, but what about *ladies?*"

Dr. Fletcher raised his eyebrows. "They all have the same anatomy, Sir Robert. In truth, Lady Kurland would've made an admirable officer's wife."

"I suspect you are right."

Dr. Fletcher awkwardly patted Robert's shoulder. "She will regain her strength, I can promise you that. It will take time, but she will get better. By the spring, she will be her old self again."

"Thank you." Robert forced a smile. "I care about her very much." He cleared his throat. "I will find out who Miss Broomfield's next of kin is, and will let you know as soon as possible."

"Thank you."

Dr. Fletcher opened the door into the parlor, where Dermot was sitting with Penelope. At least Josephine appeared to have stopped crying.

Dermot immediately rose to his feet. "Dr. Fletcher's man took your note up to Kurland Hall, sir. There has been no reply."

"Then we should be on our way." Robert

bowed to his hostess. "Thank you for caring for Josephine, Mrs. Fletcher."

"You are most welcome, Sir Robert," Penelope said.

Robert put on his hat and gloves and got into the gig beside Dermot and Josephine. He wished he had taken the opportunity to order Coleman to bring down the closed carriage, as the temperature had dropped considerably. It was, however, nowhere near as cold as the mountainous regions of France that he and his fellow soldiers had navigated during the war, so he didn't complain.

Dermot clicked to the horse, and they set off into the night. If all went well at the Greenwell residence, Robert would be back home by nine, ready to face his wife. He suspected she might have a few pointed questions for him. . . .

The sound of the study door creaking open roused Lucy from her doze by the fire, and she sat bolt upright as Robert came quietly into the room.

"Where have you been?" Lucy demanded.

He regarded her for a long moment before limping over to stand in front of the fire. His expression was drawn, and his face pinched with cold. "Didn't you get my note?"

"Your aunt *Rose* received a note and shared the contents with me, if that is what you mean."

"Did she also tell you why I wrote to her?"

"Because you didn't want me spying on you."

"Hardly that." He gestured at the seat opposite her. "Do you mind if I sit down? It's been a long day, and my leg is aching like the devil."

She waved him to the chair. "It's your house. You may sit whenever you like." She was aware that she might sound a little peevish, but he had deliberately excluded her from whatever had befallen him, and had left her alone to worry.

"Thank you." He contemplated the fire as he settled back into the chair. "It is very cold out there tonight. I think we might have snow on the morrow."

"Indeed." Lucy folded her hands in her lap and waited as patiently as she could for him to continue.

"I went down to the schoolhouse this afternoon to speak to Miss Broomfield. Dermot showed me her only reference and a letter he had just received from her last known position, where, apparently, she had been turned off without a character."

"I *knew* there was something suspicious about her." Lucy sat forward. "Did you dismiss her? Is that why you were delayed?"

"Not exactly." He finally met her gaze. "That was my intention, but when I reached the schoolhouse, someone had got there before me and had put an end to Miss Broomfield's existence."

Lucy stared at him. "You mean she is *dead?*"

"Worse than that. I believe she was murdered. Someone stabbed her with a very long hat pin."

Lucy brought her hand to her mouth. "That is . . . horrible."

"Yes." His blue gaze turned inward. "I understand that she wasn't very well liked, but someone maliciously and deliberately took her life."

Lucy shivered and drew her shawl more closely around her shoulders. "Does she have family in the village?"

"I was going to ask you the same question."

"As I wasn't involved in her hiring, I know very little about her. My father might have some information. I will speak to him tomorrow."

"As will I." Robert sighed and shoved a hand through his hair. "There is the question of the disposal of the body and her possessions."

"I will take care of those matters." Lucy paused. "Perhaps she was simply the victim of a robbery. Did you check to see if anything had been stolen?"

"From what I could tell during my brief inspection, there was no sign of a forced entry or any disruption either in the schoolroom or her private apartment. I have to assume that whoever killed her came in through the front entrance. She was sitting at her desk when she died."

"At her desk?" Lucy frowned. "So either her

91

assailant crept up on her from behind or she knew them and didn't fear them."

"Or both. Dr. Fletcher said the hat pin entered the back of her neck or thereabouts and was angled downward. There was no sign of a struggle." Robert grimaced. "So I would assume that whoever killed her was known to her and was not considered a threat." He cleared his throat. "There is one more thing. . . . She was stabbed in the eye with a quill pen."

Lucy stared at him for a long moment as she struggled to contain her repulsion. "Which somehow makes the killing far more personal than just a random act of violence."

"I agree." Robert reached into his pocket and took out some folded papers. "I found these under her hands on the desk." He passed them over to Lucy.

"He is guilty," Lucy read out. "She deserves to kno—" She looked up at Robert. "What on earth does that mean?"

"I have no idea, but it's the last thing she wrote."

Lucy smoothed a hand over the papers as a hundred thoughts jostled through her mind. Should she tell him about the letter addressed to her, or would that open up a treacherous avenue of conversation that she was unwilling to follow?

"Mrs. Jenkins received an unpleasant letter about Nicholas last week."

92

Robert blinked at her. "What does that have to do with this?"

"Nothing, perhaps, but she was not the only person to receive such a note. I have had similar complaints from several of our villagers this week. One has to wonder whether Miss Broomfield knew anything about those malicious unsigned letters."

Robert raised an eyebrow. "You are rather leaping to conclusions."

"I am aware of that, but there is something"— Lucy reread the words on the paper—"something *odd* about people in our village receiving unpleasant letters, and our schoolmistress being murdered and stabbed in the eye with a quill pen. Wouldn't you at least agree with that?"

"If you say so, my dear." His smile was tired. "Over the years I have learned not to ignore your intuition, but this does seem somewhat far-fetched."

"Then I will have to investigate the matter to my satisfaction." Lucy nodded.

"You will do no such thing," Robert retorted.

"I *beg* your pardon?"

"You are not well enough to rampage around the countryside, searching for a murderer." There was a stubborn set to her husband's jaw, one that Lucy had learned to dread. "I would much prefer it if you focused your considerable abilities on finding Miss Broomfield's family and dealing with her possessions."

"As you wish." Lucy pressed her lips together hard. "I will certainly do that."

"And you will not use this as an excuse to teach in the school, either."

She was not willing to start an argument when he had been kind enough to persuade his aunt to come on an extended visit simply to cheer her up. Such matters could simply be left to another day or conveniently ignored.

She rose from her seat. "I think I will go to bed. I am rather tired."

He stood, as well, and bowed. "I have a few matters to attend to before I can join you." He kissed her fingers. "Sleep well, my dear."

She was almost at the door before he spoke again.

"We can visit your father together after breakfast tomorrow, if that is convenient?"

Lucy turned gratefully back to him. It was a pleasure to enjoy a moment of conversation that wasn't directly related to her health or current mood. "Yes. We can ask your aunt if she wishes to accompany us. My father always enjoys her company."

"When he forgets her 'common' roots."

"He is something of a snob," Lucy sighed.

"As the son of an earl, I suppose he has that right." Robert limped over to his desk. "Although, as the grandson of a wealthy brewer, I am more inclined to be thankful for my family's source of income rather than despising it."

"Are your aunt's children really behaving badly toward her?" Lucy asked.

"Indeed, they are. She gave the girls large enough dowries to marry into the aristocracy, and now they look down on their own mother."

"That is horrible," Lucy said. "I would *never* do that."

"I know."

His smile was so full of warm appreciation, it made her yearn to go back across the room, take his hand, and lead him to bed. She hesitated, her fingers wrapped around the doorknob.

"Are you quite certain that you don't want to come upstairs, Robert? You look rather tired."

His smiled died, and he looked away from her toward the stack of books on his desk. "Alas, I have too much work to do. Good night, my love."

"Good night."

Lucy carefully closed the door and walked along the hallway to the bottom of the main staircase. The house was quiet, but Foley had left two candles at the bottom of the stairs. Lucy took one and made her way up the shallow oak steps, pausing on the first landing to look out at the moonlight streaming in through the diamond-paned windows.

The horrible desire to cry came over her again. There was no getting away from it. Her husband of three years was avoiding her company. It had been months since he'd come to bed at the same time as her. She missed that, missed sharing her last sleepy thoughts with him and lying in the shelter of his arms. . . .

She started walking again. It was not unusual for married couples to maintain separate lifestyles; she had enough relatives in the aristocracy to know *that*. She'd foolishly imagined that she and Robert were different, that they genuinely liked as well as loved each other. But the friction between them . . . The distance seemed wider every day. Even worse, there was no one she could ask about how to bridge the gap, seeing as her best friend was currently on the other side of the divide. . . .

Pushing aside such unproductive and lowering thoughts, Lucy went into her bedchamber and rang the bell for Betty. Tomorrow was going to be a busy day. If she was lucky, she would have no time to worry about anything other than the decent and Christian task of organizing the final affairs of the much-disliked but unfortunately deceased Miss Broomfield.

After sitting down at her dressing table, Lucy removed the pins from her hair. She paused to examine the ones collected in her palm. They were much shorter than the pins used for keeping a hat in place, but were still a useful weapon, if needed. Had Miss Broomfield worn a bonnet?

Lucy didn't think she had ever seen the teacher at church or in her outdoor garb, but it was fairly safe to assume she had owned at least one hat and a long pin.

Who had killed Miss Broomfield? Despite what Robert had said, Lucy believed there was information to be gathered about the unusual circumstances of her death . . . circumspectly, *of course,* seeing as her husband did not want her to involve herself in such matters.

The coincidence of the quill pen and the malicious letters could not be ignored, either— although Robert was right to suggest she should not jump to conclusions. If there were other unfinished letters in Miss Broomfield's possession or any evidence of wrongdoing, then Lucy would find them tomorrow.

"Good evening, my lady," Betty called out cheerfully as she entered the room. "Isn't it lovely that Mrs. Armitage is here to stay?"

"It is, indeed." Lucy turned to smile at her maid.

Betty picked up Lucy's hairbrush. "Now let's get you ready for bed."

Chapter 5

"Welcome, my dear Mrs. Armitage!" Lucy's father rose from behind his desk and came to greet the new arrivals. He was in his study, dealing with his usual pile of morning correspondence. As something of a renowned amateur antiquarian, who regularly published articles on obscure topics, he was often sought out for his opinion.

"You did not tell me that Sir Robert's aunt would be favoring you with a visit, Lucy."

"It was something of a surprise to me, as well, sir." Lucy smiled at her father and then at Rose. "But a delightful one."

"Indeed. Mayhap Mrs. Armitage will help put some color back in your cheeks and stop you from turning into one of those ladies who lie around complaining of ill health."

Lucy's smile faltered. "I have no intention of becoming like that, Father, I can assure you."

He patted her cheek. "Of course you don't, my dear. I was merely jesting. You know your duty is to provide Sir Robert with an heir. I am confident that if you persevere, you will achieve your aim in due course, and with God's blessing."

Robert cleared his throat. "Her *duty* is to be

well and happy, and to continue to brighten my existence. That is all I require of her."

The rector frowned. "But your family have resided at Kurland Hall for almost five hundred years! You cannot wish for such continuity to be extinguished."

"I do *have* a cousin, sir."

"A scoundrel who has been discredited and forced to leave the country." The rector shook his head. "Hardly the sort of man that any family would wish to see ensconced in Kurland Hall."

Before Robert could answer him, Aunt Rose smiled at the rector and placed her hand on his arm, then guided him gently toward the door and the parlor beyond. "And how have you been, Mr. Harrington? You look very well."

"Thank you, ma'am. I do try to keep myself in good health."

Her father almost preened at the compliment, reminding Lucy of how adept Rose was at dealing with difficult men. It was a skill Lucy lacked, particularly at the moment. She slowly let out her breath, aware that Robert was still holding the door open for her.

She gathered up her skirts and her courage and went to go past him.

His fingers closed gently on her upper arm, stopping her progress. "I meant what I said, you know."

She looked up into his blue eyes and couldn't

look away. A thousand questions threatened to overwhelm her, but she swallowed them all down. "Thank you."

He dropped a kiss on her nose and released her. "You are welcome. Let's give them a moment to chat, and then we can share the real reason for our visit."

With some difficulty, Lucy found her voice. "I'll pop into the kitchen and speak to the new housemaid. I fear she will be responsible for dealing with the disorder and clutter the twins bring with them when they arrive home."

"Poor woman." Robert shuddered.

"Indeed. I might suggest to Anna that she consider employing another housemaid over the holidays." Lucy frowned. "But it is hard to find anyone at such short notice and for a brief period of time."

"Then why don't we lend her one of our maids?" Robert suggested. "I'm always tripping over them at the hall."

"That is an excellent idea." She smiled at him. "Betty will know just who to ask."

Robert waited until Lucy was safely in the kitchen, and then turned back to the parlor, his smile dying. Damn Mr. Harrington for bringing up the subject of children. He really should know better, seeing as his own wife, Lucy's mother, had died in childbirth. The rector was remarkably blind to the distress he caused his oldest daughter. Mayhap it was time for Robert to have a quiet word with him.

He went into the parlor and bowed to Anna Harrington, who was dispensing tea to her father and his aunt. Her sunny nature was always a balm after the rector's blundering heartiness. She was a beautiful woman, and he knew Lucy worried excessively about her future prospects.

"Good morning, Miss Anna." He accepted a cup of tea from her and sat down on the couch.

"Is it true that the school is closed?" Anna asked. "Is Miss Broomfield unwell?"

Robert put down his tea. He might as well get it over with. "That's actually why I came to speak to you both today."

"Does she need help?" Anna sat forward, as if ready to fly instantly to Miss Broomfield's aid. "I have some restorative chicken broth and plenty of barley water to offer her if she is feeling unwell."

"Unfortunately, I don't think that will help." Robert turned his gaze toward the rector. "I regret to inform you that Miss Broomfield is dead."

"Good Lord," the rector said.

"Oh, my goodness!" Anna gasped. "But how?"

"I went to the schoolhouse late yesterday afternoon with the intention of speaking to her about her references and discovered she had been killed," Robert answered her.

"Killed?" The rector's face turned red. "As

opposed to dying of regrettable but natural causes? Are you quite certain?"

"Yes. At my request, Dr. Fletcher attended the body and pronounced her dead."

"But she was a young woman. Whatever happened?" Anna whispered.

"She was stabbed with a long hat pin. Dr. Fletcher believes that was enough to kill her." Robert didn't mention what else had occurred. There was no need to further distress the Harringtons. "He has the body in his keeping, if you wish to see her, Mr. Harrington."

The rector shuddered and patted his face with his handkerchief. "I'll certainly send my curate to speak a word of prayer over her departed soul."

Robert looked up as Lucy came into the room and took the seat beside him. "I was just telling your father the sad news about Miss Broomfield."

"It is indeed distressing," Lucy replied. "Do you know much about her family, Father?"

"Why should I?" The rector frowned. "She isn't one of my regular village parishioners."

"But you recommended her for the position at the school," Robert reminded him.

"Did I? I seem to remember that when the previous teacher left so abruptly, there was an urgent need for a replacement. At your urging, Lucy, I wrote to some of my university acquaintances in Cambridge for recommendations and advice."

"That's correct, sir." Robert looked encouragingly at the rector. "Would it be possible for you to share the name of the person who recommended Miss Broomfield?"

The rector looked perturbed. "I can certainly look through my correspondence from earlier this year, but pray, do not expect a speedy answer."

Anna spoke up. "I will help you look, Father. I have cataloged all your correspondence, so it shouldn't be too difficult to ascertain exactly who answered your plea for help." She nodded to Robert. "I will get the information to you as swiftly as possible, sir."

"Thank you," Robert said. "In the meantime, Lucy will ensure that all Miss Broomfield's possessions are gathered up and accounted for, in case someone steps forward to claim them."

"But what about the fact that she was killed?" Anna looked around at them all. "Should we be worried about *that?* Has our village suddenly become unsafe?"

"I will make certain that our village is protected. I also intend to find out if anyone has seen any loiterers or had anything stolen recently," Robert said firmly. "You can depend on my complete attention to this matter."

While Lucy dealt with the school, he intended to talk to every household in the village and the surrounding area by the end of the day. It was a small community, and the presence of a stranger would be noted and commented on. But like Lucy, he had a sense that whoever had killed Miss Broomfield had done so for more than simple financial gain. If his instinct was correct, finding out who it was might take quite a while. . . .

"Shall I drop you and Aunt Rose at the school-house, Lucy?"

"Yes, please."

Lucy tied the ribbons of her bonnet and allowed her husband to help her into her thick winter coat. The earlier rain had turned to sleet, and the sky was an unforgiving black. She was glad they had finally changed over to the closed carriage, but she felt sorry for Coleman, who had to sit on the box.

As they approached the carriage Robert was still talking. "I'll go back to the house, find Dermot, and start asking whether anyone else saw a man loitering around outside the schoolhouse yesterday."

Lucy blinked at him. "You *saw* someone?"

"I can't say that I did. Josephine told me that *she* had seen someone lurking there when she returned for her scarf."

Lucy paused on the step of the carriage, her hand in Robert's. "Josephine Blake?"

"Yes. She was at the schoolhouse when we arrived, and had already discovered Miss Broom-field's body."

"The poor girl! Why didn't you mention this before?" Lucy asked.

"Why should I have?" Robert asked. "She was unharmed. Dermot and I escorted her home to the Greenwells' and told her guardians what had occurred."

"Then I will certainly pay them a visit this afternoon and make sure that she has recovered from the shock." Lucy entered the carriage and took the seat next to Aunt Rose. "It must have been a terrible sight for such a young girl."

"How old is she exactly?" he asked.

"Almost sixteen."

"I would've thought her younger. She is quite petite."

Robert got into the carriage, making it creak and sway. He settled opposite Lucy, his damaged leg sticking out and catching her skirts. With a groan, he rubbed his knee and eased his booted foot back. "I do apologize. This weather is hard on my old bones."

Lucy made a mental note to ensure there were plenty of hot cloths and heat sources available at the manor house that evening to ease Robert's pain.

Within a few minutes the carriage stopped outside the schoolhouse. Lucy leaned across to release the door before her husband could do so.

"Don't get out, Robert. Aunt Rose and I can

manage perfectly well. We can easily walk back to the house from here."

"As you wish."

The mere fact that he didn't contradict her told Lucy that he was in considerable pain. She considered suggesting he leave the questioning of the villagers to Dermot but suspected he would make short work of that idea. No one doubted Robert's dedication to his tenants and those he considered in his care.

Lucy started up the steps to the schoolhouse, the key Robert had given her in one gloved hand. The door opened with a loud creak, and she quickly stepped inside. Her eyes adjusted to the dimness of the light. Apart from a couple of dropped woolen mittens on the muddy flagstone floor and what appeared to be a hat, the cloakroom was deserted.

The inner door that led into the large classroom was ajar, and Lucy pushed it open and went in. Coldness struck at her, and she hastened to set a fire in the large hearth and lit a couple of the lamps. The room was immaculately tidy and smelled of damp wool, children, and a hint of burned wood ash from the stove.

Aunt Rose, who had followed her in, walked around the perimeter, where Miss Broomfield had placed a number of embroidered biblical texts promising hellfire and damnation. "It is a fine building, Lucy. You and Robert did well."

"I would agree with you if we could have better luck with our teachers." Lucy straightened, brushed her hands over her coat, and then took off her gloves. "It is bitterly cold in here."

Rose opened the door at the back of the room. "I assume Miss Broomfield's quarters are through here?"

"There is a teacher's study and a kitchen then a staircase to the second level," Lucy called out, her attention caught by the desk where, apparently, Miss Broomfield had been slain. On one corner sat a stack of slates next to four well-thumbed copies of the Bible. On another a large inkwell held down several pieces of paper. The inkwell was missing a quill pen.

Holding one of the lamps, Lucy approached the desk and methodically opened the drawers and removed all the contents. She took the pile of items through into the kitchen at the rear of the property.

"Your Miss Broomfield was certainly a very tidy person," Aunt Rose commented as she investigated the kitchen cupboards and pantry. "I shudder to imagine what anyone would think, should I die unexpectedly. I would leave a *horrible* mess behind me. Should I remove the perishable food or leave it for later?"

"I'll send someone down to clean the rooms more thoroughly," Lucy replied as she set the contents of the desk on the kitchen table. "At the moment I think we should concentrate on assembling Miss Broomfield's personal effects and bringing them up to the hall."

"As you wish." Aunt Rose wandered through into the other room and studied the bookshelves. "It is rather hard to see anything in here on this gloomy day. The light is much better at Kurland Hall."

The fire in the closed stove in the kitchen was also out, but Lucy made no effort to rekindle it. The thought of carefully going through every single book in the study and ascertaining whether it belonged to the teacher or the school was daunting, especially in the cold. Perhaps that could wait for another day, or she could ask Rebecca or Josephine to complete the task for her.

"You are right. It is impossible to see anything in here," Lucy agreed with a sigh. "Mayhap we should concentrate on the apartment upstairs."

She went up the narrow staircase and paused on the landing. There were three doors off the small space, and they led to a bedroom, a sitting room, and a large storage cupboard with a tin bath hanging on the wall. There was an outhouse attached to an exterior wall of the building and a separate one for the children.

"Where do you wish to start?" Aunt Rose had come up behind her.

"The sitting room?" Lucy moved forward.

"There are more books in here, which I assume must belong to Miss Broomfield."

"And a very nice sewing box." Aunt Rose paused to admire the walnut-veneered box that sat beside the fireplace and the single chair. "It looks quite old. Perhaps she inherited it from her mother."

Lucy squinted at the etched brass plate on the lid of the box. "I can't read the name, can you?" She scratched at the corner. "That might be an *H*."

Rose laughed. "If you cannot see it, I don't stand a chance."

Lucy opened the box, pulled out a piece of almost finished embroidery, and read the text. "And I will judge him with pestilence, and with blood, and with violent rain, and vast hailstones: I will rain fire and brimstone upon him, and upon his army, and upon the many nations that are with him. Ezekiel thirty-eight, twenty-two."

Rose shuddered. "I'd hardly want to look at *that* over my mantelpiece every day." She continued her inspection of the room, pausing at the fireplace mantelpiece to check the clock.

"Have you noticed something odd, Aunt Rose?" Lucy asked slowly. "There are no family portraits, pictures, or even any ornaments."

"You're right." Rose spun around. "How odd. Perhaps we'll find some in her bedroom. That is a more private space."

They walked through to the next room, which was even darker than the sitting room.

"I don't see anything personal in here, either," Rose commented.

"Maybe she was estranged from her family." Lucy eyed the immaculately made bed. There was a washstand with a bowl and a jug standing beside it, a chest of drawers, and a cupboard built into the wall next to the chimney breast. She opened the cupboard door and studied the clothes folded neatly on the shelves inside. The prevailing color was black. The remaining space was filled with a small dressing table and chair. "Let's strip the sheets and place all her other possessions on the mattress."

Rose took off her pelisse and rolled up her sleeves. Despite her immense wealth, she was never averse to helping out with the most mundane of tasks.

As Lucy sorted through Miss Broomfield's possessions, it became apparent that the school-teacher had lived without much joy in her life. Her choice of reading material was mainly sermons and other edifying works, and even her needlework had a biblical bent, drawn mainly from the Old Testament.

It was the sort of joyless existence Lucy had once feared for herself. Although many would approve of the teacher's rigid morals and the lack of frivolity in her life, her choices evoked an unexpected wave of sympathy in Lucy's heart. Why had Miss Broomfield ended up alone and apparently friendless in a small village in Hertfordshire?

Lucy folded a darned petticoat and added it to the pile on the bed. The teacher had three everyday dresses in black and one church dress in dark blue.

"From the discoloration of the buttons, I suspect Miss Broomfield must have dyed these dresses at some point," Aunt Rose said.

Lucy paused in her work to consider Rose's announcement. "I wonder if she was in mourning. Not everyone can afford to have a black gown made for them. I wonder if she lost her betrothed in the recent wars."

"I suppose that could be possible," Rose agreed. "But if she *was* in mourning, one might think she would still have her sweetheart's miniature or some kind of picture of him close to her bed."

"Maybe her family didn't approve of her choice, and she wasn't allowed to have any reminders of him."

"But as she has clearly abandoned her family, why would she hide her allegiances now?" Rose pointed out.

"It certainly is a puzzle." Lucy checked the cupboard and noticed a box on the shelf, behind the last pair of walking boots. She took out the boots and picked up the box, which was much heavier than she had anticipated. "Whatever is in here?"

"Her golden treasures?" Rose smiled as Lucy put the sturdy box down on the bed. "Perhaps we have misjudged her, and she simply did not have the time to decide where to place all her personal items, and they are all in here."

"She was employed for at least five months," Lucy objected. "One might think she would have settled in by then." She attempted to open the box. "It's locked."

"Then I wonder where she put the key."

"I'll check in the cupboard." Lucy made a thorough search of the small space. "I can't find anything in here."

"Then we will simply take it to the hall and see if one of Robert's staff can open it for us. I believe Foley is rather adept at unlocking doors."

"Only because he is used to the vagaries of the locks at Kurland Hall. I swear, there is not one single keyhole that matches another throughout the whole house." With a sigh, Lucy abandoned her efforts to open the box. "I'll send someone down to pick up all these things so we can catalog them at our leisure. Is there anything we might have missed?"

"I don't think so." Rose shook her head. "Not unless Miss Broomfield had a penchant for hiding things away."

"Who knows what she might have done?"

Lucy's gaze settled on the wooden chest. "From all accounts, she made no effort to make friends in the village or share confidences. Perhaps she didn't unpack because she had already decided to leave."

"I suppose that is possible, but from what Robert told us, I doubt she would have an easy time getting another teaching post without a reference."

"Unless she intended to go back to the gentleman my father knows who recommended her. I can't wait to find out what *he* has to say about this matter." Lucy stood and brushed down her skirts. "We should get back to the hall. I'd like to visit Josephine Blake at the Greenwells' this afternoon."

Rose put on her coat and followed Lucy down into the kitchen. "Do you feel well enough to walk back, my dear? Or should I go ahead and ask Coleman to bring down the gig?"

Lucy peered out at the gloomy skies. "If we leave now and escape the rain, I'm certain I'll be fine."

To Lucy's relief, Rose didn't press the matter and merely buttoned her coat, picked up her umbrella, and followed Lucy out to the schoolroom. After making sure the fire and candles were out Lucy locked the outside door. They proceeded past the duck pond and into the High Street of Kurland St. Mary village. It was a gentle uphill walk of less than a mile, one that Lucy had made a thousand times before.

Their progress was slowed by the many people who stopped to welcome Rose back to the village, and by those who wanted to ask after Lucy's health. It was surprisingly hard to smile through some of the more pointed comments, but Lucy had learned to endure the well-meaning concern. To her relief, a lot of the chatter was directed at the unexpected closure of the school. She had no intention of telling anyone what had happened until she had spoken to Robert.

"Lady Kurland?"

Rebecca Hall, the blacksmith's daughter who worked at the school, came running out of the smithy. She wiped her hands on her apron and curtsied to Lucy.

"Good morning, Rebecca." Lucy lowered her voice. "Are you wondering why the school is closed?"

"Yes, my lady. Is Miss Broomfield unwell?" Rebecca's hair was disheveled, and her cheeks were reddened with cold. "She was in a very bad mood the last time I saw her—almost snapped my head off for putting too much wood on the fire."

"I would appreciate it if you could meet me at the schoolhouse tomorrow morning at ten o'clock, Rebecca," Lucy said. "Will your mother be able to spare you?"

"Yes, my lady. I'm not usually there during

the week, so she's been right glad to have an extra pair of hands with the little ones." Rebecca grimaced. "Not that I like it much, seeing as I don't get paid, but family is family."

Lucy had always admired Rebecca's forthright honesty and knew she could rely on her to keep a secret.

"Then I will expect you tomorrow at ten."

Rebecca curtsied again and grinned. "Yes, my lady." She drew her shawl over her head and set off toward the warmth of the smithy and her family home behind it.

By the time Lucy and Rose walked past the Queen's Head coaching inn and turned onto the main thoroughfare that led to Lower Kurland and Kurland St. Anne, Lucy was quite fatigued. The gateposts leading to Kurland Hall were a welcome sight, although the long elm-lined drive looked endless, winding away through the trees and disappearing into the gloom.

She straightened her shoulders and looked directly ahead, aware that Rose, who was at least twenty years older than her, was still chatting merrily and showing not the slightest hint of tiredness.

"Almost there, Lucy dear." Rose patted her sleeve. "A nice cup of tea and one of Cook's currant buns will soon restore our strength."

"I do hope so," Lucy replied. "If I can manage not to fall into a doze over the teapot."

"Nothing wrong with taking a little nap when the occasion arises." Rose winked at her. "I do it all the time. Living alone has its advantages."

"Do you miss your family?"

"I miss what I had when my children were young and Mr. Armitage was still alive." Rose sighed. "After his early death, I fear I overindulged our children, and now they scarcely have a good word to say about me. I overheard one of my son-in-laws referring to me as 'common but useful' on my last visit. This was just after I had paid his latest set of gambling debts because my daughter begged me to save her from ruin."

"Then I certainly wouldn't be offering to pay them again," Lucy said indignantly, her own tiredness forgotten. "What an ungrateful *rogue*."

"Indeed," Rose agreed. "It is such a relief to be here with you and Robert, where I am liked for myself and not asked for anything but the pleasure of my company."

"Your children are very foolish. If I ever come across them speaking ill of you, I will defend you with my last breath," Lucy said.

"Thank you. Robert said you were formidable. I must admit, I would quite like to see you march up to my son-in-law and ring a peal over his head." Rose pointed at the door into the walled kitchen garden. "If we go through here, will we reach the main house more quickly?"

"Yes. I was just about to suggest it."

Lucy unlatched the gate and walked through into the vegetable and soft fruit garden, which was currently under straw, waiting for winter to be over. The high brick walls kept out the rising wind and deadened all sound. It was a very peaceful spot and one that Lucy often sought out when she needed to think.

"I'll speak to Cook, organize one of the maids to go down with the gig to pick up Miss Broomfield's things, and then we can go to the Greenwells'." Lucy shook off her tiredness.

"Don't forget our pot of tea and a bite to eat." Rose opened the kitchen door, and the voices of the busy staff floated out, disturbing the quietness. "The nap, I suspect we can manage for ourselves."

For the first time that day, Lucy smiled as she stepped into the comforting darkness of the house. She must remember to thank Robert again. His aunt Rose was better for her spirits than any tonic she had ever been prescribed.

Chapter 6

It had been a remarkably frustrating morning. Robert climbed back into the gig and waited for Dermot to join him. They'd spoken to almost all the villagers and visited several of the outlying farms. Some people *had* seen strangers in the village, but none of them could agree on exactly when or what the persons had looked like.

Dermot picked up the reins of the gig. "Shall we return to Kurland Hall, Sir Robert?"

"We might as well." Robert sighed, and his breath condensed in the cold air. "We have achieved nothing of import and have probably caused more worries than we have calmed fears."

"I can't see how we could have avoided that, sir." Dermot clicked to the horse, and they moved off. "And it might make some people think about what they *might* have seen and remember more."

"I always appreciate your optimism, Dermot." Robert laid his cane against the seat. His thigh was cramping again, and his disposition was not inclined toward charity. "I am also constantly amazed at how little people notice what is going on around them."

"I did think of one more place we might ask, sir."

"Where is that?"

"The Queen's Head."

"An excellent suggestion. We can do that this afternoon. I want to make sure Lady Kurland and my aunt have returned from the schoolhouse."

"Of course, sir." Dermot took the turn into the drive and pointed up ahead. "I see one of the farm carts. Do you want me to catch it up in case Lady Kurland is on board?"

"There's no need."

Robert knew what his reception would be if his wife thought he was mollycoddling her. Sometimes she made it very difficult for him to express his concern, and while he admired her courage, he sometimes wished she'd let down her guard and allow him to comfort her.

Dermot took the gig around to the stables. Robert walked in through the front door and discovered Foley passing through the entrance hall with a full tray of tea.

"Is that for her ladyship?" Robert asked.

"Yes, sir. She and Mrs. Armitage are in the drawing room."

"Then I'll take it through to her." Robert lifted the tray out of Foley's hands, and hoped he wouldn't spill it on the way due to his uneven gait. "What time is luncheon?"

"In half an hour, sir." Foley bowed.

"Set a place for Mr. Fletcher, as well, please."

Robert went through into the drawing room and

discovered his wife and his aunt sitting on either side of the fireplace.

"Robert!" Rose smiled at him. "What a pleasant surprise."

He set the tray carefully on the table beside his aunt, surreptitiously gauging the paleness of Lucy's complexion. "I thought I'd join you for lunch. Did you manage to gather Miss Broomfield's belongings together?"

"Indeed, we did." Lucy reached for the teacup Rose offered her. "We decided to bring everything up to the hall as it was far too cold to sort it all out in the schoolhouse."

"That sounds like a sensible idea." Robert thanked Rose for the tea. "Did you find anything interesting?"

"Nothing that would indicate why someone would want to kill her," Lucy replied.

"No incriminating notes, no full confession?"

"Unfortunately not."

There was a spark of interest in Lucy's eyes, which Robert hadn't seen for quite a while. It was a pity that her interest was roused by a murder he had no intention of allowing her to investigate.

"As you well know, Robert, such matters often take time to unravel." Lucy sipped her tea.

"Indeed. What are your plans for this afternoon?"

"I intend to go and visit Josephine Blake."

"Then I might join you. I need to speak to Mr.

Greenwell about the village party, and we can introduce them to Aunt Rose."

"Splendid." Rose put down her cup. "Are they a nice family?"

"They are pleasant enough," Robert said. "Mr. Greenwell was abroad for several years in the diplomatic service. His wife preferred to let their country house and reside close to her family in south London. Now that he is between postings, they decided to open up the house in Lower Kurland again and are considering the possibility of staying there full-time."

"I wonder why he did that when his daughters are of marriageable age?" Lucy asked.

"What does that have to do with anything?" Robert frowned.

"My dear sir, if you wish to marry off your daughters, retiring to the countryside is not the best way to help them meet desirable suitors." Lucy placed her cup on the tray. "Although it might explain why the Greenwell ladies are so miserable and determined to interfere in the relationships of *others*."

Robert turned to his aunt. "Lucy thinks the oldest Greenwell girl—"

"Margaret," Lucy said.

"Has her eye on Nicholas Jenkins."

Rose sat back. "Well, if she has any sense, of course she has! He is the most eligible man in the county."

"And he is enamored of my sister, Anna," Lucy said firmly.

"Then she had better make up her mind to take him," Robert said, rising as the gong summoning them to luncheon sounded. "Or perhaps Miss Margaret will tempt him into changing his mind."

"If he *is* that fickle, then he doesn't deserve Anna."

"I'll be sure to remind him of that if he seeks my counsel."

"Please do."

Lucy took Robert's proffered hand and stood up. He was pleased to see that she was looking quite flushed and animated. If he could just keep her thoughts on her sister, Anna's romantic entanglements, and away from pursuing Miss Broomfield's killer, he would be a very happy man.

As soon as Lucy stepped into the drawing room, the entire Greenwell family converged on her and Robert with a mixture of enthusiastic greetings. She suspected that after the excitement of London, their current social existence was sadly lacking, and that any visitor would be welcome. Greenwell Manor was a small compact house built at the end of the previous century and situated on extensive grounds. It stood on the edge of the hamlet of Lower Kurland. It had been rented out for many years to a retired colonel and his wife, who had recently died.

Robert made his bow to the womenfolk and then settled into a conversation with Mr. Greenwell and his eldest son, while Lucy and Rose sat down with the ladies. Lucy introduced them to Rose and listened patiently as they discussed mutual London acquaintances and the pleasure of living in a smaller community.

"My dear Lady Kurland, it is so kind of you to bring Mrs. Armitage to visit us," Mrs. Greenwell said. "Did you come to discuss the details of the upcoming ball?"

"Actually, I came to inquire as to how Josephine is feeling today." Lucy hoped she concealed her surprise.

"Josephine?" Mrs. Greenwell looked around, as if she wondered whom on earth Lucy was talking about. "It was very kind of Sir Robert to bring her home yesterday. She did not deserve such attention."

Lucy raised her eyebrows. "You would have preferred her to walk home in the dark after suffering such a shock?"

"She does not generally walk all the way, Lady Kurland," Mrs. Greenwell objected. "She gets a ride from one of the local farmers who deliver milk to Kurland St. Mary in the late afternoon and then returns with him to our village."

"I doubt even your farmer would have waited

for her yesterday," Lucy replied. "Josephine was very distressed when Sir Robert found her."

"Being in the presence of a . . . deceased person must indeed have been worrisome for her. But she is a child with very little imagination who has already nursed her own mother through a life-ending illness. I doubt she was as upset as you might imagine."

"I would still like to speak to her, if that is possible." Lucy tried to maintain her polite smile. "I might also need her continued help as we sort out the schoolroom."

"Oh, well, if she can be useful to you, Lady Kurland, then of *course* you must see her." Mrs. Greenwell looked over at her younger daughter. "Amanda, will you go and find Josephine and ask her to come to the drawing room?"

"Yes, Mama."

While they waited, Lucy accepted a cup of tea and allowed the Greenwells and Rose to divert the conversation to more conventional subjects. The occasional burst of laughter coming from the gentlemen indicated that her husband was not encountering the same obstacles as she was with the female members of the Greenwell family.

When Josephine appeared in the doorway, Lucy rose to her feet. The girl's black hair was tied back from her face, and there were purple shadows under her blue eyes. Lucy had a sense that if she attempted to talk to Josephine with

Mrs. Greenwell present, she would not receive the assurances she required.

"I'm sure you don't want to hear Josephine repeat the story of her ordeal again." Lucy smiled at her hostess as the youngest daughter reclaimed her seat. "Perhaps I might speak to her alone?"

"But—" Margaret started to speak and then went quiet after a sharp gesture from her mother.

"That would be perfectly acceptable." Mrs. Greenwell pointed toward the far end of the drawing room, where there was a pianoforte and a small upright couch. "Will that suffice? If you need my assistance on any matter, then I am easily within reach."

"Thank you." Lucy walked over to Josephine, who was looking not only tired but also unsurprisingly apprehensive, and took her arm. "How are you feeling this morning, my dear?"

"Quite well, my lady." Josephine lowered her voice. "I did have some bad dreams about . . . *her* . . . you know."

Having seen her own share of dead bodies, Lucy could only sympathize. She sat down beside the girl on the satin-covered couch, aware of Mrs. Greenwell's curious gaze but determined to ignore it.

"Can you tell me what happened yesterday?" Lucy asked gently. "I know you have already spoken to Sir Robert, but sometimes one remembers things *after* the event that are easily forgotten during the emergency itself."

"I am more than happy to tell you everything I can, my lady," Josephine said. "Has Sir Robert found out who did it yet?"

"Not quite yet." Lucy hastened to reassure her. "But I can assure you that he will do everything in his power to apprehend the person who killed Miss Broomfield." She paused. "Are you concerned about your own safety? You did say you saw a man loitering around the back of the school when you reentered the building."

"Yes, but what if he *saw* me?" Josephine gave a convulsive shiver. "What if he thinks I know him?"

"Did you see him that well?" Lucy asked doubtfully. "If his features were indistinct to you, then it is doubtful that he saw you any more clearly."

"I suppose that is true." Josephine didn't look convinced. "All I can remember is that he was tall and wore a cap and carried something that looked like a cudgel in his hand."

"A cudgel? Perhaps he intended to break into the school and discovered the doors were unlocked and he could just walk in." Lucy patted Josephine's knee. "Are you quite certain there was no one else in the schoolhouse when you entered the cloakroom?"

Josephine's gaze became distant, as if she was

reliving the scene. "It was eerily quiet. That's what made me nervous. It is usually such a noisy place, what with the children playing and Miss Broomfield shouting. . . ." She shook her head. "I don't think there was anyone else there, but I suppose there *could've* been someone hiding in the kitchen."

"When you approached Miss Broomfield's desk, did you notice if that rear door was open or closed?"

Josephine frowned. "I *think* it was ajar, but I cannot be certain. It felt like there was a draught blowing through the whole building. I knew Miss Broomfield wouldn't like that. She was always on at us to shut the doors and keep the heat in."

Knowing how expensive it was to heat the schoolhouse, Lucy couldn't help but commend Miss Broomfield's diligence, in that matter at least.

"How was Miss Broomfield's disposition earlier that day?"

"She seemed rather distracted." Josephine bit her lip. "I don't want to get into trouble for saying the wrong thing and speaking ill of the dead, but she was very hard to please. Rebecca and I spent most of our day protecting the little ones from her."

"She was shouting at them?"

"Shouting and laying about with her cane." Josephine rolled up her sleeve to reveal a livid red welt. "I caught this one when I tried to stop her beating little Tommy Higgins."

Lucy stared at the scar, her emotions in turmoil. With every damning word Josephine spoke, her vague sympathy for the deceased rapidly diminished.

"So she was obviously upset about something." Lucy paused to frame her next question. "Did she behave any differently after the children had gone home?"

Josephine went still. "Now that I think about it, she insisted that Rebecca and I finish our work and leave as quickly as possible. That's one of the reasons why I was scared to go back for my scarf."

Lucy considered the girl. "Were you not afraid of missing your ride home if you returned to the school?"

"No, because Miss Broomfield insisted that we leave earlier than usual. I knew that if I hurried, I would be able to go back, find my scarf, and still meet Mr. Mathias in the village." Josephine let out her breath. "I wish I *hadn't* gone back."

"I'm sure you do." Lucy smiled sympa-thetically. Josephine didn't look anything like the Greenwell family, and Lucy wondered anew at the connection between them. "I was hoping that you might be willing to continue your work at the school over the next few days, but

I quite understand if the thought of returning is unpleasant for you."

Josephine gave a quick glance over her shoulder and lowered her voice. "I should *like* to continue at the school, but I'm not sure if Mrs. Greenwell will allow me to do so."

"Don't worry about that, my dear." Lucy was fairly certain she could encourage Mrs. Greenwell to comply with her more than reasonable request. "I will ask her for permission."

At that, Lucy rose to her feet and went back to the group clustered around the fireplace. Josephine curtsied and disappeared back through the door, possibly to avoid having to speak to Mrs. Greenwell.

"Thank you so much for letting me see Josephine, ma'am." Lucy took the seat next to Rose. "I do hope you will allow her to help me set matters straight in the school before Christmas is upon us."

"I'm sure she would be delighted to help," Mrs. Greenwell said. "She has some notion of becoming a governess herself in two years, when she is eighteen."

"A worthy occupation and one to which I think she will be well suited," Lucy agreed. "It is a pity that she is a little too young to take over *our* village school."

Mrs. Greenwell chuckled. "I doubt she will ever have the authority to manage a whole class,

Lady Kurland. She is far too self-effacing. Her mother was the same."

"You knew her mother?"

"Indeed. The woman's husband was distantly related to Mr. Greenwell, and when she fell on hard times, he felt an obligation to offer her and her daughter a home."

From Mrs. Greenwell's acid tone, Lucy deduced that she hadn't felt quite as welcoming or charitable toward the family as her spouse had.

"It was very good of you to take them in," Lucy said, hastening to agree with her hostess. "I'm sure that Josephine is grateful for your kindness."

"She certainly does not give herself airs or consider herself part of the family," Mrs. Greenwell said. "She knows her place."

"Indeed," Lucy murmured. "I'll send someone to collect her tomorrow morning at ten, if that will be convenient?"

"She is quite capable of walking two miles, my lady, but if you insist on cossetting her, I'll make certain she is ready."

Robert glanced over to see that Lucy had resumed her place with the ladies and that Josephine had left the drawing room. He could only guess why his wife had decided it was necessary to speak to the girl alone, but he already had his suspicions.

Mr. Greenwell cleared his throat. "Sad business about that teacher, eh, Sir Robert? And for the gal to find the body . . ." He shook his head. "She was quite shaken by the discovery, I can tell you that."

"I'm not surprised. Death is never pleasant."

"You were in the cavalry during the recent conflicts, were you not?" Mr. Greenwell asked.

"Yes. I reached the rank of major in the Prince Regent's own Tenth Hussars."

"And I understand you were ennobled by the prince himself."

Robert tried to hide a wince. "Hardly ennobled, but I am now a baronet through His Highness's good graces."

"And well deserved, too, if the stories I have heard are correct." Mr. Greenwell finished his brandy and set the glass down on the sideboard. "Will you shut the school down permanently now that you have no teacher, or will you advertise for a new one?"

"As the school is something of a special project of mine and Lady Kurland's, I doubt we intend to close it. I have a very strong belief that education for the masses can lead only to the betterment of all."

"A radical notion that many of your class would disagree with, I suspect." Mr. Greenwell's brown eyes twinkled. "I myself having traveled much around this world, and I consider an educated nation a formidable one."

"Then perhaps you might be interested in

joining our school board?" Robert asked. "As you might imagine, finding sponsors for such an enterprise in a rural environment isn't always easy."

"I would be delighted to do so." Mr. Greenwell bowed. "Perhaps you and Lady Kurland would accept my invitation to join us for dinner this coming Friday so that we could discuss the matter further?"

"That would be most agreeable." Robert paused. "However, I must warn you that my wife is an equal partner in this venture and has some very decided opinions of her own."

"I've heard that Lady Kurland is a force to be reckoned with from many admirers, Sir Robert. I would be happy to hear her speak on matters that are also close to my heart."

"Excellent." Robert took another glance toward his wife and saw she was rising from her seat and looking pointedly in his direction. "I will confirm the dinner invitation with Lady Kurland and let you know if we are available."

"Thank you." Mr. Greenwell bowed. "It has been a pleasure speaking with you, Sir Robert."

"Likewise." Robert bowed in return.

His only wish was that his host had sat down, allowing Robert to do the same. Standing in one spot for almost half an hour was never good for his damaged leg. He had to lean heavily on his cane as he made his way across to Lucy, all too aware that the Greenwell ladies were staring at him with varying degrees of disgust and sympathy.

"Are you ready, my dear?" he asked Lucy, who responded with a bright smile and a characteristically firm nod of her head. "Then perhaps we should be on our way."

He waited a moment longer for Rose to say her good-byes, and then they walked out to the front of the house, where the carriage awaited them. It took Robert two attempts to lever himself up, which didn't help his temper at all. For some reason, it felt as if his injuries were getting worse rather than better. He really should speak to Patrick about his concerns, but he lacked the courage. The thought of having to endure any more probing or well-meaning advice was intolerable.

He realized Lucy was asking him a question about the visit and returned his attention to the present.

"Yes, I certainly approved of Mr. Greenwell. He is an intelligent man with sound principles and a steady wit. I have asked him to consider joining our school board."

"Well, we will certainly need some assistance to find yet *another* teacher." Lucy sighed.

"I agree. But neither of us could have antici-pated that Miss Broomfield would be murdered." Robert grabbed hold of the strap as the carriage lurched down the drive of Greenwell Manor. "Did you speak to Josephine?"

"I did. She was still quite upset by what had transpired."

"Understandably."

"Not that Mrs. Greenwell cared one jot," Lucy added. "She is completely disinterested in Josephine. She even suggested that the poor girl was incapable of having deep feelings and didn't deserve any special treatment."

"I gather you are not impressed by the Greenwell ladies, which is a pity, because I accepted an invitation for both of us to dine there on Friday to discuss the school board."

"I suppose I'll have to come with you," Lucy said. "The opportunity to add Mr. Greenwell to our board must override my personal objections to Mrs. Greenwell and her silly daughters."

"I'm glad to hear you are willing to compromise." As the carriage made its final turn onto the county road, Robert glanced out of the window. "Do we have a moment to stop at the Queen's Head on our return journey?"

Lucy looked at Aunt Rose. "I do not have anything pressing to do for the rest of the day, do you?"

"Not at all. Are you going to check to see if the last of my luggage has arrived, Robert?"

"I will certainly do that. You're missing a hatbox, I believe?"

"Yes, dear. I left it behind in London. Genevieve promised to send it on to me."

With some difficulty, Robert lowered the window and angled his head out to shout up at Mr. Coleman. "Stop at the inn, will you?"

"Yes, Sir Robert."

Ten minutes later they pulled into the coaching yard, alongside a farmer's cart laden with turnips.

"There's no need for you to disturb yourselves," Robert said as he exited the carriage. "I won't be long."

Lucy opened her mouth as if to disagree with him and then closed it again and sank back in the seat.

In truth, once he'd spoken to the landlord about Rose's bonnets, he intended only to ask one more question, about the various comings and goings at the busy inn, and they could be on their way.

He made his way into the cramped hallway of the inn, where the owner's much younger second wife was just descending the stairs. Her low-cut bodice displayed her bosom to great advantage and was currently hovering at Robert's eye view. He raised his gaze to find her smiling at him.

"Major Sir Robert Kurland!" She reached the bottom step and curtsied to him, giving him yet another view of her bountiful breasts. "What an *honor!* What can I do for you today, sir?"

"Good afternoon, ma'am. Is Mr. Jarvis available?"

"He's in the cellar, sir. Do you want me to go and fetch him?"

Robert considered going after the man himself but doubted his leg would hold on the rickety cellar staircase.

"Pray don't disturb him. You might be able to help me instead."

"I'd gladly help you with *anything,* sir. Anything at all." She winked at him. "You don't remember me, do you, sir?"

"We've met before?"

"Indeed, we have. To be fair, it was quite a long time ago, and in London." She licked her lips. "You and your fellow officers came to the green room at the theater where I was a dancer." She lifted her skirt and pointed her toe.

"I can't say I recall—"

"No need to look so guilty, sir." She chuckled. "You weren't doing nothing more than ogling a few pretty girls. Not like some of your friends, who took things a *lot* further."

"How interesting." Robert took an involuntary step back and hit the newel post. "My aunt is expecting the arrival of a hatbox on the mail coach. Do you have any notion if it has arrived?"

"Indeed, it did, sir. I have it safe in my parlor and will go and fetch it for you directly."

She went to turn away, and Robert cleared his throat. "Before you do that, there is one other thing—"

"Don't be shy, sir." She poked him in the ribs. "Spit it out. Peg's heard it all before."

He had a sense that there was some meaning behind her playful manner that was escaping him, but he persevered, anyway. "It's quite a simple matter. Have you rented a room to any strangers this past week or seen anyone in the tavern who was alone or acting suspiciously?"

"We've seen a few new folks come through this week, but no one who stands out." She pursed her lips. "Maybe you'd better ask Ed about that. I tend to spend my time in the kitchen and ordering the staff, rather than dealing with the public. Ed don't like me showing off my charms to the clientele. He's a jealous man, you know." She elbowed Robert in the side. "And don't you worry that I'll tell him where I met *you,* sir. I wouldn't want wigs on the green over poor little me."

"Then perhaps you could ask him for me," Robert said hastily. "I'll send my land agent down tomorrow to speak to Mr. Jarvis himself."

"He's a nice-looking man for an Irishman, that Mr. Fletcher," Mrs. Jarvis commented. "Not married yet?"

"Not that I know of." Robert headed toward the door.

"Still pining over that Miss Anna in the rectory, like half the county, no doubt."

Robert paused to look down at her. "Do you really think so?"

Her smile was coy. "I have a gift for sniffing out a romance, sir. Comes from my Romany blood."

"Indeed." He offered her a tentative smile. "Do you think you could carry the hatbox out to my carriage?"

"Certainly, sir." She curtsied and turned toward the parlor. "I'll bring it right out."

Robert took his time walking back to the carriage. The yard was busy with passing traffic, and the ground was slippery with trodden straw and muck. He spoke to Alf Smith, the head ostler, and inquired after his family. He was glad to hear that one of the grandsons was seeking a position in the Kurland stables. After confirming that there was a spot available, he persuaded Mr. Coleman to come off his box and speak to the ostler himself.

By the time he was ready to climb back into the carriage, Mrs. Jarvis was walking toward him, her hands full of a very large hatbox. He unlatched the door and held it open wide.

"Your hats, Aunt Rose." He retrieved the box from the landlady and made sure it was placed in a secure position in the carriage. "Thank you, Mrs. Jarvis."

"You're most welcome, sir." She peered into the carriage, her blond curls bobbing. "Afternoon, Lady Kurland, Mrs. Armitage!"

Lucy leaned forward. "Mrs. Jarvis. How are you settling in?"

"Very well, thank you, your ladyship." Mrs. Jarvis curtsied. "And how are you, my lady? I hear you've been unwell yourself."

Lucy's cheeks flushed with color. "I am quite recovered, thank you. But I appreciate your concern."

Mrs. Jarvis looked her up and down. "You still look a mite peaky to me. You need feeding up. That's what I say."

Robert stepped forward and took Mrs. Jarvis firmly by the elbow. "Well, thank you for your help, and please don't forget to ask Mr. Jarvis about the recent activity at the inn."

"I won't forget, sir."

She picked up her skirts, displaying far too much calf, and sashayed back toward the inn. Her hips swayed as if she were promenading on a London street to attract a particular kind of customer.

Robert got into the carriage and met Rose's amused glance.

"Mrs. Jarvis seems somewhat out of place at a country inn," she said.

"I understand that *Mr.* Jarvis met her in London, and that she once had aspirations to become an actress," Lucy added. "She certainly seemed very . . . *agreeable*."

"One might say that." Robert fiddled with the collar of his coat. If truth be told, she'd made him feel rather uncomfortable.

"Did you ask her whether there had been any odd visitors at the inn?" Lucy said. "I assume you are trying to ascertain whether the man Josephine saw was a local man or a stranger."

"Unfortunately, Mr. Jarvis was unavailable, but I hope he will receive my message. I'll send Dermot down to speak to him tomorrow to make sure," Robert replied.

"Have you also spoken to the villagers who live near the school?" Lucy persisted. "Although the majority of those cottages contain our farmworkers, who are not at home in the late afternoon. What about the Hall family at the smithy? They see everyone passing by."

"Lucy . . ." Robert held her gaze. "I'm fairly certain my aunt has no interest in hearing about these matters. I can assure you that I have everything well in hand."

"But—"

Robert turned away from his wife and smiled at Aunt Rose. "What delights do you have in your hatbox, Aunt, that are so important that you insisted on having them sent down from London?"

To his relief, Lucy made no more attempts to change the conversation and listened quietly as Rose described her two new bonnets and a lace cap, which she insisted would make all the ladies in the neighborhood jealous.

When they reached the hall, Lucy waited until Rose started up the stairs before she followed Robert down the corridor to his study. She didn't bother to knock and just marched straight in to find him limping over to his desk.

"Is your leg troubling you?"

He shot her an irritated glance but didn't answer. She could tell from the hard set of his jaw that he was in pain and was refusing to admit it.

"Robert . . ."

"I am fine," he snapped as he sat down and fiddled with his pens. "Will you please stop fussing over me?"

She stopped in front of his desk and waited until she had his complete, if reluctant, attention. "Am I not allowed to discuss the matter of Miss Broomfield's death with you?"

"That's not what I said," Robert retorted. "I merely suggested that there is a time and a place for such discussions, and that my aunt would probably not wish to be part of them."

"So you *are* willing to hear my opinions on the matter."

"Of course." He put down his pen. "I always appreciate your contributions."

"Balderdash. You didn't even *ask* me whether Josephine had remembered anything about what happened yesterday."

He sat back and looked up at her, one eyebrow raised. "Probably because I assumed you were going to tell me, anyway, in your own good time."

"No. You hoped I wouldn't," Lucy retorted. "You *hoped* I'd sit quietly and not ask any questions to anyone about anything ever again!"

"That is somewhat of an exaggeration, my dear." He lined up the pens on his desk. "You are not well. You agreed with me that you would not involve yourself too deeply in this matter. In fact, you *promised* me—"

"I did no such thing! I promised not to attempt to run the school."

"You knew what I meant." His blue gaze was steady and unflinching. "You are already exhausting yourself organizing a ball and a village party. You have guests to care for, and your twin brothers are coming home for the holidays. Owing to your father's somewhat selfish disposition, I suspect that *we* will be entertaining them at the hall for the duration of the holidays."

"I am quite capable of managing all these things," Lucy said firmly.

"I *know* you are, which is why I'm suggesting you focus your energies *on* those things and stop chasing after a murderer!" He shoved a hand through his dark hair. "Am I being unreasonable to expect you to take *care* of yourself?"

She raised her chin. "You are certainly being *very* high-handed."

"I am your husband. If I'm not allowed to tell you that you are attempting too many tasks, then who is?"

"Perhaps you might consider that I know myself well enough to make those decisions without help from you."

He flung out his hand. "Which means that regardless of my position on the matter, as usual, you will go your own way and ignore me."

Good gracious. Now he was as cross as she was. Lucy pressed a hand to her heart and took a deep breath. Was he right? Her father could probably quote many instances from the Bible that showed where her obedience lay. But if she gave in and kept quiet, she would wither away, and then what?

"Are you *ordering* me not to take any interest in Miss Broomfield's death?"

He was silent for so long that she almost forgot to breathe.

"No." He sat back, one arm resting on the back of his chair. "I refuse to be cast as the villain in this play."

He sounded so defeated, her resolve wobbled.

"Thank you for that at least."

His gaze dropped to the ledgers piled on his desk. "Is there anything else you wish to say to me? Otherwise, I would like to get on. I have the end-of-the-year accounts to wrestle with."

"I know you will not believe me, but I truly do not wish to fight with you." He didn't look up, so Lucy continued. "I just want to make sure that whoever killed Miss Broomfield is brought to justice."

"As you said." He continued perusing the accounts sheet. "I'm sure that is what we all wish for."

"And I know that you will do everything in your power to make that happen."

"Indeed."

"Then can you not allow me at least some share in the endeavor?"

"I've already told you that I won't stop you doing whatever it is you're going to do, anyway."

She bit her lip. "That makes me sound so . . . contrary."

"You are contrary." He still didn't look up. "You turn my concern for you into something to be fought over and mauled to death."

"No," she whispered. "That's not what I mean to do at all."

There was a brisk knock on the door, and Dermot came in, carrying a pile of papers. He stopped dead and looked from Lucy to her husband.

"I do apologize for interrupting you, Lady Kurland, Sir Robert. I will come back later." He turned on his heel, but Lucy was already moving past him.

"I was just leaving. Please stay. I'm sure Sir Robert would be delighted to talk to you."

Chapter 7

"Mag I come in?" Lucy looked up from her letter writing to discover Robert at the door of her sitting room. He looked as tired as she felt, and seeing as they had barely exchanged more than a dozen words since their disastrous argument the day before, she was somewhat surprised to see him. She'd deliberately waited until he'd left the breakfast table before partaking of her own meal. It was not like her to be such a coward, but she had a sense that she had offended him deeply, and she had no notion of how to fix the issue without surrendering to his demands.

"Of course."

He entered the room and took up a position on the hearthrug in front of the fire, reminding her forcibly of her father. "I wish to clarify something I said yesterday."

Lucy turned in her chair to look at him but didn't speak. She hated being at odds with him and had felt sick to her stomach all night.

"Aunt Rose reminded me that you had taken possession of Miss Broomfield's belongings and that you were intending to sort through them today."

"That is correct." Lucy raised her chin. "Would

146

you like me to relinquish the task to her entirely, or should I simply make a bonfire and dispose of everything in one fell swoop?"

A muscle twitched in his cheek. "I was going to say that I have no issue with you dealing with her effects. In truth, I would appreciate your help in the matter."

"Oh." Lucy twisted her hands together in her lap. "That is very . . . gracious of you."

"As you said yesterday, I also do not wish us to fight." He inclined his head. "If you do find anything interesting in your search, I would appreciate it if you would let me know."

"I will certainly do that," she said, hastening to reassure him. "And thank you again."

He went, as if to leave, and she held up her hand. "There is one more thing. . . . I arranged to meet with Josephine and Rebecca in the schoolhouse this morning so that they could help me go through the rest of the books in the study and upstairs."

"Then meet them, and make sure that they are the ones doing the work and that you are just supervising." He nodded and turned, as if to leave.

Lucy rose to her feet and rushed across the room to take Robert's hand. "Thank you."

He raised her hand to his lips and kissed her fingers. "Make sure you wrap up warmly. It is bitterly cold out there."

She cupped his cheek with her palm. "I am sorry for being such a troublesome wife."

"No you're not." His smile was reluctant but still very welcome. "But I can't say I didn't know what I was letting myself in for when I proposed to you, can I?"

"You were certainly well aware of my faults."

"As you were of mine." His blue gaze grew serious. "We can do much better than this, you know."

Lucy swallowed hard. "I realize that I am not the most congenial of partners at the moment. I will try to do better."

"As will I. My temper is never at its best during the cold winter months." He released her hand. "If you are to meet with your young charges at the school, you had best be on your way. Have you arranged for the carriage to take you, or do you intend to walk?"

"I'm taking the carriage." She gave him a grateful smile. "Aunt Rose is visiting Anna at the rectory, so I will take her there first."

"Excellent. Perhaps I will see you this afternoon." He nodded and left the room, while Lucy resumed her position at her desk.

She attempted to finish writing her letter, but the ability to concentrate had deserted her. Beneath his somewhat irascible exterior, Robert was a good man, and she was being foolish by challenging him over everything. The problem was, she didn't know *why* she kept doing it. . . .

She had always questioned her father about everything and had suffered the consequence of his irritation with her throughout her childhood and beyond. He much preferred Anna, who dealt with him in a far more sympathetic manner. Even though he'd encouraged Lucy to expand her education and read widely, he'd never appreciated it when she displayed her knowledge.

Robert liked her just as she was . . . or he had until recently, when she'd twice failed in her wifely duty of giving him an heir. Not that he'd ever say that to her, but the thought of his obnoxious cousin Paul inheriting Kurland Hall couldn't possibly sit well with him. She was almost thirty. Most of her friends had three or four children by now. Even Penelope and Sophia, who had married comparatively late like her, had succeeded where she had failed.

Grace and Dr. Fletcher had assured her that her ability to conceive had not been compromised by her previous miscarriages. She was not convinced they were right, and seeing as Robert had avoided her bed for the past few months, the chance of proving them right was far from settled.

With a sigh, Lucy gave up on her letter writing and put her pen away. She still had a lot to accomplish before Christmas Day. There were invitations to write and the festivities to organize. If she focused on the things she *could* accomplish, maybe she would feel better about the things that currently eluded her.

After leaving Rose at the rectory, where she was warmly greeted both by the rector and Anna, Lucy was driven to Lower Kurland. Josephine was ready to depart, meaning that Lucy didn't have to deal with the Greenwell ladies. She did leave a message to confirm their dinner arrangements for the upcoming Friday.

Josephine was well wrapped up against the cold and seemed disinclined to talk on the short journey back to the village. Lucy wondered if the girl was worried about reentering the school. She decided not to say anything to draw attention to the matter, in case she made things worse.

To her surprise, when they alighted from the carriage, the outside door to the school was already unlocked. She pushed it open and went inside, Josephine trailing behind her, to find Rebecca Hall already setting a fire in the main schoolroom.

"Good morning, Lady Kurland," Rebecca called out cheerfully. "I thought I'd start a fire. This place is as cold as a tomb."

"I didn't realize you had a key to the building, Rebecca," Lucy said.

"My father made a copy of both the front and back door keys for Miss Brent." Rebecca grinned. "She was always worried she would lock herself

150

out. We keep them in the smithy in case they are needed."

Lucy wondered if Robert was aware of that, but decided not to question Rebecca too closely, as there was a lot to do.

"I tried to start a fire in the kitchen, as well, my lady, but the chimney wasn't drawing properly, so I stopped."

"I remember Miss Broomfield telling me that one of the chimneys was blocked," Lucy said. "I told her I would have someone come down and see to it."

"There's probably a bird's nest fallen in there, or something has died," Rebecca commented, with all the practicality of a girl raised in a farming community. "Can't smell anything rotting, though."

"Thank goodness," Lucy murmured as she passed through the schoolroom into the kitchen behind. "Come along, Josephine."

Rebecca carried on chatting as she pulled out a chair and waited for Lucy and Josephine to sit down at the small pine table. She reached out to poke her friend's arm. "Did you really find the body, Josie? Was it scary?"

Josephine shuddered, and Lucy hastened to intervene.

"Yes, Josephine did discover that Miss Broomfield was dead. It was hardly a pleasant experience."

Rebecca nodded sympathetically. "Did her heart stop, my lady? My father always reckoned her temper would get the better of her. The way she used to get all red in the face and start shouting at everyone . . ."

"I don't think that's how she died, Rebecca," Lucy said. "In truth, Dr. Fletcher thinks she was killed."

Rebecca's hand flew to her mouth. "Oh, Lordy! Who would've thought that would happen here in Kurland St. Mary?"

"It is certainly unusual," Lucy conceded. "Sir Robert is attempting to discover the culprit. I have complete confidence in his ability to resolve this matter in a timely and satisfactory manner."

"Of course, my lady." Rebecca nodded. "Can I tell my parents about this?"

"I'd rather you kept it to yourself until we have apprehended the villain who did this." Lucy held Rebecca's brown gaze. "Do you think you could do that?"

"I'll try, my lady, but I'm not very good at keeping secrets." Rebecca shifted in her seat. "My dad says I have a big mouth."

"Then if you can't remain silent, mayhap I can tell your parents and swear them to secrecy."

Lucy was fairly certain that the news was already known throughout the village. Keeping a secret in Kurland St. Mary was virtually impossible.

"You could try, my lady, but my mum does like a good gossip." Rebecca looked even more doubtful than Lucy felt. "What about Josephine's family? Do they know?"

"Sir Robert informed the Greenwells when he took Josephine home after she discovered Miss Broomfield was dead." Lucy sat back. "Do you think we could move on to discussing what needs to be done in the schoolhouse?"

After setting Rebecca and a subdued Josephine to sorting out the books on the shelves in the study, Lucy went up the stairs to the teacher's private apartment. She had a sense that she was missing something important, some clue to Miss Broomfield's enigmatic personality, some sense of the woman who had lived amongst them without a friend or an acquaintance who had even noticed she was dead.

She turned a slow circle on the landing, taking in the silence and the lack of even a hint of remaining fragrance or essence of the schoolteacher. It was almost as if Miss Broomfield had divested herself of any hint of who she really was before she'd embarked on her teaching career in the village.

Perhaps Lucy was being foolish and she would form a different picture of Miss Broomfield once she'd sorted through her personal effects. Last night, after speaking to Robert, she'd read the letter from the school in Cornwall that Dermot had placed on her desk stating that the teacher had been dismissed for unbecoming conduct. The letter had only made her more curious as to what *exactly* had transpired. Surely, Robert wouldn't object if she wrote to the headmistress with some questions of her own?

She wandered into the bedroom and studied the sturdy bed frame and the bare mattress. A small crucifix hung over the bed. It certainly didn't belong to the fittings Lucy had provided for the apartment. She must have missed it in yesterday's gloom. Had Miss Broomfield been a Roman Catholic? It might explain why Lucy had rarely seen her in the parish church. She had to climb onto the bed and steady herself before she was able to reach up and remove the cross from its nail. There was a small piece of twine wrapped around the base, and it secured something wrapped in paper to the back of the wood.

She placed the crucifix in her pocket to examine later. She could only hope she had discovered the key to the locked box she had found in the cupboard the day before. Just as she was about to get down, from her superior vantage point, she noticed something concealed on the top of the chest of drawers.

Climbing down from the bed, she contemplated how to reach the object, and she ended up standing on the rather wobbly chair that usually stood in front of the dressing table. She was fairly certain Robert wouldn't approve of her current actions, but he couldn't see her and would never know, as long as she didn't fall and break her neck.

She retrieved the flat velvet box and sat down on the side of the bed to open it. The clasp gave easily. Lucy gasped as she took in the beautiful diamond and ruby necklace and earrings nestled in the satin. Why would a woman who chose to teach at a rural village school have such expensive jewelry? Had she inherited them from a family member, or was their appearance more sinister?

If someone knew about the jewels, they might well have considered a robbery worth the effort. . . .

"Lady Kurland?"

Lucy slammed the lid of the box shut, hid it beneath her skirts, and turned toward the stairs, which Rebecca was already ascending.

"Yes, Rebecca? Is something wrong?"

"No, my lady. I just wanted to ask you what will happen to the school." Rebecca smoothed her hands over her apron. "I, like a lot of the children around here, don't want it to close down. Even with a teacher like Miss Broomfield, it was worth coming every day to help the little ones and learn something new for myself."

"Was Miss Broomfield difficult to work for?" Rebecca bit her lip, and Lucy carried on speaking. "I would appreciate your honesty in this matter. Nothing you say can harm Miss Broomfield now."

"She had a bit of a temper, my lady, and she didn't seem to like teaching, if you know what I mean." Rebecca shifted from one foot to the other. "She kept saying we were all too stupid to learn, and that there was no point in trying to better ourselves, because we would never be good enough."

Lucy kept hold of her temper with some difficulty. "I hope you know that what she said wasn't true."

"Oh, I knew that, my lady." Rebecca made a firm gesture with her hand. "Miss Brent told me differently, and I still visit her at her new home. Did you know she's increasing? A baby a year after marriage." Rebecca chuckled. "She's very happy."

"I'm glad to hear it," Lucy replied. "Did you tell her that Miss Broomfield was having a deleterious effect on the children at the school?"

"I did mention it eventually." Rebecca fleetingly touched her cheek. "I had a cut under my eye from the tip of Miss Broomfield's cane. Miss Brent asked me how it happened. She intended to speak to you and Sir Robert when she saw you at the Christmas service." Rebecca paused. "Oh, my lady! What are we going to do about the carols? The children are so looking forward to singing in front of the whole village."

"They are?" Lucy questioned.

"Indeed. Some of the little ones are going to be heartbroken if they don't perform." Rebecca hesitated. "Do you think Josephine and I could keep practicing the carols with the children? It would be only for a week or so more, and we wouldn't try to teach them anything else."

"I don't see why not, as long as you are supervised." Lucy considered the idea. "As long as Sir Robert doesn't object to using the school for this purpose."

It would also mean that she would have to pop in occasionally to oversee the girls, which Robert could hardly object to, either—could he?

"How did Miss Broomfield seem the last day you saw her?" Lucy asked.

Rebecca looked thoughtful. "She was in a terrible mood. The little children were cowering in their seats while she prowled around the room like a cornered cat lashing out with its claws."

"Did she say why she was angry?"

"Not to me, my lady. After my dad came up to the school to have a little chat with her about how she used her cane, she wasn't as mean to me as she was to Josephine."

Knowing that Josephine had no family to protect her made Lucy fear that Rebecca was right.

"Did she say anything in particular to Josephine that you can recall?"

Rebecca looked over her shoulder, as if fearing either the teacher or Josephine would overhear her. "Miss Broomfield said that Josephine must be some rich gentleman's by-blow, and that made her and her mother sinners."

Lucy frowned. "Why would she say such a horrible thing?"

"Well, Josephine does live with the Greenwells, who are gentry, and even she admits that she isn't closely related to them." Rebecca lowered her voice. "Miss Broomfield liked to listen to all the gossip. Some of the smaller children would tell her all kinds of things."

Lucy considered Rebecca's words. In truth, through the children in her care, Miss Broomfield had had intimate access to the daily lives of almost every family in the vicinity. If she was the type of person who liked secrets, she must have been in her element. But had she used that information for other purposes?

"Did Miss Broomfield ever get you to deliver messages to anyone?" Lucy asked.

"Occasionally, my lady, but only in the village."

"Were you ever sent as far as Mrs. Jenkins's house or up to Kurland Hall?"

"I don't think so," Rebecca said doubtfully. "But I wasn't the only one who ran messages for her. Do you want me to ask Josephine?"

"There is no need. I can ask her when I go down to the kitchen. Have you finished sorting the books in the study yet?"

"We still have a few left. Some of them have names printed inside them, and we weren't sure who they might belong to."

"I'll come and look at them. Lots of people donated books from their libraries to help the school, so I should recognize those names."

"Imagine having your own library." Rebecca sighed. "I have three books tucked away on a shelf where my brothers can't get at them."

"You are more than welcome to come up to the hall and borrow a book from our library, Rebecca."

"Really, my lady?" Rebecca's brown eyes widened. "You have *hundreds* of books in there! I saw them that day I came up to speak to Sir Robert."

"And they are all available to you." Lucy paused for a moment to consider some of the more lurid classical literature housed in the library. "As long as you receive my or Sir Robert's approval."

"Thank you, my lady!" Rebecca bobbed a curtsy. "I can't wait to tell my dad. He'll be so proud of me."

"Now, why don't you continue your task downstairs, and I will join you in a few minutes."

Rebecca clomped down the stairs, leaving Lucy

to put the jewelry box in her pocket and complete her search of Miss Broomfield's bedroom. Now knowing the teacher's habit of concealment, Lucy paid close attention to less obvious parts of the furniture but found nothing more interesting than an embroidered handkerchief that had fallen to the floor behind the bed.

She moved through to the sitting room and, dispensing with formality, sat on the floor to go through the books on the shelves built below the window. The books were more personal in nature, consisting of many volumes of sermons, a well-worn copy of the Bible, and a travel guide to the county of Hertfordshire. Tucked right in at the end was a leather-bound edition of Rudolph Ackermann's monthly *Repository of Arts, Literature, Commerce, Manufactures, Fashions, and Politics*, which seemed positively frivolous compared to everything else. Why had Miss Broomfield kept this particular book?

After ascertaining that everything else was the personal property of Miss Broomfield, Lucy placed the books in a box, with the Ackermann's on the top, for removal up to the hall. There was nothing else to investigate in the living quarters, so Lucy made her way downstairs to help the girls.

To their credit, they had almost completed their task, leaving just a small pile of books for Lucy to examine on the kitchen table. She easily recognized most of the families who had donated the books to the school, but two names eluded her. After instructing the girls to place everything but the books belonging to Miss Broomfield back on the shelves, she asked Rebecca to bring down the box she had left on the landing.

It was now almost noon, and Mr. Coleman would be returning to take her home to Kurland Hall. Knowing her father's delight in having company, she suspected Rose would be having her midday meal with the Harringtons and wouldn't be returning for some while after that. The rector had proclaimed Robert's aunt to be a woman of sound mind and high intelligence and seemed to enjoy her company immensely. To Lucy's surprise, Rose seemed to agree.

"The carriage is here, my lady." Josephine spoke for the first time in quite a while.

"Thank you." Lucy pointed at the various boxes on the kitchen table. "Perhaps you could both help me carry these out?"

Lucy had barely left the schoolhouse before Mr. Coleman relieved her of the box she was carrying.

"I'll take that, my lady. Sir Robert doesn't want you exerting yourself."

"Thank you." She willingly relinquished her load. Despite what Robert might fear, she had no intention of getting into an argument with her staff every time they showed their concern for her.

She waited until Rebecca closed the schoolroom door behind her and held out her hand.

"Do you have your key?"

"Yes, my lady." Rebecca took it out of her pocket. "Shall I lock the door?"

"Yes, please, and then give the key to me. I'd rather keep them safely at the hall. You can accompany me in the carriage, Rebecca, and I will call in on your father and retrieve the other one."

"All right, my lady." Rebecca started for the carriage. "Come on, Josephine. Don't stand around in the cold."

Mr. Coleman winked at the girls as he handed them up into the interior of the carriage. "Miss Blake, Miss Hall."

Rebecca giggled, and even Josephine managed a smile.

"Lady Kurland."

"Thank you, Mr. Coleman. Can we stop by the smithy first and then proceed to the Greenwells'?"

"As you wish, my lady." He shut the door and then climbed back on his box.

It took only a minute or so before they were stopping outside the smithy. Rebecca was already wrestling with the carriage door.

"I'll get the key, my lady. There's no need for you to get out," she said.

Lucy placed her hand over Rebecca's and showed her how to release the door latch. "Josephine can definitely stay here in the warm, but I intend to get out and speak to your father. Perhaps you can locate the key while I do so?"

"As you wish, my lady." Rebecca hurried down the step without waiting for Mr. Coleman to assist her and ran toward the smithy, shouting as she approached. "Dad! Her ladyship wants a word with you!"

Lucy winced. Even though she knew Rebecca was shouting so that her father could hear her over the sound of his furnace, she was still extremely loud.

The banging abruptly ceased, and the smithy emerged from the depth of his workshop, wiping his hands on his stained leather apron.

"Miss Lucy! I mean Lady Kurland. How are you today, lass?"

"I am very well, thank you." Lucy had known the Hall family her entire life and stood on easy terms with them. "I wanted to thank you for allowing Rebecca to aid me at the school. She has been extremely helpful."

Mr. Hall grinned. "I'm glad to hear it. She's a handful that one but smart as sixpence. Shame she wasn't born a boy, because then at least I'd know the smithy would be in good hands after I'm gone."

"I'm sure your Sam will do an admirable job."

"God willing." Mr. Hall didn't sound convinced. He leaned in a little closer. "Is it true the schoolteacher is dead?"

"Indeed, it is," Lucy replied.

"She wasn't very old, but illness can strike at any time. Was it a lung sickness?"

"No. She was stabbed in the back of the neck."

"Well, I never." Mr. Hall's mouth dropped open. "Right here in Kurland St. Mary. Under our very noses?"

"Apparently. Have you noticed any strangers loitering around here in the past few days, Mr. Hall?"

"There are always a few passing through the village, like, but most of them don't linger. I had one gentleman stop at my smithy the other day so that I could fix his bridle. He did go off for a wander around the village while I soldered the ring closed again."

"A gentleman?" Lucy asked. "Did he say where he was from?"

"He said he was heading for London. I didn't tell him he was a fool for doing so in this weather, but after seeing the state of his horse, I did wonder if he'd make it."

"Did you notice which way he went when he left the smithy?"

Mr. Hall scratched his head. "I can't say I did, Miss Lucy. I told him there was an inn on the far side of the village, if he changed his mind and decided to stay for the night. It was already getting dark when he left me."

"Thank you."

"If I think of anything else, I'll be sure to pass the message on to you or Sir Robert." Mr. Hall looked over his shoulder as Rebecca came out to join them. "Her ladyship says you've been very helpful, daughter. Shame that the school will be closing now that the teacher's gone."

Rebecca's smile disappeared, and Lucy hastened to intervene.

"The school will be closed only temporarily. We fully intend to find another teacher with the utmost urgency so that we can reopen after Christmas." Mr. Hall opened his mouth, but Lucy continued speaking. "In fact, I will still require Rebecca's help over the next week or so, while the children practice their carols for the Christmas service at the church. I do hope you will allow Rebecca to assist me in this matter."

"That's up to her mother, my lady."

"Mum's fine with it," Rebecca interjected with a grin. "I just asked her."

"Then that's all settled." Lucy gave Mr. Hall her most confident smile. "We will, of course, pay Rebecca's salary in *full* for the next two weeks." She nodded at the girl. "I will send you a message when I have spoken to Sir Robert about the carol service."

"Thank you, my lady."

"Now I must be on my way. It is always a pleasure to speak to you, Mr. Hall. Do you have that key for me, Rebecca?"

Rebecca's smile disappeared. "I was just going to tell you, my lady. It's not there. Someone must have taken it."

Chapter 8

After dropping Josephine off at the Green-wells', Lucy returned home and ate a hearty lunch. Robert was still out with Dermot, and Rose had sent a note to say she would be returning in time for dinner and not to worry about sending the carriage for her. For the first time in a while, Lucy didn't feel tired enough to require an afternoon nap and instead decided to tackle Miss Broomfield's personal effects.

She'd asked for the boxes from the school to be placed in her sitting room, along with everything else she'd gathered from the teacher's apartment. The house was quiet, and for once the sun was shining, making everything more cheerful. Lucy decided her first task would be to write to the headmistress of the school in Cornwall who had dismissed Miss Broomfield. The letter would probably take a while to reach the remote area, so the sooner she wrote it, the better.

A fresh box of writing paper from the stationer's in Hertford awaited her on the table, and she remembered the small matter of the invitations for the ball. If she were in London, she would have saved time and had them engraved, but there was no such service in the countryside, so they would all need to be handwritten.

That thought prompted another one as she put on her spectacles. She moved her daybook to one side to reveal the anonymous letter she'd received the previous week, and compared it to the letter Mrs. Jenkins had shared with her. The paper used by the writer was different, but the handwriting was similar enough to make Lucy curious. After opening her desk drawer, she found the pieces of paper Robert had taken from under Miss Broomfield's hands the day she died, and compared them to the others. . . .

"Goodness me," Lucy breathed. "The script is quite similar."

Was it possible that Miss Broomfield, the gatherer of secrets, was behind the poison-pen letters? Had she sat behind her desk every day, listening to the children in her care gossip, and used that information for her own nefarious means?

"But why?" Lucy whispered.

What pleasure had Miss Broomfield gained from hurting those in Kurland St. Mary? Lucy took off her spectacles. Why would anyone do such a horrible thing? Had Miss Broomfield been envious of Lucy and Mrs. Jenkins? She had lived in the village for only a few months and hadn't even met Lucy formally until just before her death.

After placing the letters in a pile, Lucy rose to her feet and went over to the box that contained the contents of Miss Broomfield's desk. If there were any more clues to the mystery, she would surely find them there.

Robert put his head around the door into Lucy's sitting room and discovered his wife sitting on the floor, surrounded by piles of paper, her spectacles on the end of her nose. She looked up and beckoned him in, her expression so animated that he almost wanted to cheer.

"Robert, do come in. I have spent the past hour examining the contents of Miss Broomfield's desk, and I have discovered some interesting things."

He sat on the chair nearest to her and leaned forward to take the papers she offered him. In his present state of discomfort, if he attempted to sit on the floor, he might never get up again.

"What have we here?"

"The papers you found the day Miss Broomfield died, a letter written to Mrs. Jenkins, and one written to me. Compare the handwriting. Does it look similar?"

Robert spent a moment reading the letters and then looked sternly down at his wife, his good humor fading. "When did you receive this abomination of a letter?"

She bit her lip. "I believe it was last week."

"Why didn't you *tell* me about it?"

"I fully intended to, but—"

He interrupted her. "Only after you'd attempted

to discover who sent it? Lucy, for God's sake! When will you learn?"

"It wasn't that simple, Robert." She raised her chin. "I was *upset*. I didn't want anyone to know the contents of that letter. It was only when Mrs. Jenkins told me she had received an unpleasant communication *herself* that I began to wonder if there was something suspicious going on."

In the interests of harmony, he tamped down both his exasperation and the desire to reassure her that the letter writer was wrong, and focused on the matter at hand. "It seems as if your assumption was right."

"Yes. And would you agree that the papers you took from Miss Broomfield are written in a very similar style?"

He held up the last sheet of paper and squinted at the script. "It is hard to say when they contain so few words, but I will give you the benefit of the doubt. Are you suggesting that it was *Miss Broomfield* who wrote those unpleasant letters to you and Mrs. Jenkins?"

"Yes." She searched his face, her expression grave. "It might also explain why she died."

"You believe Nicholas Jenkins killed Miss Broomfield, then?"

"No! Of course not."

"Then you killed her, or was it me, defending your honor?" Robert placed the papers on her desk.

"What if we weren't the only people she wrote to?" Lucy asked. "*Someone* killed her and then stabbed her in the eye with a quill pen. Doesn't that suggest that they wanted to make a point?"

"Sly, insidious letters might be hurtful, but they are scarcely worth killing someone over, are they?" Robert reasoned. "If you'd done the right thing and shown me that letter, and I'd found out it had come from Miss Broomfield, I would've gone down to the school and had a few words with her—maybe threatened her within the rights of the law—but I certainly wouldn't have killed her."

"But what if she wrote other letters that weren't so easy to ignore?"

"There is always that possibility," Robert said, conceding the point. "Perhaps we need to ask if anyone else received a letter from her."

"As if anyone is likely to come forward now, knowing that Miss Broomfield is dead and they would be the prime suspect in her murder," Lucy said gloomily.

"Unfortunately, you have a point." He sighed. "Perhaps we should attempt to keep the matter of the letters separate from Miss Broomfield's death until we are certain she was the culprit."

"That sounds far more practical." Lucy nodded. "In truth, I cannot understand why she would have taken Mrs. Jenkins and me in such dislike after such a short acquaintance. I doubt either of us had done her any harm."

"From all reports, Miss Broomfield seemed to be the kind of woman who disliked everyone. She even managed to annoy Dermot, which is quite a feat. Have you found anything else that confirms your suspicions?"

"Not really." She grimaced and made a sweeping gesture encompassing all the other pieces of paper on the floor. "These items are all from her desk and are mostly concerned with checklists and notes for her classwork."

"As you might expect. I doubt she would keep copies of her offensive scribblings in her desk."

"Which begs the question of why you found her writing one there." Lucy frowned. "Miss Broomfield insisted that Josephine and Rebecca leave early that last day. Maybe she was writing a letter and intended to pass it over to the person who ended up killing her."

"It's a possibility," Robert agreed. "Or maybe she was just busy writing and wasn't expecting anyone to come and call on her. At this point, we simply don't know."

"Several people saw a man loitering around the school that day, and Mr. Hall at the smithy says he repaired a bridle for a gentleman who went for a walk around the village while he waited for the ring to be fixed," Lucy said.

"It might be the same man who stayed at the Queen's Head last week," Robert said. "Dermot and I were just speaking to Mr. Jarvis about that

172

very matter. The gentleman's name was Mr. John Clapper. Mr. Jarvis thought he was visiting family in the area and was on his way back to London when his horse's bridle broke."

"Clapper?" Lucy considered the name. "I don't know any family in the vicinity with that name, although we could ask my father. He does hold the parish records."

"With all due respect, George Culpepper, the curate, is far more familiar with the local population than your father will ever be."

"That is true. I will ask him if he knows any Clappers next time I am at the rectory." Lucy went to rise, and Robert took her hand to help her up. "I do have one more thing to show you." She went over to her desk and picked up a flat velvet case. "I found this hidden in Miss Broomfield's bedroom."

"Hidden?" Robert opened the lid and blinked as the diamonds and rubies inside caught the sunlight. "Good Lord."

"I know." Lucy stood beside him, and they both stared down at the jewels. "I wonder why she was hiding them."

"Possibly to keep them safe," Robert said.

"Or to conceal them from their rightful owner," Lucy suggested.

Robert frowned at her. "I know you disliked Miss Broomfield, but you seem awfully keen to ascribe some very serious crimes to a dead woman who can't defend herself."

"I am not saying she *did* steal them. I am just speculating as to why she might have kept them hidden away."

Robert retrieved his spectacles, put them on, and examined the clasp of the necklace more carefully. "There is probably a maker's mark on here somewhere. There are very few jewelers who would be capable of producing a set of this high quality. I suspect that with a little investigation, we could find out who made them and to whom they were originally sold. I'll set Dermot on it this afternoon."

"That would certainly be helpful." Lucy nodded. "In the meantime, could you keep the jewels in your strongbox?"

"Certainly. What else did you find in the school? A hidden passage and a treasure trove?"

Lucy shuddered. "God forbid." She pointed at the table. "There is another box, which is locked. Goodness knows what we will find inside that one."

Robert frowned. "If Miss Broomfield had the means to conceal the jewelry securely, then why didn't she do so?"

"That's an interesting point." Lucy hid a yawn behind her hand as she walked over to the door. "I am due to meet with Anna and Aunt Rose in less than an hour, so I fear my investigation into the locked box will have to wait."

"Then perhaps you should rest for a while before they arrive?" Robert suggested.

"Actually, I am feeling quite rested."

Robert couldn't decide if he was delighted to see Lucy so animated or alarmed about the reasons behind it. Surely, if she kept her promise and did not exert herself too much, he would have nothing to complain about. And at least it gave them something to talk about other than the state of her health.

"There is one more thing. . . ." Lucy hesitated by the door.

"What is it?"

"Rebecca told me that the children are going to be terribly disappointed if they don't get the opportunity to sing at the carol service."

"So?"

She smiled up at him, her brown gaze so sweet, he was immediately suspicious. "I said that if you gave your permission, she and Josephine could use the schoolroom to continue to rehearse."

"That sounds . . . perfectly acceptable."

"Thank you." Her smile was a thing of beauty. "I will let the girls know." She blew him a kiss and whisked herself out of the room.

He had a sense that he had been bamboozled, but couldn't decide quite how. It was not an unfamiliar feeling in his long and sometimes contentious relationship with his wife, but he was almost glad to have her matching swords with him again. All he could do was continue to keep an eye on her and hope for the best.

• • •

"Paper is expensive." Lucy looked up from writing her umpteenth invitation. She was seated in the drawing room with Anna, Sophia, and Rose while they laboriously wrote out the invitations to the Christmas ball. It was not a particularly arduous task, merely a necessary one.

"What's that, my dear?" Aunt Rose inquired.

"I was just thinking out loud." Lucy put down her pen. "If you have to write a letter and don't order your stationery from town, like we do, where do you get the paper?"

"You can purchase it by the sheet in the village store," Anna said. "But you are correct. It certainly isn't cheap. And even if you can afford to buy the paper, a lot of our parishioners do not have the ability to write well enough to compose a letter."

"And it isn't cheap to send a letter, either," Sophia piped up. "Unless you can get it franked by a peer."

"I'd forgotten that," Lucy said. "Father often wrote letters for people and paid to send them out with our own mail at the rectory."

"Mr. Culpepper continues to do so," Anna said. "He has also started a class in the evenings to teach some of the local men how to read and write."

"What an excellent notion." Lucy stretched out her cramped fingers. "Does our father not object to George filling his house with common laborers?"

Anna smiled. "The class is held in the school in the evening twice a month. Your delightful husband gave his permission."

"Is it?" Lucy shook her head. "I had no idea. I wonder what Miss Broomfield thought of that!"

"She was vociferously and vehemently against the idea." Anna's smile disappeared. "I know that one should not speak ill of the dead, but she made her feelings on the subject very clear both to Father and me."

"So Father didn't like her very much, either," Lucy commented.

"I don't believe he did, my dear." Rose folded another sheet and wrote the address on the outside before folding the edges into a neat packet. "The rector has some very forward notions about the education of man. I believe that in retrospect he regretted his decision to support Miss Broomfield's employment at the school."

It was more likely that her father regretted the attention being directed at him for his poor judgment. He was certainly unlikely to apologize to his family. Lucy felt no need to explain that to Rose, who, like Anna, always saw the best in everyone.

If Mr. Culpepper had been using the school for his meetings, and Miss Broomfield had objected to them, it meant that not just the village children had been exposed to her unpleasant behavior. Had someone who gained access to the school taken the opportunity to search the teacher's apartments and maybe discovered she was worth robbing, after all?

Lucy didn't like to think of anyone she knew behaving in such a way, but she had learned to her cost that people were sometimes prepared to do anything to protect themselves and their secrets. Or had the teacher sat upstairs, listening to the men talking, and gleaned more secrets to use against her neighbors? It would seem possible.

She had a sense that Robert would remind her not to get ahead of herself, but it was hard not to speculate when they knew so little.

"Did Miss Broomfield ever mention her family to you, Anna?" Lucy asked as she took up her pen again.

"No. As I mentioned before, she barely tolerated my presence or spoke a word to me. She thought I was silly and frivolous." Anna shuddered. "I don't think she had any family in this area. She often complained that there was nothing of worth in Kurland St. Mary."

"Apart from a well-paying position and accompanying accommodation," Lucy huffed. "One might think that with her spotty past, she would've been grateful for the opportunity."

"I think she believed we were all beneath her—even Father, who *is* the son of an earl. She did

178

mention having lived in London at some point, but that's all I remember." Anna looked over as the clock on the mantelpiece chimed the hour. "Mr. Culpepper is coming to collect me soon, Lucy. We have some church business to attend to in Lower Kurland."

"Then I will take the opportunity to speak with him." Lucy counted the number of invitations. "Thank you all for your help. We will have these finished by tomorrow."

"Thank goodness." Sophia groaned. "I'd forgotten how boring it is. Andrew's secretary does all these things for me now."

"I could have asked Mr. Fletcher," Lucy acknowledged, "but he is writing all the invitations for the village party, and I didn't think it was fair to burden him with these, as well."

"Between the four of us, we have managed quite nicely," Rose said. "And shared an enjoyable afternoon."

"That is true," Sophia agreed. "I am quite willing to return tomorrow and resume my duties. Andrew is bringing the children over to ride, so I will have plenty of time on my hands while they are all tearing around the countryside. It was very kind of Robert to offer them his horses."

Foley came in and bowed to Lucy. "Mr. Culpepper is here for Miss Anna, my lady."

"Thank you, Foley. Will you ask him to come in for a moment?"

"If you wish, my lady. Shall I make some more tea?"

"That would be most welcome." Lucy made sure her inkwell was stoppered and went to sit by the fire.

George Culpepper came in and made an awkward bow to the assembled ladies before turning to Lucy. He was a slight young man with a kind face and a shock of reddish brown hair that he had never quite tamed.

"You wished to speak to me, Lady Kurland?"

"Indeed." Lucy waved him to the chair opposite hers. "I wanted to reassure you that despite Miss Broomfield's death, your work at the school can continue without pause."

"That's excellent news, my lady." He sat down. "I was rather worried that with the building being closed, my students would not be able to study."

"How many men do you tutor at the moment, Mr. Culpepper?" Lucy asked.

"It varies depending on the time of year and the weather. A lot of the men come from the surrounding areas, and if the roads aren't passable, then they can't come. But generally, there are at least six of them."

"Do you use the supplies at the school? Their ink, paper, and books?"

"Yes, my lady. Is there a problem?" Mr. Culpepper twisted his hands together. "Sir Robert and the rector said that I might do so."

"Where does the school get those items from?"

"I believe some are ordered by Sir Robert and the rector, and others are donated by local families. I use the children's slates to teach basic penmanship, and then move on to writing on scrap paper that I collect from the villages." He hesitated. "Am I doing something wrong? Did Miss Broomfield complain about me again?"

"I understand that she was unwilling for the school premises to be used for such a venture," Lucy said.

"I pray for her soul, but she certainly wasn't a great believer in the notion of education for the masses, I can tell you that." He sat forward, his expression eager. "There is nothing quite as remarkable as watching a man learn to read a newspaper or form his letters. He then becomes the arbiter of his own fate."

"Indeed." Lucy considered her next question. "Did Miss Broomfield ever interact with any of your students, or did she keep to herself?"

Mr. Culpepper made a wry face. "She occasionally came down to berate us for being too loud and coarse, but otherwise she kept to herself."

"Did she know all the men who were present?"

"Most of them had children who attended the school, but not all of them. The men who had children tried to be respectful toward her, but some of the younger ones were less likely to heed her words and occasionally mocked her—not that I allowed such behavior in her presence, my lady—but behind her back."

"Do you have a list of the names of the men who attend your classes?"

"I can certainly write one out for you, but with all due respect, I also wonder why you would need that information." He lowered his voice. "Does this have anything to do with Miss Broomfield's demise?"

Lucy didn't fault him at all for defending his students. In truth, she admired his tenacity and his desire to protect the men he was educating.

"It is more of a precautionary measure to ensure that everyone who had access to the schoolroom has been accounted for. I promise you that the only person who will see the information will be Sir Robert, and you can be certain that he will use it wisely."

"I'm sure he will. I will get that list to you by the end of today." Mr. Culpepper sat back. "Is there anything else I can assist you with, my lady?"

"Do you know of a family called Clapper in the villages?" Lucy asked.

"Clapper?" Mr. Culpepper considered. "I don't believe so, but I can inquire, if you wish."

"There was a gentleman of that name staying at the inn the other night who said he was visiting family in Kurland St. Mary." Lucy smiled at the curate. "I couldn't think who it might be. If you do come across the name, I would appreciate the information."

"As you wish, my lady. I can also check the parish records, if that would help. Are you concerned that this man was up to no good? I would much rather it was some random visitor to our village who attacked and murdered Miss Broomfield than one of our own, wouldn't you?"

"Absolutely." Mr. Culpepper made as if to rise, and Lucy held up her finger. "There is one more item I believe we need to discuss. Miss Dorothea Chingford."

"Ah, yes." A slight blush rose on the youthful curate's smooth cheeks. "Do you think Dr. Fletcher and his estimable wife would be willing to entertain my suit?"

"I don't see why not. You are a man of upstanding character, with a secure position and an excellent standing in your local community. You may tell the Fletchers that you have the blessing of Sir Robert and myself. I think Dorothea is a very lucky young woman."

"Thank you, my lady." Mr. Culpepper smiled fully for the first time. "The rector has also agreed to stand as a character reference for me."

"Then what is stopping you?" Lucy couldn't help but ask.

"It's *Mrs.* Fletcher, my lady. She keeps telling

Dorothea that she could do much better for herself."

"Mrs. Fletcher's acerbic disposition means that she is never satisfied with anything. I would discount her opinion and go ahead, anyway." Lucy resolved to have a word with her contrary friend at the earliest opportunity. "Why not settle things with Dr. Fletcher and then propose to Dorothea during the Christmas ball?"

Mr. Culpepper's face got even redder as he contemplated that idea. "I . . . will do that!" He shot up out of his chair. "I will go and see Dr. Fletcher immediately!"

Lucy rose, as well. "May I make a suggestion? Mrs. Fletcher will be attending me here in approximately an hour. Perhaps you might prefer to wait until then."

Chapter 9

George Culpepper doesn't know any family in the parish who is named Clapper."

"Neither did Dermot." Robert speared himself a slice of ham. He and Lucy were sharing a luncheon before the Stanford family arrived to spend the afternoon with them. "I suppose the Clapper relative could be a married female."

"He said he will check the parish records for me and write a note containing the names of all the men who attend his class in the schoolhouse for your attention."

"How very efficient. I suspect your father would be lost without him."

His wife looked much better today: the color had returned to her cheeks, and she was remarkably animated. Despite his continuing misgivings, he had to allow that the investigation had certainly rejuvenated her.

"Mr. Culpepper also intends to propose to Dorothea Chingford during our ball."

"My. He has been busy. Does *Mrs.* Fletcher know about this?"

"She does. I told Mr. Culpepper to speak to Dr. Fletcher when Penelope is not at home."

"A wise decision." Robert put down his knife. "From what I can see, Dorothea will make

George Culpepper a very comfortable wife."

"I agree. I intend to ask Father to offer them the cottage in the village next to the vergers."

"Don't I own that?" Robert looked up from his plate.

"No. It's part of church property and thus in the rector's gift." Lucy poured them both a cup of coffee.

"While you are busy matchmaking, have you made any progress with your sister and Nicholas Jenkins?"

"I have not." Lucy sighed. "Nicholas is not the sort of man to be pushed into anything, and my influence upon him is very slight. Mrs. Jenkins wishes him to marry Anna, but she, too, is worried about driving him too hard."

"Do you think Anna is inclined to favor his suit or not?"

"I'm not sure . . . ," Lucy said cautiously. "She certainly considers him a good friend and an excellent example of a gentleman. Why do you ask?"

"Because someone suggested to me the other day that Dermot was rather enamored of your sister."

"Mr. *Fletcher?* Who on earth suggested that?"

"Mrs. Jarvis at the Queen's Head."

"And you believed her?"

Robert shrugged. "She seemed fairly certain that she was right, and to her credit, since she mentioned it, I have noticed that Dermot can hardly take his eyes off your sister whenever they are in the same room together."

"Goodness gracious." Lucy shook her head. "Who would've thought that? Next time they are both present, I shall have to observe them more closely."

"Just observe them. Don't mention it to Anna, will you? Poor Dermot would be mortally embarrassed."

"I am not *quite* that green, Robert." She paused. "Although, my father would not look favorably upon such a match. The Fletchers are Roman Catholics."

"That is true."

"I found a crucifix in Miss Broomfield's bedroom."

Robert blinked at the sudden change of subject. "Are you suggesting she might have been a Catholic? I had many soldiers of that particular persuasion in my ranks, and they fought just as well as the next man. As long as Miss Broomfield didn't attempt to convert the children's parents to the Church of Rome by influencing the children I cannot see it causing harm."

"I think we would have heard from the villagers if any such thing had happened." Lucy used her napkin. "I was just surprised to find the crucifix there. It was the only personal item Miss Broomfield had added to her rooms."

"No knickknacks? No ornaments or pictures?" Robert asked. "That *is* odd."

A tapping on the glass drew his attention to the large windows that opened out into the garden.

"Is that Grace Turner?" Robert beckoned her to enter.

Lucy turned in her seat. "I believe it is."

Robert rose to his feet, came around the table, and bowed. "Good afternoon, Miss Turner."

Grace stopped and looked him over as if she were purchasing a horse at Tattersalls. "Good afternoon, Sir Robert. Is your leg bothering you today?"

He frowned at her. "Good Lord, woman. Don't you start. As you well know, my joints are always painful during the winter months."

She continued to examine him, her head to one side and her bonnet almost sliding off the hair hanging down her back. "It's more than that, though, isn't it? You are holding yourself as if you are in fear."

He glowered at her. "Don't be ridiculous."

She raised her eyebrows and turned to Lucy. "Do you think he is in pain?"

"Well, he certainly has been very short tempered recently," Lucy agreed.

"If my temper is *short,* madam, it is because you constantly shred it." He bowed. "If you have both finished dissecting me, I shall leave you in peace to discuss me further at your leisure."

Grace smiled at him. "My, you are magnificently snooty today, sir. I am quite overawed."

"That *was* my intention."

She sketched a curtsy. "I humbly beg your pardon."

"Indeed." Robert raised an eyebrow. "Why are you here, anyway?"

She produced something out of her pocket. "I thought you should see this."

Robert took the scrap of folded paper, opened it, and read the contents out loud. "Everyone knows you are a witch and a betrayer of your family. One day you will burn in hell."

Grace shrugged. "It was stuck under my door the other night." She raised her gaze to Robert's, and he registered the hurt in her eyes. "It's the truth, but it still hurts."

"It is a highly distorted version of the truth," Robert replied. "You know that."

Lucy came to put a tentative hand on Grace's shoulder. "When exactly did you find it?"

"About five days ago, just after we spoke about the other letter. Why?"

Lucy exchanged a glance with Robert, who replied to Grace. "Because four nights ago Miss Broomfield was killed."

"I heard about that." Grace nodded. "She wasn't well liked by the villagers or their children. She carried much darkness in her heart." She paused. "What does she have to do with this unpleasant letter?"

"We are wondering if she was the author of the notes," Robert said. "What most people don't know is that Miss Broomfield died at her desk, stabbed in the eye with her own quill pen."

"That hardly sounds enough to kill her." Grace didn't sound particularly impressed.

"That was just the finishing touch. She was stabbed in the back with a hat pin. There was no sign of a struggle."

"So it was probably done by someone who had a personal grievance against her, rather than by a random passerby or a robber?"

"That's what we believe. Your note is very similar in tone to the ones Mrs. Jenkins and my wife received. Can I keep this so that we can compare the handwriting?"

"Of course you can. I don't want the foul thing in my house." Grace glanced curiously at Lucy, who had gone still. "You didn't mention that you had received a note, as well."

"I was going to tell you," Lucy said hesitantly as Robert belatedly remembered everything her letter had implied about Grace's dislike of her. "I just wasn't sure—"

"My wife's letter suggested that you hated her and were out for revenge," Robert said. In his opinion, there was no point in avoiding the issue.

Grace grabbed Lucy's hand. "You do know that is a lie, don't you?"

"Of course." Lucy squeezed Grace's fingers. "I must confess that, initially, it was something of a shock, but I soon realized you were not capable of keeping such hatred from anyone, let alone me."

"What a horrible thing to say to you!" Grace exclaimed. "If Miss Broomfield *was* the author of these notes, it is a good thing she is deceased, or I might be proving that I am indeed a witch."

"There's no need for that, Miss Turner," Robert hastily interjected. "We've had enough problems with witchcraft in this village without you starting it all up again."

The look she gave him was not reassuring. But he owed a debt to Grace Turner, and he was ever mindful of it in his dealings with her. Their relationship was certainly unorthodox, but he suspected they both enjoyed the sparring. She owned her cottage, earned her own living, and had little interest in the ways of the gentry, so he had no say over anything she did. And Lucy liked and trusted her, which was even more important.

"I will leave you two ladies to talk." Robert bowed. "Don't forget that the Stanfords will be here at one, will you, my dear?"

"I'm not intending to stay, Sir Robert." Grace smiled at him. "I have to go into the village and see your doctor friend. Sometimes we discuss our patients and squabble over how best to treat them."

"Well, for heaven's sake, please don't mention my name," Robert said as she winked at him. "The last thing I need is for you all to gang up on me." He left the room, but her voice carried out into the hall.

"If you insist on ignoring our advice, what else do you expect?"

"Some respect in my own community?" Robert muttered as he made his way to his study, encountering Foley by the main staircase.

"Ah, Foley. Have you made sure Mr. Coleman is ready for our guests at the stables?"

"I have indeed, sir." Foley bowed. "He is expecting the children and greatly looking forward to it. I suppose there is not much opportunity for the Stanfords to ride much in London."

"Which is why they will enjoy a good romp around the countryside with their father while Mrs. Stanford visits with my lady."

"Do you intend to ride out with them, sir?"

Robert's smile faded. "Not today. My leg is not in a cooperative mood."

Sometimes he grew tired of all the interest in his shortcomings. He nodded and kept going until he reached the sanctuary of his study, where the only person who would bother him before their dinner engagement with the Greenwells would be Dermot. And thank goodness for that.

• • •

Lucy gathered the folds of her fur-lined evening cloak more tightly around her shoulders as an icy draught circled through the carriage. Foley had insisted on putting foot warmers on the floor, and for once she was grateful for his consideration.

Robert settled beside her, one hand braced on the back of the seat, and Andrew Stanford took his place beside Sophia. They had decided to go to the Greenwells' house together to save the horses. Lucy also hoped it might take Robert's mind off the necessity of traveling in a closed space, which never sat well with him, since he'd almost been crushed by his own horse at Waterloo.

Having to make polite conversation with their guests should ease his disquiet, and the journey would be over in no time. She had no idea who else the Greenwells had asked to dine, but she hoped it wasn't too large a gathering. It had already been a long day, and she would rather not have to exert herself too much.

Robert had a tendency to become a little impatient with some of the local gentry, those who cared more about their horses than the current state of their country, and she wasn't in the mood to apologize for him. But at least he appeared to have found an ally in Mr. Greenwell. If that was the case, then Lucy would willingly put up with the female members of the family.

The carriage arrived at the Greenwell residence, and they descended and entered the house. It was surprisingly warm, and Lucy was almost willing to relinquish her cloak. To her relief, there was a not too large group of people gathered in the drawing room. She recognized Mrs. Jenkins and Nicholas, and after greeting her hostess, she went over to speak to her elderly neighbor.

"What a pleasure to see you here, ma'am." Lucy smiled down at the diminutive old lady, who wore a purple satin gown with a matching turban. "Did Mr. Greenwell ask you to dine because you are also a member of our school board?"

"I assume so." Mrs. Jenkins jerked her head in Nicholas's direction. "Although I suspect Mrs. Greenwell had some motivation of her own."

The two Greenwell sisters were on either side of Nicholas and were chattering away like magpies. Margaret, the oldest of the pair, actually had her hand on his sleeve in a very overfamiliar way.

"Is your sister, Anna, attending this evening?" Mrs. Jenkins asked. "I know the rector is coming."

"My father is bringing Mrs. Armitage. They should be here very shortly."

"How kind of him."

"We could not fit everyone in the same carriage, so he came to our rescue and offered to bring her instead."

Just as she spoke, her father and Rose came in through the door, and Mrs. Jenkins went over to speak to them.

The dinner bell rang, and Mrs. Greenwell took Robert's arm as Mr. Greenwell came toward Lucy.

"Good evening, Lady Kurland. May I escort you in to dinner?"

"Thank you."

Lucy placed her hand on his sleeve, and they proceeded through the double doors into the dining room, which easily seated a dozen. Mr. Greenwell drew out her chair for her and waited until Lucy settled into her seat. There was an older man opposite her whom she did not recognize.

"May I introduce you to my wife's uncle Frederick Halston, Lady Kurland? He is a justice of the peace in London and is spending the festive season with us."

"It is a pleasure to make your acquaintance, sir."

Lucy smiled through the candlelight, but the man merely grunted something unintelligible back. Used to dealing with curmudgeons from her days shepherding her father's flock in the rectory, she turned her attention to her host and began a very agreeable discussion about the state of the Kurland St. Mary school and their quest for a new teacher.

"Yes, Sir Robert and I both agree that the ability to read and write is the key to improvement in any individual." Lucy set aside her dessert plate and waited as the footman refilled her glass of Madeira.

"What a very dangerous statement to make, Lady Kurland."

"I beg your pardon?" Lucy looked up into the eyes of Frederick Halston who sat opposite her. It was the first time he had directly addressed her all evening.

"I suggested that your naive remarks about the value of an education are dangerous."

"*Dangerous?* How so?"

"The only reason the poor should be taught how to read is so that they can examine the Scriptures and understand their place in a godly society." He regarded her over the top of his spectacles. "As to the subjects of writing and arithmetic, such knowledge might produce in them a distaste for the more laborious occupations in life."

"And why would that be an issue, sir?" Lucy asked, aware that the rest of the diners had stopped talking and were listening to their conversation. "Surely, it is for the betterment of society if *all* its members are well informed."

"My dear Lady Kurland, your sentiments, of course, do you credit, but perhaps the logic of the situation is beyond your feminine comprehension." His smile was kindly. "With all due respect, ladies are not known for the power of their reasoning, which is as it should be."

"Oh, good Lord. Now he's in for it." Lucy was fairly certain that was Robert muttering as she smiled back at the older man.

"What exactly do you fear from an educated population, sir?" she asked.

"Because such a thing would be prejudicial to the morals and happiness of the working class. If we educate them, Lady Kurland, we would teach them to despise their lot in life, and then who would do their work? How would they survive?"

"By doing more educated work? There is always work for the desperate, so I suspect those lower jobs would readily be filled."

"I agree there is already plenty of employment for the lower orders," Mr. Halston said firmly. "Instead of teaching them to be subordinate to their betters, such skills will make them more difficult to control, and *then* where will we be?"

"Forced to listen to them? Forced to acknowledge the inequality of our current political system?" Robert's abrupt questions fell into the silence. "There are schools in the factories in the north. I helped found the ones in my own business enterprises. Why shouldn't there be schools in the more *rural* areas of the country?"

"And what have those northern schools unleashed, Sir Robert? Men who are reading seditious pamphlets, vicious books, and publications against Christianity. Is that what you want? A working class that is insolent to its superiors and likely to overthrow its betters? That is *treason,* sir. I cannot think you mean what you say."

Robert leaned forward, his gaze locked on the older man. "I certainly want a more equal system of government, and if educating a country's citizens helps that occur, then I, for one, am all for it."

"It is not right," Mr. Halston blustered. "Rector, I appeal to you. Does not the Bible state very clearly that every man has his place?"

"The rich man in his castle, the poor man at his gate?" Mr. Harrington smiled. "Indeed, but I have to admit that like Sir Robert, I do not believe that teaching children to read and write means the end of civilization as we know it."

"I suppose you'll both be suggesting we should educate women next," Mr. Halston said gloomily. "Or how about a vote for every man?" He looked over at his nephew. "You have surprisingly radical friends, Edward."

"Apparently so." Mr. Greenwell bowed to Lucy, his eyes twinkling. "Revolutionary indeed."

Mrs. Greenwell abruptly rose to her feet, her gaze on Lucy. "Perhaps the *ladies* should withdraw and leave the gentlemen to their politics."

With a resigned sigh, Lucy stood and headed

for the door. As she passed Robert's chair, he caught hold of her hand and kissed her gloved fingers.

"Well done, my dear. I do apologize for inter-rupting, but I wanted the poor man to save some face before you eviscerated him."

She didn't stop to chat, but his approval of her out-spokenness warmed her heart and steeled her against the disapproval she suspected she would garner from the Greenwell ladies.

When she reached the drawing room, she spotted Josephine pouring tea and coffee and made a point of speaking to her before returning to face the barrage of disapproval on the opposite couch. It was comforting to have Rose and Sophia sitting on either side of her. Mrs. Jenkins had already fallen asleep by the fire.

Mrs. Greenwell drew herself up, visibly flustered. "As I was just saying to Margaret, Lady Kurland, and I am sure that you will confirm my instincts, such political outbursts from ladies are not *generally* the norm at the dinner table."

"I quite agree." Lucy sipped her tea. "I do apologize if I offended you."

"Then perhaps you might choose to enlighten us as to why you felt the need to express such an opinion in the first place?"

"Why should I not? Surely, my opinion is as valid as any man's." Margaret Greenwell tittered behind her fan, and Lucy continued. "Both my father and my husband were present at the table, and neither of them chose to censor me."

"But do you not think it unbecoming in a woman to *parrot* the views of a man when she clearly does not have the knowledge to understand the nuances of such information for herself?" Mrs. Greenwell persisted.

"Why should Lady Kurland not understand anything?" Sophia said sweetly. "She is remarkably intelligent, you know."

"So I have heard." Mrs. Greenwell was far from mollified. "Lady Kurland is something of an 'original.' But surely you must agree with me, my dear Mrs. Stanford, as a fellow mother, that such outpourings are not the kind of talk one wishes to hear in one's own unmarried daughters."

"Why ever not?" Sophia asked.

"Because men do not generally choose to marry bluestockings or radicals."

"More fool them." Sophia smiled. "I can assure you that there are gentlemen out there who *do* want to marry intelligent women. I am proof of that, as surely is Lady Kurland. Neither of our husbands feels the need to stifle our opinions."

"Then perhaps you should feel privileged that your husbands *allow* you such independence of thought." Mrs. Greenwell's smile was thin.

"I shall continue to teach *my* daughters that obedience to their parents and to their future husbands is paramount to their success in life."

Sophia winked at Lucy as Mrs. Greenwell walked over to ring the servants' bell, and whispered, "I suspect I will not be invited back again."

"How nice for you. I will have to endure her and her daughters for years to come," Lucy complained under her breath. "I must remember to thank my husband for the privilege of being allowed a single thought of my own."

Sophia concealed a chuckle as Margaret glared at her. "I'm fairly certain Sir Robert would appreciate that immensely."

On the way back to Kurland Hall, the Stanfords went with the rector, and Rose rejoined Robert and Lucy in the carriage. After a happy day out riding, Mr. Coleman had already taken the children home to Sophia's mother. It was bitterly cold, and bright moonlight streamed down from the ink-black sky, illuminating the barren fields and trees lining the road from Lower Kurland.

Robert was secretly very fond of Andrew's two children and had enjoyed the opportunity to spend some time with them. Alex had become an accomplished horseman, and his little sister, who had once been as scared of horses as Robert, was coming along nicely, as well.

During his career in the cavalry, he'd never really thought much about children. His focus had been on surviving the next battle rather than on what went on at home. He couldn't deny that the thought of his feckless cousin Paul inheriting the Kurland estate and his title filled him with dread. The estate would be gambled away and dismantled within a year, and his tenants would be scattered. He would never admit it to Lucy, but she knew him well enough to understand it would be a bitter pill to swallow.

She sighed and leaned in closer, her head coming to rest on his shoulder as her eyes closed. Her familiar lavender scent surrounded him as he eased an arm around her shoulders and anchored her against his side. The only time he had ever come close to hitting his father-in-law was when he'd suggested that Robert should not concern himself about the consequences to his wife's health of another pregnancy, seeing as a man could "always marry again."

But he didn't want to marry again. He wanted *this* wife—this obstinate, redoubtable, intelligent treasure of a woman.

Sometimes life came down to making a choice. He'd learned that on the battlefields of France, and in this instance, he'd rather keep Lucy than some imaginary child. He bent to drop a kiss on her unsuspecting head and caught Aunt Rose's approving gaze.

He shrugged. "I have learned to appreciate the moments when she sleeps."

Rose's warm chuckle, and the elbow in his ribs from his obviously not quite asleep wife, made him smile and feel very hopeful for the future.

Chapter 10

I have this for you from Father." Anna held out a piece of paper. "It is the name and direction of the professor in Cambridge who recommended Miss Broomfield for the teaching post."

"Please thank Father for the information, although I suspect you found it for him." Lucy took the paper. "I will write to this professor directly."

They were seated in her sitting room, finishing off the last of the invitations and dividing them into batches for the stable boys to deliver. Dermot had informed her that the invites to the village party had also gone out, and that everyone was very excited at the prospect of an afternoon's entertainment.

"Did Dermot mention where he intended to purchase all the toys and games for the village children's gifts?" Anna asked.

"I assumed he would go to Hertford. Why?"

Anna pointed at the address she had just given Lucy. "I wonder if we could go to Cambridge instead? It should be manageable in a day, even in this weather."

"That is an excellent idea." Lucy pondered the notion. "I'm sure Robert would understand the necessity of my supervising Dermot's choices and expenditure."

"I'm sure he'd be very suspicious, but as long as I went with you, how could he possibly complain?"

Lucy counted the ways but kept her counsel. "I will write to this professor immediately. If he seems inclined to be helpful, then I will consider your plan to go to Cambridge."

"It would also be nice to do some Christmas shopping in a proper town," Anna said wistfully. "Have you any gifts to purchase yourself?"

"I don't have anything for Aunt Rose, as she was an unexpected addition to our household, but I have everything else well in hand."

"Of course you do. You are one of the most organized people I know." Anna placed the last letter on the pile. "I am looking forward to seeing the twins. I wonder if they have grown again."

"It wouldn't surprise me." Lucy smiled fondly at the thought of her rambunctious twin brothers. "Despite all my earlier worries, school does seem to agree with them. I suspect they will spend most of their visit in our stables, bothering Mr. Coleman, but at least he will keep them within the boundaries of civility."

"At least they have each other at school." Anna sighed and set down her pen. "That must be comforting."

Lucy considered her sister's downcast face. "Is there anything wrong, Anna?"

"Father received a horrible letter," Anna said

in a rush. "It was written on a scrap of paper that somehow got mixed up with George's mail. George gave it to me this morning."

"So you have no idea when it was actually delivered?"

"No."

"What did it say?"

Anna gulped down a breath. "That Father was a heartless sinner who would burn in hell for his wickedness."

"Did you show it to him?" Lucy asked.

"No. I didn't want to upset him. I thought it best to bring the matter to you." Anna pressed a hand to her heart. "When Mrs. Jenkins received a similar letter, you promised that Robert would investigate the matter."

"Robert *is* investigating, but we are still no closer to discovering who the culprit is," Lucy said carefully. "We did wonder if it was Miss Broomfield."

Anna blinked hard. "The *teacher?* But she's dead."

"Which is why I asked you when the letter arrived." Lucy opened her desk and drew out the other three letters. "So far we have these." She passed them to Anna. "There is a similar theme."

"They are certainly all horrible." Anna passed them back, as if she didn't want them in her possession. "Why would anyone be so . . . *spiteful?*" She raised her beautiful eyes to Lucy's.

"Should I show the letter to Father and tell him about the others?"

"There is no need for you to do that, Anna. When Robert discovers who wrote them, he will naturally inform our father."

"Thank you." Anna took a deep breath. "I hate it when people I love are hurt by such unnecessary things. Father has been very kind to me since I returned from London unwed. He does not deserve to be treated so harshly."

Lucy bit back her first response and tried to be diplomatic. "In truth, Anna, you deserve his thanks for taking on the responsibilities of the rectory when you should be setting up your own home and nursery."

"I am more than willing to stay at home." Anna hesitated and then spoke in a rush. "I know you think I should marry Nicholas, but I am afraid of the responsibilities of marriage and all it entails."

Lucy took Anna's trembling hand in her own. She had never seen her sunny-natured sister so upset before. "Which particular part of marriage?"

"The *wedded* part of it . . . the idea of constantly having children, of . . . *dying,* like our mother did. I remember that day, Lucy. I remember the sickly coppery smell of death, of her *screaming* and begging God to ease her pain. I remember our father galloping away on his horse, leaving us to deal with everything. . . ."

"I . . . didn't realize you had been so deeply affected by what happened," Lucy said hesitantly. "You were so *young*. But you must know that childbirth doesn't always end like that."

"I have attended plenty of births since I returned home, and I cannot say that I have learned to enjoy the experience or have changed my opinion," Anna said firmly. "Look at you, Lucy. You almost bled to death last time you attempted to provide Robert with an heir, and I'll wager you are more than willing to try again."

"I hardly bled to death," Lucy remonstrated. "I will not lie and tell you the experience was pleasant. The thought of having Robert's child makes what I suffered worthwhile."

Anna shuddered. "I do not understand how you can be so brave."

"Hardly brave," Lucy pointed out. "Women have been giving birth since Adam and Eve. And if you have found . . . *contentment* in a relationship with a particular man, the thought of having his child somehow makes sense of the dangers. Mayhap you simply haven't met the right person yet."

"There was a man . . . a gentleman in London . . . whom I thought I might come to care for." Anna looked past Lucy and out of the window.

"Is this the naval officer Aunt Jane mentioned in her letters?" Lucy asked.

"Yes. Captain Harry Akers."

"Then perhaps we should consider returning to London next year for the Season so that you can meet this man again."

"He rarely comes back to England these days." Anna sighed. "And in truth, I don't think he would wish to see me. I told him not to attempt to contact me ever again."

Lucy stiffened. "Did he behave in an inappropriate manner to you?"

"No. He simply kissed me."

"And you don't consider that ungentlemanly?"

"Not when he asked for permission and I gave it." Anna's faint smile died.

"Did he attempt to force you in some way?"

"Not at all. He was the perfect gentleman."

Lucy tried to gather her thoughts. "Some kisses can seem . . . rather *intimate* at first, but—"

Anna waved away her words. "I know that."

"Then what happened to make you send him away with a flea in his ear?"

"I *liked* his kiss. That's what scared me, Lucy." Anna gulped down some air. "It made me think that I might be persuaded by my own desires into a relationship that would only end up exactly where I feared, with me pregnant and afraid."

Lucy stared at her sister. What on earth could she say to assuage Anna's very real fears? She had seen many women die during childbirth and couldn't deny the risks.

"If you did ever become pregnant, you know

that Dr. Fletcher and Grace would do everything in their power to make sure you survived the experience."

"I know." Anna found a smile. "Mayhap you are right, Lucy, and I have not met the right man yet. Surely, there must be a gentleman who already has enough children and would be content with a friend and companion."

"If you wish to look after a man like that, you might as well stay in the rectory," Lucy said tartly. "You deserve more."

"And a man, especially one of our class, deserves an heir," Anna snapped back, her color visibly heightened. "You, of all people, should know that."

"Yes, indeed." Lucy busied herself with her pens and paper. "Did you bring the letter Father received with you?"

Anna rose from her seat and went over to the settee where she'd placed her reticule. "I have it here." She brought the note back to Lucy and reached for her hand. "I am sorry. That was cruel. I did not mean to upset you."

"You didn't." Lucy patted her sister's hand. "And I was a little blunt with you, so I probably deserved it. Have you considered telling any gentleman who you might be interested in marrying how you feel about not having children?"

"I doubt such a conversation would go well."

Anna sat back down with a thump. "But I will keep your suggestion in mind. It would certainly scare off some of my suitors, which would not be a bad thing. Sometimes I wonder whether I should become a teacher or a governess like Miss Broomfield and simply fade into the background."

"I doubt you could fade away. All the ladies would be jealous of your beauty, and the sons would consider you fair game."

"I suppose that is true," Anna said. "Then maybe a teacher rather than a governess."

"Miss Broomfield didn't seem to enjoy the experience very much. I would hate to see that happening to you."

"I wonder *why* she was so bitter," Anna mused. "Did she lose the love of her life, was she ruined, or was she running away from something?"

"You read too many gothic novels," Lucy grumbled. "Maybe she just wanted to be a teacher to gain independence from her family."

"Women of our class are neither encouraged nor allowed to be independent. Lucy, you know that. And Miss Broomfield did have a very upper-class diction and a distinctly commanding air about her."

"She did, didn't she?" Lucy said, slowly remembering the lavish set of diamond and ruby jewelry. "Perhaps she was escaping from something, after all. . . ."

"Have you finished sorting through Miss Broomfield's possessions?" Anna pointed at the pile of boxes on the table. "I can stay for another hour or so if you need help. Father is taking Mrs. Armitage on a tour of the three churches today, and I don't expect them back until late this afternoon."

"I would appreciate some help." Lucy abandoned her desk and joined Anna at the table. "There is one large box that I haven't opened yet, because there is no key, but I also found this." She held up the crucifix.

"How very popish."

"There is something tied to the back of it. It was concealed against the wall." Lucy patiently picked at the twine wrapped around the base until she was able to unfold the paper and reveal a key beneath it. She held it up to Anna, who was busy dragging the heavy strongbox to the edge of the table. "I was right. It is a key."

"Then let's hope it fits." Anna stood back as Lucy inserted the key into the lock.

"It's too small." Lucy tried again, with no success. "I will have to ask Foley if he can help us. He is something of an expert on locks."

As if he had known he was required, Foley chose that moment to arrive with the tea tray and a selection of cakes the cook wanted "Miss Anna to try."

After Lucy explained the problem, he approached

the box and studied it, his head to one side, like a bird's.

"With your permission, my lady?" Foley drew a key ring out of his pocket that positively bristled with keys of all shapes and sizes. "One of these might work. If it does not, we'll require the assistance of James, our first footman. His father was a locksmith, and young James learned the rudiments of the trade."

"And if James can't help, there's always Joseph Cobbins from the stables," Lucy murmured to her sister. "His ne'er-do-well father was an expert at breaking and entering."

None of Foley's keys worked, so Lucy rang the bell for James and waited patiently as Anna poured them both some tea. She couldn't help but wonder what was in the box, and what the key she *had* found was for. Knowing Miss Broomfield's habit of concealment made her think she must have missed something when she searched the school before.

She had arranged for Josephine and Rebecca to open the school on the following day to rehearse the carols with the younger children. While she was supervising the session, she would have time to reexamine the teacher's quarters and see if she had missed anything. The key wasn't very large, but the fact that Miss Broomfield had deliberately concealed it made it seem important.

Unless it was for another box, a box concealed in the one James had just managed to open with a combination of one of Foley's keys and a hoof pick. . . .

"Thank you so much, James." Lucy smiled at the footman.

"You're welcome, my lady." He stepped back and nodded at Foley. "I'll be going back to the kitchen now to help with setting up dinner."

"Thank you again." Lucy waited until Foley followed James out of the door before cautiously opening the lid of the box.

"This feels like velvet." Lucy drew out what appeared to be some kind of dark green shoulder cape and wrinkled her nose. "It smells rather musty." She set it on the table, beside the box, and peered into the interior of the box. "Oh, my goodness."

"What is it?" Anna exclaimed.

"Look." Lucy reached in and picked up four flat boxes, which were surprisingly heavy. "I think they are jewelry cases."

Ignoring Anna's squeak of surprise, Lucy continued to remove another layer of shallow boxes and one large, deep ornate wooden one.

"Shall we look inside?" Anna asked.

"I don't see why not." Lucy opened the first box to reveal a double strand of pearls with a carved ivory pendant at the center of the chain. "This is beautiful."

Leaving Anna to sigh over the contents of the smaller boxes, Lucy turned her attention to the ornate wooden box she assumed was an actual jewelry casket which had a small key in the lock. On the blue satin lining inside sat a multitude of rings, earrings, and brooches, which sparkled and glowed even in the dullness of the winter afternoon.

Anna met Lucy's gaze. "Where on earth did Miss Broomfield get these things?"

"Perhaps she inherited them from her mother."

"But why was she working as a teacher? Just one of these pieces is worth five *years* of her salary. Why didn't she just sell everything and live off the income?"

"I don't know," Lucy finally said. "None of this makes any sense at all."

Hours later, after Anna had returned to the rectory and Lucy and Robert had eaten dinner with Aunt Rose, Lucy was still no nearer to understanding Miss Broomfield's peculiar behavior.

She waited impatiently as Robert methodically went through the hoard of jewelry, whistling under his breath as he held up some of the more elaborate pieces, such as the delicate tiara.

Eventually, she had to ask. "Why do you think Miss Broomfield had all this wealth concealed in her cupboard?"

"I have no idea." He set down the last piece.

"I suppose she might have wanted to keep the pieces for her future children."

"While teaching in a school and not even attempting to attract a husband of any kind?"

"Or maybe she was simply attempting to keep her legacy safe."

Lucy sat at her desk. "I suppose it does provide a good reason why someone might want to kill her."

"But no one is this community would've known or suspected that she was rich," Robert countered.

"What about that Mr. Clapper who visited the smithy on the day she died?"

"We don't even know if he was acquainted with Miss Broomfield. Mr. Hall didn't say he asked any questions about who lived where in Kurland St. Mary, or anything useful like that."

"I should ask Mr. Jarvis if he remembers Mr. Clapper saying anything when he stayed at the Queen's Head."

"He didn't seem to know much." Robert smiled. "Better ask Mrs. Jarvis. She's the one with all the gossip."

"I will." Lucy stared at the boxes piled on the table. "There is one odd thing, though."

"What is that?"

"The diamond and ruby necklace I found on top of her chest of drawers."

"Ah yes." Robert perched on the edge of the

desk and looked down at her. "Why was that piece in a different place to all the rest of her loot?"

"Perhaps she was contemplating selling just that one item. Or giving it to someone."

Robert raised an eyebrow. "So now you suspect she was paying someone off? Who? The mysterious Mr. Clapper, I presume."

Lucy sniffed. "You are the one who used the word *loot,* as if she had somehow accrued all the valuables in a less than honest way."

"If we are bent on discussing outrageous scenarios, my dear, as is your wont, then we cannot ignore the fact that she might have stolen every damn thing and made off with it."

"I suppose that would explain why she was hiding her wealth." Lucy sighed. "This is *most* confusing. I must write to my father's friend in Cambridge tonight and hope that he can provide us with more information."

"In the meantime, I'll call Dermot to come and help me lock up this treasure trove in our strong room." He slowly straightened up and grabbed his cane. "We can rely on him to be discreet and keep this information to himself."

"Do you need my help?" Lucy inquired.

"No. You write your important letter, and I will ensure that it is delivered as quickly as possible on the morrow."

"Thank you." Lucy hesitated. "I had a long

conversation with Anna today about her marriage prospects."

"And?"

"She fears having a child."

"An understandable dilemma." He went toward the door, his gait awkward even with his cane.

"I don't think I managed to reassure her about the matter, either."

"How could you, considering what you have been through this last year?" He looked back at her from the door, his face in shadows.

"I do not regret what has occurred." She held his gaze. "I only wish the outcome had been . . . better."

"Indeed."

"Do you think there are gentlemen who might consider marrying a woman and not expect her to have children?"

"I doubt it. What man would choose to marry if he *didn't* want an heir?"

"I see." Lucy looked down at her lap. "What about for companionship and respect and . . . love?"

He came back in and gently closed the door. "If you are trying to tell me something, could you be more specific?"

She blinked up at him. "What ever do you mean?"

"If you are suggesting that our marriage is built on friendship, respect, and love, then I would have to agree with you. I would also agree that it can remain like that if that is your choice."

"I was talking about *Anna*."

"Are you sure?" He didn't look angry, just tired. "I promise that I will not stop loving and liking you, regardless of your decision. Just let me know, won't you?"

With an abrupt jerk of his head, he turned on his heel and left, leaving Lucy openmouthed.

Had he thought she was suggesting she no longer wanted to share his bed? Was he really that *foolish?* He was the one who had been avoiding her for the past few months! She half rose from her seat and considered running after him, and then remembered what had happened the last time she chased him into his lair.

She sat down again, her hands entwined together on her lap, her whole body trembling. Should she consider what he was offering her? Was he merely suggesting an arrangement that he had already started to implement in his own subtle way? An arrangement that many couples of their social class arrived at and agreed with?

Taking a deep breath, Lucy turned her attention to the letter she had to write. If Robert came back with Dermot to take the boxes away, she would pretend not to see him at all.

Chapter 11

The next morning, Lucy decided to start her day by visiting the Queen's Head. She'd slept badly, too aware of Robert gently snoring on his side of the bed, as if he didn't have a care in the world. She knew him well enough to know that he wouldn't force further discussion on the issue of whether she wished their marriage to remain celibate but would leave her to make her own decision and communicate it to him when she was ready.

But she had no answer for him, just a sense that her heart was actually hurting, and that it was somehow difficult to concentrate. She didn't like to fail at anything, and marriage was no exception.

As it wasn't market day, the inn was relatively quiet. It was a chilly but bright morning, and she'd chosen to walk down to the village, as much to give her something to do as to avoid having to rouse Mr. Coleman from the stable. Having taken her breakfast in bed, Aunt Rose had agreed to meet her at the rectory at noon, when the twins were expected to arrive home.

She was looking forward to seeing her brothers, who would be sure to keep her busy, with their boundless energy and propensity for getting into trouble. Over the years they had come to regard Robert as something of a hero, probably because unlike their indolent father, he was more than happy to order them around and expect instant obedience. For some reason, they appreciated that. Lucy would never quite understand men.

"Lady Kurland?"

Lucy walked into the inn to find Mrs. Jarvis just emerging from the kitchen. The inn was over two hundred years old, with neither a straight ceiling nor a flat floor within its black beams and wattle-and-daub walls.

"Good morning, Mrs. Jarvis. I wonder if I might have a moment of your time?"

"Good gracious, my lady, of course you may!" Mrs. Jarvis curtsied. "I was just thinking of going up to the hall to speak to Major Kurland myself." She opened the door into one of the private parlors and ushered Lucy inside. "Not that he's Major Kurland anymore now, is he? Of course, when I knew him, he wasn't even that!" She chuckled, sending her blond ringlets bobbing under her lace cap.

Lucy turned to face her. "You knew Sir Robert before you moved to Kurland St. Mary?"

"Oh, yes, my lady. Didn't he mention it to you? The naughty boy. I met him in London about sixteen years ago, when I was a dancer in the theater, and he and his officer friends came backstage to ogle the performers."

Lucy managed a smile. "How strange that you ended up living in the same village."

"I know." Mrs. Jarvis winked. "I can't say he was pleased to see me, but I'm not here to cause trouble. You can have my word on that, my lady."

"That's . . . very good of you." Lucy sank into a chair in front of the fire. "Do you have a message for Sir Robert that I can deliver for you?"

"No need for that now." Mrs. Jarvis took the seat opposite Lucy. "You can tell him yourself. He was asking whether that Mr. Clapper who stayed here had shared any information about why he'd been in the village, seeing as the name wasn't familiar to Sir Robert."

"I believe my husband said you'd confirmed that Mr. Clapper stayed the night but that no one spoke to him beyond the basic civilities."

"Which was how matters stood until Bertha, my second chambermaid, came back to work today after staying home to look after her poor mother." Mrs. Jarvis shook her head. "Thirty-nine years old and birthing her fifteenth child, and Bertha's the oldest and only seventeen."

"The Pilcher family?"

"Yes, my lady, that's right. Well, as I said, Bertha came back today, and she was the one who tidied up after Mr. Clapper the night he stayed here. She was telling me that he was quite a chatty man, but a little likely to pinch her bottom, if you take my meaning, and—"

In a vain attempt to stem the flow of words, Lucy held up her hand. "So Bertha spoke to Mr. Clapper. What did he say to her?"

"I was just getting to that, my lady. Bertha said that Mr. Clapper was a solicitor, and that he lived in Cheapside, in London."

"Cheapside?" Lucy tried to locate the area in her memory. "I don't think I ever visited anyone there."

"Probably not, my lady. It's not exactly a fashionable part of town, is it? Filled with cits, merchants, and bankers."

"Did Mr. Clapper mention why he was in Kurland St. Mary?"

"Now, Bertha did ask him, which she shouldn't have done, seeing as I tell my girls not to be too nosy about our clients, just in case they end up getting themselves into trouble, and he said it was confidential client business, whatever that means."

"Presumably, he came to see someone in the village involving a legal matter," Lucy said. "I wonder who it was. Could I speak to Bertha directly? Mrs. Jarvis, would you mind?"

"I'll see if I can find her for you." Mrs. Jarvis stood and retied her apron strings around her ample waist. "Now, you stay there beside the fire, and I'll find you something hot and warming to bring the color back to your cheeks. I didn't hear your carriage, or I would've come outside to welcome you. Did you walk? I'll wager Major Kurland doesn't like you doing that when you're not well."

"I'm quite well," Lucy said.

Mrs. Jarvis made a tutting sound. "That's just like a lady to pretend all is fine. The whole village knows of your sadness, Lady Kurland, and we all wish you nothing but the best of health in the upcoming year."

"Thank you. I really am—"

"And don't you worry about Major Kurland looking elsewhere for his oats, because if he were, I'd be the first to know, and I haven't heard a whisper, so he's still as loyal as can be—which I would expect from a gentleman of his standing. And you've been married only three years. Give him another ten, and then he might be gallivanting across the county, with your blessing."

Mrs. Jarvis winked before she disappeared out of the door, leaving Lucy feeling like a ship caught in a storm. Had Mrs. Jarvis implied that Robert didn't have a mistress—*yet?* She'd forgotten that the village school wasn't the only place where gossips gathered.

It hadn't even occurred to Lucy that Robert might already have provided for his own needs . . . and she certainly couldn't believe that he would do so in his own village. But her father had maintained a similar arrangement for many years, so perhaps she could be wrong.

Lucy undid the buttons of her pelisse as the heat from the fire warmed the air around her. And why hadn't Robert mentioned his prior acquaintance with Mrs. Jarvis? He'd certainly seemed slightly ill at ease the last time they'd visited the inn. What exactly had their relationship been? She could hardly ask Robert. The fact that Mrs. Jarvis had ended up in Kurland St. Mary could be viewed either as unlucky chance or as quite deliberate.

Chastising herself for the unruly and non-sensical direction of her thoughts, Lucy turned as the door opened. A short round female came in and curtsied to her.

"Lady Kurland? I'm Bertha Pilcher."

Lucy smiled. Bertha had the distinctive red hair of her father and the freckles to match. "How is your mother faring since the birth of her child?"

"Oh, you know her, my lady. She's already back working in the fields, the little 'un strapped to her back."

"I will visit her as soon as I can."

"She'll like that, my lady. She's always pleased to see you. Miss Anna sent a lovely basket of knitted baby things from the rectory this morning."

"I'll make sure to tell her that the items were well received." Lucy redirected her thoughts. "I wanted to ask you about a gentleman who stayed at the inn last week—a Mr. Clapper. Do you remember him?"

"Yes, indeed, my lady. I was just telling Mrs. Jarvis that he was a mite fond of patting and pinching my backside. Eventually, I stood on his toes, and he became a bit more gentlemanly after that!"

"I understand he was a solicitor from Cheapside, in London."

"Yes, that's right, my lady. He was boasting about what a fine house he lived in and how many aristocratic clients his business had." Bertha sniffed. "Not that I believed him, my lady. He was no fashion plate. His shirt cuffs were fraying, and his coat was so old, it had patches on the elbows."

"Did he give you any hint about why he was in Kurland St. Mary?"

"Just that he was here on business, to see a lady."

"A *lady?* Are you quite certain he said that?"

"Yes, indeed. Does it matter?" Bertha asked. "I suppose there aren't that many people in our village who don't conduct all their business through Jacksons Solicitors in Hertford. Who needs a fancy solicitor from London?"

"I suspect you are right." Lucy frowned. "Did he say anything else?"

"About why he was here?" Bertha shook her head. "Not really. He did seem pleased as punch about having secrets to keep, though."

"He certainly sounds like an extremely

annoying man," Lucy murmured. "Thank you for your help, Bertha, and please give your mother and father my best regards and congratulations on the birth of their latest child."

"I'll do that, my lady. Now, is there anything else I can aid you with?"

"You have already been most helpful." Lucy smiled at the girl as she curtsied and left the room.

Mrs. Jarvis appeared almost immediately and placed a glass containing some kind of steaming hot liquid at Lucy's elbow. "Whiskey and honey with a touch of my own apple cider and ginger to warm your cockles, my lady."

"It certainly smells delicious." Lucy took the glass in her gloved hands and sniffed appreciatively. "Thank you."

"Now, you drink it all down before you go," Mrs. Jarvis ordered. "Are you walking back to the hall, or have you errands to run in the village?"

"I'm meeting my sister and Mrs. Armitage at the rectory, so I don't have far to go." Lucy suspected that the landlady was about her age, if not younger, but she couldn't find it in herself to object to being mothered for a moment. "My younger brothers are arriving home from school today."

"Oh, that's right. Major Kurland told me last time he popped in for a chat. How lovely for you." She beamed at Lucy. "My son is coming down from London to celebrate the festivities with us this year. You'll meet him at the party on Christmas Eve."

"I didn't realize you had a son, Mrs. Jarvis."

"He works in a brewery in London. That's how I met Mr. Jarvis. I was there meeting my son one day, and he introduced me to Mr. Jarvis, who was a widower in want of a wife." She winked at Lucy. "And seeing as I'd always had my eye on a move to the countryside, I was more than willing to lend an ear to his proposal."

"How . . . convenient for you both."

"Seeing as Mr. Jarvis hasn't got a son to take over this place, he's hopeful my boy might be interested. He's a big lad of almost sixteen and well suited for this kind of work. Knows his ale, as well."

"That sounds like an excellent plan." Lucy finished her drink in one long overheated swallow. The whiskey burned a searing and not unpleasant path straight to her stomach. "I had better be on my way. Thank you so much for your hospitality."

"You're welcome, Lady Kurland."

Mrs. Jarvis opened the parlor door and gestured for Lucy to follow her out into the main hallway. The fragrant smell of baking pies wafted out from the depths of the inn, followed by a wave of stale ale and hops from the public bar.

"Now, you take care, my lady." Mrs. Jarvis patted Lucy's shoulder. "It's icy underfoot."

"I will. Thank you." Lucy buttoned up her coat and made sure that the ribbons of her bonnet were tightly tied before she ventured outside. The wind had picked up, but there was no sleet or snow to worry her. "Good-bye, Mrs. Jarvis."

She set off down the street toward the rectory, hunching her shoulders against the slice of the breeze that tugged at her clothing. There was no sign of a carriage in the circular drive in front of the rectory, which meant that her father and brothers had not yet returned.

Mr. Clapper had met with a woman in either Kurland St. Mary or one of the surrounding villages. Seeing as the only women of property Lucy knew had all lived in the area for as long as she had, Lucy was fairly certain that Mr. Clapper hadn't been visiting one of them. Which left Miss Broomfield, who had closed the school earlier than usual and had been in a foul mood with her students the entire day.

It seemed only logical that the teacher had met with the so-called solicitor, but for what purpose? Surely, an inquiry directed to Mr. Clapper would help clear up any lingering doubts as to whether he'd been in the village to see Miss Broomfield or not. But how to find him? Would a letter suffice, or would she need someone to go to London and find him and his offices in Cheapside?

Robert would certainly not approve of her traveling to London in the current weather, but would he see the necessity of sending someone to check the dubious evidence Lucy had so far gathered? Normally, she would have *persuaded* him to do so, but she wasn't sure she had the energy for another fight at this juncture.

She let herself into the rectory and stamped her muddy boots on the well-worn mat in the scullery before taking off her bonnet and pelisse and entering the kitchen proper. Her sister, Anna, sat opposite the cook at the kitchen table, with a list in her hand. She looked up as Lucy entered, and offered her a bright smile.

"Good morning, Lucy. Mrs. Armitage is arranging flowers in the dining room, and I'm consulting with Cook as to the increase in food required to deal with the arrival of two growing boys."

"Don't you worry about that, miss." The cook smiled. "I have plenty of provisions in store for now and for the Christmas season."

"Thank goodness for that."

Lucy joined them and helped herself to a cup of tea from the pot on the table. She had not lived at the rectory for three years now and had gradually learned not to interfere in Anna's decidedly informal way of managing her staff.

Anna turned to look at the kitchen clock. "Father said that he hoped to be back by midday, but that it depended on the state of the roads and the weather. Mr. Pugh, the shepherd, told me he expects it to start snowing any day now."

"And Mr. Pugh is usually right about such matters." Lucy sipped her tea. "As long as we can hold the afternoon party, and the ball on Christmas Eve, I shall be happy."

"I assume several of the guests will be staying overnight after the ball?" Anna asked. "I know that Robert asked Father if he could accommodate some of his friends. Are you still considering your trip to Cambridge?"

"The letter went out only today. I'll wait and see whether I receive a reply within the next few days. I suppose the professor might go away for Christmas."

"I do hope not." Anna turned toward the window. "I think I hear the carriage." She stood up and took off her apron while patting her hair. "Come on, Lucy. Let's find Mrs. Armitage and greet the twins on the front step."

After a tumultuous hour spent with her twin brothers and a luncheon with her father, Lucy was tired but content. Her brothers had grown even taller and had not changed one bit, which made her very happy. She had practically brought them up after their mother died at their birth, and secretly considered them her own. Sending them away to school had at first seemed cruel, but they seemed to be thriving.

She'd already arranged for them to come and spend the following day up at Kurland Hall, where she knew Robert had plans to entertain them. Her smile faded as she turned out of the rectory gate and continued down through the village toward the school. Despite insisting he had no time for children, Robert was remarkably patient both with the twins and the Stanford children. He would make an excellent father. . . .

Lucy pushed that thought away and considered her recent conversation with Mrs. Jarvis at the Queen's Head. Andrew Stanford was a lawyer in London. Perhaps he would know of a way to ascertain if Mr. Clapper really did practice the law and live in Cheapside. She would write a note to Sophia when she got home, and would ask his opinion on the matter.

"Afternoon, Lady Kurland."

Startled, Lucy looked over her shoulder to see one of the Kurland Hall farmers grinning at her from his cart.

"Good afternoon, Mathias. Are you headed home?"

"No. I'm off to the blacksmith's, my lady. I was wondering if you would like me to take you up?"

Lucy considered the length of the High Street

and smiled gratefully at Mathias. "As I am going to the school, that would be most helpful."

He came down to help her climb up onto the driver's bench and then clicked to his horse to restart.

"My horse is throwing a shoe. Don't want him to go lame. Sir Robert wouldn't like that."

"No, indeed, he would not." Lucy settled her skirts and held tightly to her reticule. The wind had picked up considerably, and there was now a hint of rain in the air. "Do you think you could send a message up to the house on your return?"

"Of course, my lady."

"Will you tell Foley to send the carriage down to the school to collect me at five o'clock?"

"I'll do that."

"Thank you."

From her high perch, she had already noticed a couple of children heading for the schoolhouse and that the front door was ajar. She'd sent the key down to the smithy earlier. Rebecca Hall was nothing if not efficient and would make a remarkable teacher one day. Lucy wasn't quite so sure that poor Josephine had the necessary force of manner to persuade a roomful of children to obey her. She might do better as a governess. In two years' time, when the girls were eighteen, Lucy would make sure that whatever they chose to do, they received the necessary support and references.

"Here you are, my lady." Mathias stopped the cart and came around to lift Lucy down. "I'll pass on your message."

"Thank you." Lucy hesitated by the cart. "If you are still in the vicinity when the children come out of their rehearsal, please do not hesitate to take any of them home."

"I'll do that, my lady." He touched his hat to her. "Afternoon."

Lucy made her way into the school, pausing at the door to allow her eyes to adjust to the dim lighting. For the first time in over a week, there was the joyful sound of young voices in the building. In the center of the classroom, Rebecca had cleared a space to allow the dozen or so children present to stand grouped together. Their ages ranged from five or six to around fourteen.

Josephine stood beside Rebecca, her expression serious as she attempted to quieten some of the more raucous elements. She smiled down at one of the little girls and took her hand.

Rebecca clapped her hands. "Everyone be quiet, and let's start with 'While Shepherds Watched Their Flocks.' "

"Washed their socks," piped up one of the boys, and everyone giggled.

Rebecca gave the little boy a hard stare. "Don't sing that in church, or Sir Robert will scowl at you."

"And you'll cry like a baby and pee your breeches!" said the boy next to him.

There was more laughter, and for the second time that day, Lucy allowed her spirits to lighten and laughed along with them.

Rebecca's head shot up when she noticed Lucy by the door.

"Lady Kurland!"

All the children turned to gape at her. Most of them were smiling, but a couple hid behind their larger peers, perhaps fearing she had come with the aforementioned Sir Robert.

"Please carry on." Lucy gestured at Rebecca. "I'd love to hear you all sing." She took a seat at one of the desks and sat up straight, her hands folded on her lap.

"Ready then?" Rebecca counted to three.

To Lucy's amusement, the little boy who'd made the joke about the socks proved to have the most beautiful voice, and it soared over the others like a lark. The second carol, "Adeste Fideles," proved a little more difficult for the children, because of the different language, but they muddled through it quite successfully.

When they finished, Lucy drew off her gloves and applauded. "That was very nice. A little more practice, and I don't think Sir Robert will be scowling at anyone. In truth, you might even make him smile."

"Thank you, Lady Kurland," the children chorused.

Lucy rose from her seat. "I'll leave you to

continue, girls, while I attend to some matters in the teacher's study. Leave the key on the desk, Rebecca. I will lock the door when I leave."

"We won't be much longer, my lady," Rebecca said. "It's getting dark, and I promised we'd get the little ones home safely before it rains."

"Mr. Wilson is at the smithy with his farm cart. He is more than willing to take anyone home after his horse's shoe is repaired."

"Thank you, my lady."

Lucy walked through to the back of the school, leaving the door ajar as the children launched into another chorus of the second carol. After a cursory glance around the study, she climbed the stairs to the teacher's quarters and considered what to do next. The faint sound of the children singing permeated through the shadow-striped floor and petered out.

If Miss Broomfield had hidden something, where might it be? Lucy went into the bedroom, took the chair from the dressing table, and set it in front of the chest of drawers again. Was it possible that she had missed something on top of the cupboard? She stepped up on the chair and reached up with one hand, but her fingers encountered only a layer of dust, and she reluctantly stepped down. She checked inside the chest of drawers and the closet in the wall, but there was nothing.

The singing started again, and she hummed

along as she turned her attention to the storage cupboard, where a hip bath hung on a hook on the wall and other bulky items sat on shelves. She hadn't looked through the storage cupboard on her previous visit, but she knew she had no choice but to investigate it now. With a sigh, she started pulling things from the shelves.

After a long while, when she was beginning to feel quite fatigued, she stepped back onto the landing, having found nothing of import, but having improved the appearance of the storage cupboard beyond recognition. The school was now silent, the children long gone, and dusk was falling.

With a weary sigh, Lucy headed for the last of the rooms. She had to open the curtains just to be able to see. There was a bookcase and a little cupboard to explore. She attempted to move one of the armchairs, but it was too heavy, so she returned to the bedroom to collect the small chair she'd used before.

A door banged somewhere down below, and she went still, her gaze seeking the clock on the mantelpiece. Was it already five o'clock? She knew Mr. Coleman wouldn't hesitate to come into the school if she didn't appear on the step at the correct time. The clock wasn't ticking, as she had forgotten to wind it on her last visit.

She peered out of the window, but the view wasn't helpful. She couldn't determine if the carriage had arrived at the front of the building or not. She certainly hadn't heard anything. Glancing down at the chair, she placed it in front of the cupboard set high in the wall over the bookshelves and climbed on the seat. She opened both the doors wide and scanned the lower shelf.

It was quite hard to see. She reached up and her fingers brushed against something that had fallen flat on the very top shelf. She stood on tiptoe, trying to get a proper grip on whatever it was, as one of the chair legs wobbled on the uneven surface of the tiled fireplace. A draught of air behind her made her attempt to look over her shoulder, and then everything shifted. She started to fall, her hand clenched around whatever she had found on the shelf.

The last thing she remembered was hitting the floor, narrowly avoiding the falling chair, before her prize was ripped from her grasp and she fell into blackness.

Robert glanced impatiently around the empty schoolroom and marched through into the teacher's study. There was no sign of Lucy. It was only by chance that he had encountered Foley in the hall at home and discovered that his wife was no longer at the rectory with her family, where she was supposed to be, but in the school. He'd told Foley he would drive down and bring her home himself. He had no idea why she'd decided to go to the school, but he had his suspicions.

"Lucy?" he called up the stairs. His irritation died when a faint groan floated down to him. "Lucy!"

His breath caught in his throat as he stumbled up the stairs. The door to the sitting room was open, and his wife lay in a tangled heap on the floor. He hurried over to her, discarded his cane as he knelt down on the floor, and then gathered her into his arms.

She opened her eyes and blinked at him. "Robert. What are you doing here?"

"Saving you, apparently." He scanned her dazed face and then noted the overturned chair. "Did you fall?"

She wrinkled her nose. "I'm not sure."

"How can you not be sure?" Robert tried not to snap, but it was difficult. "You're lying on the floor, damn it."

"I thought I heard someone coming up behind me, and I tried to turn my head. The next thing I knew, I was falling."

"You probably heard me calling your name downstairs and overbalanced."

"No. I most certainly did not." She met his gaze. "I'd just checked to see if Mr. Coleman had arrived, and there was no sign of a carriage. Did you walk down?"

"I came in the gig. Can you sit up?"

Lucy winced as he drew her into a more vertical position. "I was feeling around the top shelf of the cupboard and found something. I had to stand on tiptoe to reach it, and that's when the chair was knocked from under me."

"Probably because you caused it to fall."

She showed him her hands. "Then how come whatever I found has disappeared?"

Robert stared at her. "Are you quite certain you had a good grasp on whatever it was and didn't simply leave it up there?"

"If you let go of me, I can easily remedy that by checking." She attempted to push away from him, but he stopped her by the simple expedient of picking her up and placing her in one of the armchairs.

"Stay there. I'll look."

He righted the chair and, with some trepidation, climbed up. His superior height meant he had no trouble seeing all the shelves, and they were definitely bare.

"There's nothing up there." He took his time returning to the floor and winced as his booted left foot hit the floor. "Are you sure you didn't just drop whatever you found?" He pointed at an object close to the fireplace. "Is it that?"

She didn't immediately reply, and he turned back to see why, only to discover she'd gone quite pale.

"Are you going to swoon?" Robert asked urgently.

She shook her head and moistened her lips with her tongue. "That flatiron wasn't there earlier."

"What are you saying?"

"Perhaps I should be more grateful that you arrived when you did, Robert." She raised her troubled gaze to meet his. "The person who pushed me off that chair might have intended to use that iron to put an end to me."

Chapter 12

"The important question is, what did I have in my hand that made someone contemplate killing me?" Lucy asked.

She was tucked up in bed while her husband paced their bedroom, his expression brooding. He'd driven her home, delivered her into the arms of Aunt Rose, and left her to take her dinner in peace on a tray in bed. Despite falling on the floor, Lucy had suffered nothing worse than a bruised hip and shoulder. She suspected she might feel worse on the morrow.

Robert spun around to stare at her in a rather intimidating manner. "The *important* thing is that, as per usual, you decided to wander down to the schoolhouse without telling anyone where you were going, and exposed yourself to unnecessary danger."

"You make it sound as if I was being deliberately underhand. I *did* send a message to Foley, and Anna knew I was going to the school. I was merely supervising the children while they learned the carols for the Christmas service, which you agreed I could do," Lucy pointed out in her most reasonable tone. "You are just annoyed because I got hurt."

"Of course I am annoyed! Wouldn't you be?"

She set her dinner tray aside. "I would be furious if I had discovered you in the same situation. You know that. But I hope I would try to be *reasonable* about *why* it happened, instead of glowering at you as though you were deliberately trying to inconvenience me."

He shoved a hand through his already disordered hair. "Lucy . . ."

"I apologize if I scared you, but we did learn something valuable." She sat forward, her braided hair sliding over her shoulder. "There is obviously something we are missing from our knowledge of Miss Broomfield. Did she have an accomplice who helped her steal the jewelry or sells it on for her? Or did someone mistake me for her in the darkness?"

"And attempt to kill her *again?*"

"Mayhap this second person was unaware of what had happened to Miss Broomfield. Or perhaps it was someone who received one of her letters and wanted to kill her, as well."

Robert sank into the chair closest to the bed and regarded her through his steepled fingers. "You are incorrigible."

"I believe you have mentioned that before."

"Your flights of fancy continue to amaze and befuddle me."

She risked a smile. "Thank you."

"All right," he said abruptly. "Let's agree that whatever you had in your hand has gone, and that whoever saw you in that room thought you had found something of importance."

"Agreed."

"Can you remember anything about what you found?"

Lucy considered. "It felt like a packet of letters or something similar."

"Maybe letters that Miss Broomfield had written and had not yet sent out?"

"Possibly. I didn't find any evidence of her letter writing in her desk or her private apartments."

"Then why would your would-be assailant want those letters?"

"That's an excellent question." Lucy looked approvingly at her husband. "Why indeed? What if she *did* have an accomplice? Maybe someone who delivered the letters for her and didn't want to be found out?"

"But by all accounts, Miss Broomfield hadn't made any friends in the village."

Lucy frowned. "That's true. Rebecca said that Miss Broomfield sometimes asked the children to deliver notes for her, but she couldn't recollect anyone traveling up to the hall or out to Mrs. Jenkins."

"We can certainly ask the children individually, but I doubt any of them are likely to have tried to murder *you*. We know all their families."

"What if it was one of the men who attended the evening class?"

"From what I've heard, I doubt she would've condescended to *speak* to any of them, let alone treat them as an accomplice."

"Then what is going on?"

"That, I cannot tell you." Robert rose from his seat. "May I suggest you take some of that cordial Grace prepared and put yourself to bed?"

Lucy concealed a yawn behind her hand. "I am quite fatigued."

He came over to kiss her on the forehead. "Sleep well."

"I will." She offered him a smile. "I have the ladies of my planning committee coming here tomorrow, so I promise I will not stir from the house all day."

"Good." He turned to the door. "Knowing where you are does help maintain my sanity."

"The twins will be here, as well."

"I know." His smile was resigned. "I'm expecting them at the crack of dawn. Luckily, Dermot is willing to take them out with him on estate business, which will occupy them for most of the day." He headed for the door. "Good night, my dear."

"Robert . . . is your leg really troubling you?"

He looked over his shoulder at her. "What does that have to do with anything we have just discussed?"

Lucy spoke in a rush. "It's just that I hate to

see you in pain, and I think you are concealing something from me because you believe I'm too frail to deal with the issue, which I am not, I can assure you."

He returned to sit on the side of the bed and cupped her chin, his thumb grazing the corner of her mouth. "It's true that I don't want to worry you, but I don't *know* what's wrong with my damned leg. I'm praying that whatever it is will settle down once this bad weather is over."

She searched his face. "Then will you promise to tell me if things do not improve?"

"I suspect that will be blatantly obvious," he said dryly. "If my temper is any indicator of my state of health, you'll know what to expect, and you won't allow me to get away with behaving like a bear for too long."

"I will certainly hold you accountable." She smiled into his dark blue eyes.

"I'd expect nothing less."

The next morning, Lucy returned to her sitting room after breakfast and wrote a note to Andrew Stanford about Mr. Clapper before turning to the morning post. Buried in the pile of acceptances to the ball that she'd laid to one side, she found another letter. After breaking the seal, she unfolded the single sheet and put her spectacles on to read the small cramped script.

My Dear Lady Kurland,

As to the matter of Miss Broomfield and her tenure at my school, I regret to learn of her demise, but I cannot say I regret dismissing her. She proved to be a very strange individual indeed, with her insistence on the less "respectable" aspects of the Bible and her conviction that most of her students were destined for Hell. A conviction she felt necessary to convey to them at every opportunity, leading to some distress amongst our younger, more vulnerable girls.

One can only hope that she did not behave in the same manner during her time at your school. I fear, because of your correspondence, that perhaps she did. She did not ask for a reference when she left the school, perhaps guessing that I would have nothing good to say about her.

The final straw was when one of our older girls informed me that Miss Broomfield had threatened to write to her parents and tell them of her "immoral" ways. This was simply because the poor girl received a set of earrings from an old but unmarried male friend, which she foolishly wore to dinner one evening. Miss Broomfield relented only when the girl offered her a very nice emerald ring in exchange for her silence.

Since Miss Broomfield left, more students have come forward with tales of her spite and bitterness toward those more fortunate than herself. I can only wish that God will have mercy on her soul. Her version of our blessed Savior would perhaps mean she would not embrace such mercy, but rather would enjoy the eternal fires of Hell she wished so often upon others.

If you need a new teacher for your school, Lady Kurland, I have two very promising young ladies who would be ready and willing to start in the new year. Both of them are a credit to our school and would be a credit to yours.

Yours sincerely,
Agatha Pemberton
Headmistress, Pengaron School, Cornwall

Lucy put the letter down and stared into space.

Not only had Miss Broomfield terrorized her students with her religious leanings, but she'd also attempted to blackmail one of them. . . . And it wasn't as if she had needed money. Her treasure trove of jewelry gave lie to that. Unless all the jewelry had been stolen from others? Was it possible that one of Miss Broomfield's letters had also threatened to blackmail someone in Kurland St. Mary?

But whom?

A knock at the door made her jump. She turned to see Dermot Fletcher smiling at her.

"Good morning, Dermot." Lucy beckoned him in.

"Good morning, Lady Kurland. I have received a letter from the jewelers in London to whom I sent details of that diamond and ruby necklace you found." He held it out to her. "They have a record of making the set for a family named Hillcott that lives in the county of Norfolk."

Lucy took the proffered letter and read it through. "I wonder if that is where Miss Broomfield's family resides."

"Do you wish me to write to the jewelers and ask for the full address?" Dermot frowned. "I'm not sure if they will be willing to share such private information."

"If you mention that we are seeking the surviving members of the deceased's family, they might be more willing to open their books. Make sure the letter comes from Sir Robert, in his capacity as justice of the peace. That should do the trick." Lucy handed him back the letter. "How are your plans for the Christmas party coming along?"

"Very well, my lady. Miss Anna Harrington has been most helpful in identifying the needs of each family and the number of children who will require some kind of gift."

"I'm glad that she was able to assist you." Lucy couldn't help but notice the admiration shining from Dermot's green eyes as he mentioned her sister. "I understand that you are about to take my twin brothers out for the day. I am most grateful for your forbearance."

"I enjoy their company. They are spirited but are still willing to listen to reason—occasionally."

Lucy smiled. "Thank you again, and do not hesitate to treat them as if they were your own."

"You are most welcome, my lady." He turned to leave and then paused. "I forgot to mention that I saw Mr. and Mrs. Stanford's carriage coming up the drive. They will probably be with you shortly."

Lucy rose and smoothed her skirts. "Then I will accompany you out to the entrance hall and greet our guests."

She found Sophia just taking off her cloak and bonnet, and Andrew relinquishing his hat and gloves into Foley's tender care.

"Ah, Lady Kurland," Andrew called out. "Just the person I was hoping to see."

Lucy led the way into the drawing room, where there was already a roaring fire, and waited until her guests were seated.

"We thought we'd come early, before you became engulfed in the plans for the ball,"

Sophia said. "I showed Andrew your note about the solicitor in Cheapside."

"And do you know whether it might be possible to locate Mr. Clapper?" Lucy addressed her question to her friend's husband.

"It is definitely possible. I'll write a note to my clerk and ask him to search the man out. It shouldn't take him that long, and seeing as I am away, there is very little else for him to do. Do you wish to send your Mr. Clapper a letter enclosed in mine?"

"That would certainly speed up the process of discovery." Lucy nodded. "I will do so immediately."

After an enjoyable lunch, for which they were joined by Rose, Robert, and Dermot, the men went off to discuss business, leaving the ladies to await the arrival of Mrs. Jenkins, the Greenwells, and the party from the rectory, including Penelope and Dorothea, who had no carriage of their own.

It took quite a while for everyone to settle down, enjoy a comfortable gossip, and partake of a selection of refreshments. Mrs. Greenwell was at her most gracious and spent a lot of time speaking to Mrs. Jenkins and asking pointed questions about Nicholas and his whereabouts.

After matters concerning the ball were settled to her satisfaction, Lucy went to order another pot of coffee and came back into the drawing room to the sound of Margaret Greenwell holding court. There was no sign of Mrs. Greenwell or Mrs. Jenkins, who she suspected had gone to the retiring room.

"Well, Miss Harrington? Do you have anything to say for yourself?"

Anna's cheeks were flushed, but knowing her sister, Lucy decided to stay where she was and let her defend herself.

"As I have no idea of what you are referring to, Miss Greenwell, perhaps you would be so good as to enlighten me."

"My mother received a letter yesterday suggesting she should investigate my conduct!"

"And what on earth does that have to do with me?" Anna sounded more amused than worried.

"You know very well what it has to do with you," Margaret huffed. "I am sick and tired of elderly spinsters who have had their chance to marry criticizing those of us who haven't yet achieved that state. It was bad enough when Miss Broomfield had the nerve to suggest I should dress more appropriately, and now *this*."

Lucy took a step forward. "Miss Broomfield criticized you?"

"Indeed, she did. I met her when she came to interview Josephine for the position at the school, and I immediately disliked her judgmental ways. In truth, I told Josephine not to take the job, but

252

she has always been something of a doormat and willingly agreed to allow that woman to order her around. Not that she fared any better. I believe she and that Rebecca Hall both received anonymous letters criticizing them, as well."

"Are you suggesting that my *sister* wrote all those letters?" Lucy asked.

"She and Miss Broomfield probably. They had much in common." Margaret looked down her nose at Anna, who was now visibly trembling. "Miss Harrington is probably afraid that she will lose her last suitor to me."

Anna rose slowly to her feet. "If a gentleman cannot remain faithful to a lady and can so easily be led astray, I wouldn't want him, anyway."

"You always appear so 'saintly,' Miss Anna, but I know the truth about you," Margaret sneered. "I heard the gossip about why you *really* returned from London without a husband."

"That is *quite* enough, Miss Greenwell." Lucy stepped in between her sister and Margaret. "If your mother was here, I am sure she would be mortified by your disgraceful display of manners. How *dare* you come into my house and speak in such disparaging terms to my sister?"

"It's all right, Lucy." Anna touched her sleeve. "Miss Greenwell is entitled to her opinion. The fact that she is quite wrong about everything says far more about her character than it does about mine, wouldn't you agree?"

"I most certainly would." Lucy held Margaret's gaze for a moment longer, until the girl dropped her eyes. "Jealousy and envy are never becoming, Miss Greenwell, and have a tendency to embitter the offender, affecting their looks, disposition, *and* ability to snare a husband."

"Whatever is going on?" Mrs. Greenwell's voice came from behind Lucy at the door. "Margaret?"

Lucy turned to her guest. "Perhaps it might be better if you took your eldest daughter home, Mrs. Greenwell. She will not be welcome in this house until she is willing to apologize to my sister."

"Margaret? Whatever have you done?" Mrs. Greenwell asked.

"What about the ball?" the quieter, younger Greenwell daughter whined to her sister.

Margaret's defiance crumbled as she glanced at her mother's shocked expression and then back to Lucy. "I . . . apologize for my remarks, Lady Kurland. I was upset about this attempt to stain my character and misspoke."

"Apologize to Anna, not me," Lucy said. "If she is willing to forgive you, I will overlook your behavior. It is the season of forgiveness."

Margaret turned with some reluctance toward Anna, who raised a pointed eyebrow and managed not only to smile but also to look composed as Margaret stumbled through another apology.

"My dear Lady Kurland." Mrs. Greenwell's flustered voice rose as she rushed over to Lucy. "I do apologize for Margaret's behavior. She was deeply upset when I received that anonymous letter, and I fear her emotions overcame her."

"The letter wasn't signed?"

"No, and it was delivered by hand. Mr. Greenwell gave it to me yesterday, and I must say that it did overset my spirits for quite a while."

"As anything like that would." Lucy tried for a sympathetic tone. "Is it true that Josephine also received a letter?"

"Did Margaret say so? She would probably know better than I would. She and Josephine are quite close in age." Mrs. Greenwell lowered her voice. "Please forgive her, my lady. If she is unable to attend the ball or any other event hosted by you and Sir Robert, her reputation will suffer *terribly*."

Lucy had a few pointed remarks about that but, in the spirit of the season, chose not to utter them. Anna was right. If Nicholas did realize he preferred Margaret, it might be a good thing for everyone.

"If Anna is satisfied with her apology, then I will accept her decision."

"Thank you, Lady Kurland." Mrs. Greenwell clutched at her hand. "It is hard enough to be buried in the countryside with two daughters of marriageable age without offending the only decent society around us."

"Then perhaps you might speak to your daughter about how she chooses to present herself in that society." Lucy couldn't quite forgo the opportunity to make a point.

"Do not worry on that score. I intend to." Mrs. Greenwell cast her eldest daughter a sharp look. "I do hope you and Sir Robert will grace us with your presence at the hunt breakfast on Friday."

"I believe we will be attending."

Robert had no intention of riding to hounds. He considered the sport barbaric. But as the local magistrate, the largest landowner, and a ranking member of the gentry, he was honor bound to attend and at least acknowledge his neighbors.

"Then we look forward to seeing you." Mrs. Greenwell bobbed a quick curtsy and gathered up her daughters. "Good day, Lady Kurland, and thank you for your forbearance."

"Forbearance, my foot!" Penelope said loudly enough for the retreating Greenwell ladies to hear in the hallway as they left. "What an extremely rude young woman. I would never have been allowed to speak so forcefully in my day."

Lucy returned to her seat by the fire and looked over at her friend. "My, what a short memory you have, Penelope."

"I might pride myself on being forthright, Lucy, but I am *never* rude."

"Miss Greenwell was very rude," Sophia said, reluctantly agreeing with Penelope. "In truth, her annoyance and desire to deflect blame on Anna seemed rather out of proportion to the supposed insult she had suffered."

"Unless the note had some truth in it," Lucy said slowly. "Has Nicholas made any mention of Margaret annoying or accosting him in private, Mrs. Jenkins?"

"Not that I know of," Mrs. Jenkins said. "I haven't seen her climbing out of one of my windows in the middle of the night, either."

Lucy smiled. "Then I wonder what upset her."

"Perhaps she is just one of those females who allows her jealousy to dictate her actions. We've all met such women." Sophia shrugged. "Anna is far more beautiful than Margaret will ever be, and much admired."

Lucy glanced over at her sister, who was blushing. "She is indeed."

"Well, I must be on my way." Mrs. Jenkins levered herself out of her chair and placed her teacup on the table beside her. "I think under your able direction, Lucy, the ball will be wonderful, and the villagers' party even better."

"I sincerely hope so, and I could never have managed this by myself." Lucy went to take the old lady's hand. "Thank you for coming and for your wise and practical counsel."

Penelope came over and smiled at Lucy. "We

will take Mrs. Jenkins home in the rectory carriage with us."

"Thank you." Mrs. Jenkins said.

Lucy didn't point out that Penelope didn't actually live at the rectory or own the carriage. She'd had quite enough disagreeableness for one day.

Once Lucy had spoken to Anna and reassured herself that her sister was unaffected by Miss Greenwell's behavior, she waved them all off and walked arm in arm down to Robert's study with Sophia at her side. For once, she was quite keen for her friend to leave so that she could talk to Robert about the extraordinary behavior of Miss Margaret Greenwell.

"So Margaret Greenwell said her mother received an anonymous letter *yesterday?*" Robert asked.

He was sitting with Lucy in his study, by the fire, after they had shared their evening meal with both the Stanfords and the twins. It had been a remarkably entertaining evening, and his wife had enjoyed it immensely. It had been good to see her happy and laughing again.

"Yes. And Mrs. Greenwell confirmed that she had indeed received a letter that suggested her daughter had behaved inappropriately." Lucy sighed. "I wish I could get my hands on the original. Judging from Margaret's reaction, I suspect it was rather more pointed than that, don't you?"

"Probably." Robert frowned. "And then Margaret suggested that *Anna* was the letter writer and had been in cahoots with Miss Broomfield all along?"

"Exactly." Lucy sat forward, her hands clasped together on her lap. "Margaret is the first person to suggest that Miss Broomfield wrote those letters."

"Apart from us."

"Obviously, but we have gathered the information to make that conjecture. But don't you think it is strange that Margaret arrived at that conclusion on her own? She also said Rebecca and Josephine had received letters, too."

"It certainly is odd that she made that assumption."

"Maybe she knows *exactly* who wrote the letters."

Robert studied her face. "You think *Margaret Greenwell* wrote them?"

"Why not?"

"Because . . . why *would* she? And do you really think she killed Miss Broomfield?"

"What if Miss Broomfield discovered something about Margaret—maybe something Josephine innocently mentioned at school—and Miss Broomfield attempted to blackmail Margaret?"

"But—"

Lucy carried on speaking over him. "If Miss Broomfield successfully blackmailed someone before, why wouldn't she try it again?"

"I'm sorry, my dear, but I cannot see Margaret Greenwell as a murderer."

"Why *not?* Miss Broomfield was killed with a hat pin. Anyone could've done it."

"Because you haven't got a single shred of evidence to make this case," Robert pointed out. "This is *pure* supposition."

"But what if I found some evidence?"

"Then I would have to believe you. In the meantime, perhaps we should focus on identifying Miss Broomfield's family and locating Mr. Clapper, who might or might not have come to Kurland St. Mary to meet with her."

"You still believe it was Mr. Clapper who killed her?" Lucy asked.

"I would certainly prefer it to be him. I like Mr. Greenwell and would hate to have to haul one of his children off to the county court sessions."

"Oh. I didn't think of that." His wife contemplated her joined hands before looking up at him again. "I promise I will conduct my inquiries with the utmost of delicacy."

"And you will promise not to do anything reckless. Agreed?"

She sighed. "If I must."

"You must for the sake of my sanity." Robert reached over to squeeze her hand. "Despite everything, I *am* rather fond of you."

"Then I will endeavor to keep in your good graces."

"There's one thing you've forgotten," Robert said as he rose to help himself to a glass of brandy.

"What is that?"

"Seeing as Mrs. Greenwell received her letter only yesterday, we can no longer safely assume that Miss Broomfield is our letter writer."

"Which is why I think it has to be Margaret," Lucy said firmly. "Or maybe Miss Broomfield paid someone to deliver the letters before she died. It is *so* confusing. And the Greenwells aren't the only family that has recently returned to the village. What about our new verger? What about Mrs. Jarvis at the Queen's Head?"

"Now you are becoming ridiculous." He had no intention of discussing Mrs. Jarvis with his wife. She might decide to question the loquacious landlady, and goodness knows what Mrs. Jarvis would say. He returned to his seat. "Why is it that the simplest matter becomes a tangled mess whenever we are involved?"

"We haven't had any peculiar deaths in our village for three years," Lucy pointed out. "This is an *exception*."

"And we still can't completely discount the

notion that this was just a random act of violence and will never be solved." Robert sipped his brandy.

"I detest not knowing what really happened."

"I know you do, which is why I also know that you will pursue this matter until it is solved to your satisfaction."

Lucy sat up straight. "You make it sound as if I am the only person who cares about such things, when you are just as invested."

"I'm the local magistrate. I *have* to be involved. It is my duty to bring the guilty to justice."

"And as your wife, I am merely *supporting* your efforts."

He raised his glass to her. "Which just goes to show that I am a very lucky man indeed."

Lucy rose quietly from the bed, lit a candle, and went down the creaking oak staircase. She'd been unable to sleep. Her mind was too busy circling around the extraordinary events of the day. If Miss Broomfield hadn't written the letters, who had? She knew it couldn't have been Anna, which left exactly whom?

Was Mr. Clapper responsible for the delivery of the letters? Had Miss Broomfield's blackmail scheme encompassed a wider area than just Kurland St. Mary? It might make sense that Miss Broomfield had set the diamond and ruby necklace aside to pay off her accomplice. But if

Mr. Clapper had known about the jewelry and killed Miss Broomfield, why hadn't he stolen the rest of it when he had the opportunity?

And there was Margaret Greenwell, a young woman with a fiery temper and an obvious disdain for those around her. She either knew more about the matter than she was letting on or had jumped to some remarkable conclusions. But as Lucy had pointed out to Robert, the Greenwells weren't the only newcomers in the village. Lucy paused to set the candle on the desk in her sitting room. The fire had died, and she stirred the embers and added a couple of lumps of coal.

It was time to acknowledge the fear lurking in her heart. What *about* Mrs. Jarvis? She had apparently known Robert in his youth. Had she come to the village deliberately? She certainly had access at the inn to the best gossip in the county. But what possible reason could she have for wanting to kill Miss Broomfield or for sending out vile letters to her fellow villagers?

There was no connection between the two events, and she was probably being silly at the thought that at some time in his past, Robert had . . . dallied with Mrs. Jarvis. Did she want Mrs. Jarvis to be guilty of something because she could not countenance the idea of another woman having once been important to Robert?

But he hadn't acknowledged that he'd known the woman earlier. . . .

Lucy sighed and wrapped her shawl more tightly around herself, her gaze falling on the box of books she had brought back from Miss Broomfield's abode. She moved the candle closer and picked up the well-worn black leather Bible and flipped through the pages. Miss Broomfield had underlined several passages and had written notes in the margins in her neat script.

It didn't take Lucy long to realize that the version of the Bible Miss Broomfield preferred wasn't the familiar King James one, but something called the Douay-Rheims Bible. She would have to ask her father what that implied. She suspected it might be the Roman Catholic version.

It was too dark to read exactly what the teacher had written. Lucy suspected she would find no comfort in Miss Broomfield's particular brand of religion. It was probably why the teacher had attended the services at the Kurland St. Mary church only reluctantly. Her father's genial brand of Anglicanism would hardly have interested Miss Broomfield.

There were a couple of bookmarks placed within the pages. One was leather and depicted the St. Peter's Basilica of Rome in embossed gold. The second was from the Shrine of Our Lady of Walsingham. Both decidedly popish sites.

"Walsingham . . ." Lucy murmured. "Isn't that

in Norfolk, where Miss Broomfield's family might be from?"

She placed the Bible back in the box and on impulse picked up the bound copy of *Ackermann's*. Inside there were about three full volumes of the monthly periodical. Considering what she knew about the teacher, it seemed a remarkably frivolous thing for Miss Broomfield to have kept.

Lucy sat down by the fire and leafed through the illustrations, fashion plates, and articles. One of the pages was turned down at the corner, so she paused to investigate the engraved hand-colored image of what appeared to be a large country house. Holding the book close to the light, she squinted to read the small print at the bottom of the illustration.

"Hillcott Hall in the county of Norfolk." Lucy frowned as she tried to remember where she had heard that name before. "The jewelers in London," she whispered. "The diamond and ruby set was made for the Hillcott family."

Chapter 13

Robert surveyed the gathering of the hunt in front of Greenwell Manor and tried not to look intimidated either by the variety of barely controlled mounts or the baying pack of dogs being marshaled by the hound master. It was a typically cold December morning, and the ground was icy underfoot. Perfect hunting weather unless you were a farmer, a fox, or a coward like him.

He knew his refusal to continue the tradition of holding the Christmas hunt at Kurland Hall had offended and puzzled his neighbors. But he had no obligation to explain his position to anyone except his wife, and she at least fully supported his stance. He glanced down at her as their carriage drew up at the side door of the house. She often reminded him of a little brown sparrow. She'd been quiet at breakfast, her thoughts far away—something that worried him almost as much as the idea that he should get on a horse and lead the charge across the barren countryside.

She also hadn't slept in their bed all night. There'd been no time to ask if all was well as they hurried to make themselves presentable to represent the Kurland family at the traditional hunt meet. Andrew was bringing his children, and Dermot had already set off with the Harrington twins to join the ranks of the riders. Robert would have to make an effort to find the boys, to ensure that they were safely mounted and were well aware of the dangers of misbehaving in such company.

That meant moving through the sea of horses without betraying his crippling anxiety for all to see. Most of his peers thought his injuries were the reason he couldn't ride to hounds. They would've been incredulous if he'd tried to explain that after five years the fear was so much worse. He still had nightmares about being trapped and almost suffocated under his horse in the French mud at Waterloo—and about coming so close to losing his leg completely. . . .

"Robert?"

He jerked his attention back to his wife, who had one hand on his arm and was patiently waiting for him to unlock the carriage door.

"I do apologize. I was woolgathering." He found a smile somewhere. "May I help you descend?"

As it turned out, he was lucky enough to spot the twins on the outskirts of the teeming scarlet-coated crowd and had a stern word with them about not cramming his horses or showing themselves to disadvantage. With Andrew and

Dermot guiding the group, he knew they were in safe hands. There was no sign of the rector, who, as the current master of the hunt, had many responsibilities to fulfill before he could lead the riders out. His father-in-law was an accomplished horseman and would completely forget his sons existed the moment the horn blew.

After making the effort to greet his neighbors, who all made a point of telling him how much they were looking forward to the ball later that week, Robert escaped to the front steps of the mansion, where Mr. and Mrs. Greenwell stood welcoming their guests. Footmen were distributing cups of warmed punch and cider to anyone who wanted one, and Robert gladly accepted a glass.

"Good morning, Sir Robert!" Mr. Greenwell called out to him. "I was just speaking to your delightful wife. I believe she has gone inside to find Mrs. Stanford and Mrs. Jenkins."

Robert shook Mr. Greenwell's hand. "Good morning, sir. You seem to have attracted a good crowd. Are you riding yourself today?"

"I intend to, as do my daughters. And later this morning my good lady will drive out in her carriage and bring sustenance for all of us— depending on our luck, of course!" His gaze swept over Robert and lingered on his cane. "You don't care to ride to hounds?"

Robert tapped his left boot with the tip of

his cane. "Unfortunately, my leg is too badly damaged to risk taking another fall."

"That is a shame. I hear you were quite a sight in your hussar uniform, leading a battle charge."

"Whoever told you that?"

Mr. Greenwell bowed. "One of my second cousins had the honor of serving under you during the war. He said you were an exemplary officer and always led from the front."

"Hardly." Robert was never comfortable discussing his wartime antics. "What was your cousin's name?"

"Blake. Grenville Blake." Mr. Greenwell lowered his voice. "His sister was Josephine's mother."

"Ah."

"Morning, Mr. Greenwell." The rector strode up the steps and nodded to Robert. "All ready for the off, then?"

"If you are, Mr. Harrington." Mr. Greenwell relinquished his tankard of ale to one of the servants. "Let me just inform my wife."

Mr. Harrington's gaze swept the assembled company. "Quite a gathering today, eh, Robert? Don't you wish you were joining us?"

"I can't say that I do, sir."

The rector chuckled and prodded Robert in the ribs with his riding crop. "Always with the dry wit. You hide your regrets very well, sir, very well indeed. A credit to your family and your upbringing. Lucy did very well for herself by marrying you, very well indeed. Now I must be off."

He nodded and stomped down the steps toward the groom holding his horse, shouting to everyone to form some kind of orderly line. Nicholas Jenkins acknowledged Robert as he rode by on a very flashy hunter that Robert would have coveted greatly when he was younger. Mr. Greenwell strode past Robert, his hat tucked under his arm as he tried to pull on his gloves.

"Good hunting," Robert called out to him.

"Thank you, sir."

A second later the horn blared, and the entire cavalcade took off, hounds baying, the hard riders at the front, and most of the ladies and the children at the rear. The twins' faces, full of excitement, flashed by, making Robert remember when he had once lived to hunt and had driven his parents mad by demanding better mounts. He'd thought nothing of falling or breaking a bone or two. The thrill of the chase—the pulse-pounding excitement of pursuit—had made his heart sing.

But not anymore.

He slowly ascended the steps, his left leg dragging and throbbing with the new searing pain he was becoming accustomed to. His place was with the ladies who chose not to hunt and with the elderly, who had better things to do with their remaining days than risk life and limb in the saddle.

Today, for some reason, watching the hunt stream out in all its loud, raucous glory bothered him far more deeply than usual.

After enjoying the lavish breakfast Mrs. Greenwell had provided for the hunt, Lucy settled herself in the drawing room with Sophia. It was a pleasant room with a southerly aspect and a large fireplace that produced a great deal of much-welcome heat. In Lucy's opinion, the furnishing and draperies needed updating, but she was certain that Mrs. Greenwell would get around to that at some point.

The Greenwell girls had gone out with their father, so there was a lack of pettiness in the air, and the general conversation was warm and lively. Penelope had opted not to attend the hunt, although Dr. Fletcher was there in case anyone needed medical attention. There was usually a fair sprinkling of injuries, especially when the weather was so foul and the ground underfoot treacherous even for the most spirited of horses and experienced of riders.

Not being considered quite gentry, Dr. Fletcher was ensconced in the kitchen, and Robert had gone directly to speak to him. Despite his best efforts, Lucy knew such gatherings were difficult for her husband, and she tried not to bother him too much about minor matters. She still hadn't told him what she'd discovered the previous night. Would a letter to Hillcott Hall provide more information about Miss Broomfield, or would it be better to pursue the professor in Cambridge?

"Lucy, are you feeling quite the thing? You are very quiet."

She shook herself out of her reverie and turned to Sophia with a smile. "I do apologize. I didn't sleep very well last night."

"Andrew said that the letters to his clerk went off this morning and that he expects an answer within a day or so."

"That is very good of him."

"Why do you want to talk to this Mr. Clapper?"

"We think he might have some connection with Miss Broomfield. We haven't been able to locate any members of her family yet to advise them of her demise."

"How sad," Sophia sighed. "From all I have heard, she wasn't the most pleasant of women, but to die alone and be forgotten? I would not wish that on my worst enemy."

"Perhaps Mr. Clapper will be able to shed some light on this matter," Lucy said. "Otherwise I fear that you may be right. It is so unusual for a woman of her class to be cast . . . *adrift* like this. Even if a family goes into debt and loses everything, there is usually *someone* willing to take in a female relative."

"And work them to death." Sophia shuddered. "Remember how Penelope and her sister narrowly avoided such a fate? But maybe Miss Broomfield *wanted* to be left alone. She certainly made no effort to make friends, did she?"

"But striking out on your own . . . I consider myself a strong, independent, intelligent woman, Sophia, but I don't know if I could've done what Miss Broomfield apparently did."

"I certainly could not have left my mother behind," Sophia agreed. "Let alone my little dog, Hunter." She paused. "Is it possible that her family was the one doing the casting out? Maybe they issued an ultimatum to her—expecting her to comply—and she simply chose not to obey them."

"She certainly appeared contrary enough to do just that," Lucy agreed. "But still, it was a big step to take."

"Well, then, let's hope the ubiquitous Mr. Clapper can be found to answer all our questions." Sophia patted Lucy's hand.

Mrs. Greenwell appeared in the drawing room and smiled at the collection of ladies stationed around the fire. "I have cards set up in the parlor if anyone wishes to play, and the library is at your disposal. At noon I will be taking a picnic luncheon out to the riders, and anyone who wishes to join me is welcome to do so. Otherwise, please make yourselves at home."

Lucy smiled agreeably at her hostess. With Margaret and her sister out of the house, she fully intended to.

After Mrs. Greenwell departed with some of the guests and the picnic food packed in large wicker hampers, Sophia confided her need to take a nap and settled into a concealed nook in the library. Lucy made sure her friend was comfortable and then quietly made her way up the staircase to the upper story of the house.

It was very peaceful. The majority of the staff was either busy preparing food in the kitchen or was away from the house, serving the picnic with Mrs. Greenwell. Even Josephine had gone with their hostess, meaning Lucy didn't have to worry about encountering the girl as she took advantage of everyone's absence.

It didn't take her long to work out which bedroom belonged to Margaret Greenwell. Although her maid had obviously been in and had tidied up, there was still an air of confusion in the chamber, with scarves and hats thrown randomly on the bed, along with an afternoon gown that Margaret presumably intended to change into when she returned from the hunt.

From the state of it, Lucy was fairly certain that no one would notice her intrusion in the room. Aware that she might not have too much time before Robert came looking for her, she sat down at Margaret's dressing table and methodically went through the contents of her drawers.

In the bottom drawer she discovered a journal and placed it on her lap. Was it honorable to open it and read what the younger woman might wish to be kept secret? Robert would certainly be appalled, but this was a matter of *murder*.

Her gaze was drawn to a piece of paper sticking out of the book. It was not as if she would share anything she read with another person—unless it was pertinent to the death of Miss Broomfield or the discovery of the writer of the poison-pen letters. . . . She opened the book at the page where the paper stuck out, and quickly scanned the words on the single sheet.

Your daughter is in love with her own sister's husband. Shame on you and your depraved family. You will all burn in hell.

Lucy gasped and covered her mouth. The note was eerily similar to the ones she had already seen. She had all but forgotten that Margaret had an older, married sister. But what on earth did the note mean, and why had Margaret reacted so strongly to such an obvious lie?

"Margaret couldn't possibly have written that," Lucy murmured to herself and then hesitated. "Unless she chose to write something so fantastically wrong that she knew no one would believe it if the note ever came out."

Was it an attempt to protect herself? To claim that she couldn't have written the other letters, because she'd received one?

"But this one arrived *after* Miss Broomfield's death," Lucy reminded herself. "*This* one is an anomaly."

She glanced down at the journal. Did she even need to read anything else? Wasn't this ridiculous note a clear indication that Miss Margaret Greenwell was indeed the author of the other anonymous letters?

But it still didn't explain *why*.

After carefully replacing the letter in the journal, Lucy slid them both back into the drawer and closed it. If ever she'd needed Robert's cool head and composure, it was now.

"So tell me about the pain. Is it in your hip, your thigh, or your calf?" Dr. Fletcher said as casually as if he'd just asked the correct time.

Robert gave his old friend his best irritated glare. "I thought we were discussing the merits of French brandy over champagne?"

"We were, but I can't help but notice how hard it is for you even to sit comfortably. You're squirming on your chair like a schoolboy." Dr. Fletcher raised his clear gaze to meet Robert's. "So which is it?"

"My thigh." Robert smoothed a hand over his buckskin breeches. "It feels like a smoldering powder keg is going off in there."

"That bad, eh? And when were you going to mention this to me? When you lost the ability to walk again?"

"Probably." Robert shrugged. "I assumed there was nothing that could be done about it."

"You're the lord of the manor, not a trained physician, Major. How about you do your job and allow me to do mine?" Dr. Fletcher hesitated. "After Christmas will you let me take a look at you?"

"If I must. But please don't involve my wife in this."

"Hard not to when she's the one who's been badgering me to examine you."

"She has, has she?" Robert sighed. "I suppose I should be pleased she cares enough to notice."

"Lady Kurland is a formidable woman," Dr. Fletcher said. "And by the way, she looks much improved these past two weeks."

"Yes, despite organizing the ball, the party, and worrying about Miss Broomfield's death, she looks remarkably healthy."

"Then perhaps you should make the effort to regain your health, as well?"

Robert scowled at him. "I've said I'll allow you to practice your macabre profession on me. Now can we change the subject?"

"Of course." The doctor's grin contained more than a hint of complacency. "Would you like to wager which one of the Harrington twins breaks his collarbone first today?"

The door into the kitchen opened, and one of the footmen came running in.

"Dr. Fletcher? Can you come with me immediately? There's been an accident in the upper copse. I have a gig waiting outside, sir."

"I spoke too soon." Dr. Fletcher rose and grabbed his large bag, hat, muffler, and coat. "I assume you won't wish to accompany me, Sir Robert?"

"No thank you. I've seen enough carnage to last me a lifetime." Robert grimaced. "I'll go and find my wife and assure her that I intend to subject myself to your approval in the New Year."

He left the kitchen and walked back into the main part of the house. A large grandfather clock ticked away in the hall, but there was no sign of the other guests. As he paused in indecision, a woman came flying down the stairs. It took him only a second to recognize his wife.

"Oh, Robert, there you are. I was just coming to find you." She grabbed his hand. "Where can we go that's quiet?"

"Let me recap. You went into Margaret Green-well's *bedchamber?*" Robert asked.

"I knew you were going to cut up stiff about this, but please listen. I—"

"Lucy, that is *trespass*."

"No it is not. Mrs. Greenwell said to treat the house as our own."

"You know that's not what she meant." He sank into the nearest chair. "Go on. Tell me what other horrors you have perpetuated."

"I *happened* to see her journal. . . ."

He gave a strangled groan and buried his face in his hands.

"And I saw the letter that was *purported* to have come from the anonymous writer."

He slowly looked up at her. "Purported?"

She sank down on her knees in front of him. "It said that Margaret was in love with her older sister's husband, and that the whole family would burn in hell."

"Then it sounds remarkably similar to the other efforts."

"But it arrived *after* Miss Broomfield's death. What if Margaret wrote the letter to avoid any suspicion falling on her?"

"We were hardly suspicious of her in the first place!" Robert demurred.

"The idea that she is in love with her sister's husband is rather far-fetched, don't you think?"

"No more so than the suggestion that your father should burn in hell, or that Grace Turner betrayed her family." He hesitated. "Wouldn't you agree that there is a grain of truth in each letter? Something deliberately meant to hurt the recipient?"

Her voice wobbled when she thought about the claim that she would remain barren. "Yes, I suppose that is correct."

"I wonder if we could find out if this particular rumor is true."

"I am not sure how." Lucy pursed her lip. "Even I would vacillate about asking *that* question out loud."

"And it still leaves us with the conundrum of what happened to Miss Broomfield."

Lucy put her hand on his knee. "What if . . . Margaret received the letter much earlier from Miss Broomfield and killed her for exposing her secret?"

"And then made sure her mother saw the letter?" Robert frowned. "Why would she do that?"

"To make absolutely sure that no one would think she was *responsible* for killing Miss Broomfield."

"Your reasoning is becoming somewhat torturous, my dear."

"I know." Lucy sighed and rose to her feet. "You're right." She paced the room, her hands locked together at her waist.

Her husband looked up at her. "You're *agreeing* with me?"

"I'm agreeing that I do not know what to do about this muddle. Don't you think that someone should be held responsible?"

"Of course I do. But what if it really is as simple as Miss Broomfield wrote the notes for her own purposes, and someone *killed* her for reasons connected to her wealth?"

"But nothing was stolen." Lucy paused. "Maybe because Josephine came back unexpectedly to the school, and whoever it was didn't have time to search for the jewels? That would also explain why I was knocked off my chair and almost beaten with the flatiron."

"Yes, indeed," Robert said slowly. "You might have something there."

"But why stick the quill pen in Miss Broomfield's eye if it wasn't connected to the letters?"

"I don't know." Robert stood and came toward her. "Let's go and join everyone else and see if they know what time the hunt will return."

Eventually, driven out by too much female chatter, Robert left Lucy in the company of Sophia and walked out toward the stables. He still had no idea who had killed Miss Broomfield, and Lucy's snooping had merely addled the pot. As he walked, he lit one of his cigarillos and enjoyed a quiet, contemplative moment of peace.

There was no sign of the returning riders, and Mrs. Greenwell hadn't come back, either. The flatness of the land in Hertfordshire meant the hunt could cover a significant amount of ground in one outing. Mrs. Greenwell might have to travel several miles out of her way on the winding country roads to locate them.

Robert was almost ready to turn back when an all too familiar sound caught his attention. He stubbed out his cigarillo and turned toward the fields at the back of the stables, his gaze trained on the bushes and hearing the thundering of hooves. His gut tightened as a riderless horse burst through the field hedge and careered across the grass right toward him.

Instantly, the world around him narrowed to that one sight, to the fact that he should run and hide, but his feet were nailed to the ground, and there was no escape. His breath deserted him as he flung out an arm and grabbed the trailing reins. Instinct and well-rehearsed memory made him jerk the horse's head toward its tail to contain the kicking and bucking steed within the tightest circle he could manage.

He hung on, his shoulder burning, as the horse at first resisted and almost knocked him off his feet. He managed to grab a better hold on the actual bridle and exerted more pressure by throwing his whole body weight forward.

"Hold on, sir! I'm coming!"

The welcome sound of running feet came from behind him. He didn't dare turn his attention away from the horse and hung on as a second set of hands joined his and brought the horse to a sudden shuddering stop.

"It's all right, India." The groom's calming voice worked its spell on Robert, as well as the horse. "Well done, sir."

Robert attempted a shrug. "I didn't have much choice, seeing as the mare was heading straight toward me. Do you know this horse?"

"Aye. It belongs to Miss Margaret." The groom's worried expression deepened. "I wonder what became of her."

Robert made his way back to the house. Every bone in his body was aching, and he was shaking as images from his past clashed and collided with what he forced himself to remember was the present. He paused before he went into the drawing room, and took several deep breaths. His neighbors already thought he was odd. Displaying his fear in front of them would only confirm their prejudices.

Lucy looked up as he came in, and immediately came across to him, her gaze concerned.

"Is everything all right?"

He took her hand and kissed her fingers. "Is Mrs. Greenwell back yet?"

"No. Why?"

He lowered his voice so that only she could hear him. "Patrick was called out to an accident earlier, and I just found Margaret Greenwell's horse running for the stables."

"Without her?"

"Exactly."

Lucy pressed her fingers to her mouth. "Goodness me. I do hope she isn't hurt."

Robert placed her hand on his sleeve and drew her away from the fire toward the large picture window at the rear of the room. "We won't know until Patrick returns. I suppose Miss Margaret might have grown tired and taken a seat in her mother's carriage for the return journey."

"And abandoned her horse?"

"I know." He grimaced. "It doesn't look good, does it?" The sound of voices out in the hallway made him look over to the door. "I hear a carriage. Shall we go and see what has transpired?"

They both turned and exited the drawing room, then walked down the long corridor to the front hall. The front door was flung wide open, letting in the cold air. Dr. Fletcher was issuing orders over the sound of female weeping and general upset.

"Bring her in carefully, please, gentlemen. Mrs. Greenwell? Can you direct the men to the correct bedchamber, please?"

"It's this way." Mrs. Greenwell was sobbing into her handkerchief as she led the men carrying the inert body of Margaret Greenwell up the stairs.

"Is she dead?" Lucy whispered.

"I don't know. I'll have to ask Patrick," Robert murmured as he tightly gripped Lucy's hand. "Let's not give up hope just yet."

Chapter 14

"Well, at least Margaret is alive."

Lucy looked up from her coddled eggs to find that Robert hadn't even opened his newspaper and was instead tapping an impatient tattoo on the side of the coffeepot.

"Dr. Fletcher has been unable to rouse her. He insists that she is best left to sleep for as long as she needs to. I've seen such cases before." Lucy sighed. "Sometimes the patient wakes up and has no memory of what happened to them, and sometimes . . ."

"They never wake up," Robert said, finishing for her. "I saw the same thing during the war."

"Such an unfortunate thing to have happened right before the Christmas festivities. We can hardly ask the Greenwell family any embarrassing questions now."

"Indeed."

"I wonder, should I cancel the ball?"

Robert raised an eyebrow. "I don't think us holding a ball will make any difference to Margaret's recovery, do you?"

"I meant more as a mark of respect."

"She isn't dead yet. I'm going to drive over and speak to Mr. Greenwell this morning. I'll ask his opinion on the matter, if you wish."

Lucy gave him a searching look. "Only if you can ask in a *subtle* manner that will not place him in a difficult position."

"I'm sure I can manage that."

Lucy doubted it, but she had no time to argue the matter through, and gentlemen were often far more blunt with each other than a lady could get away with.

"I'll write a note to Mrs. Greenwell and ask if there is anything I can do to help," Lucy said. "I would go myself, but I have much to accomplish today."

"It's all right. Rose is going to accompany me."

"Thank goodness for Aunt Rose. She really has been a godsend." Lucy sat forward. "Robert, I *do* wish she would consider coming and living with us permanently."

"You really mean that?" Robert studied her. "I would certainly like it. Shall I ask her opinion on the matter?"

"Yes, please. She has the ability to get along with everyone—even my father."

"So I noticed." Robert poured himself more coffee. "Then that's settled." He opened his newspaper and started to read.

"The morning post, my lady." Foley offered her a silver tray piled high with letters.

"Thank you." Lucy took a moment to separate out new replies to the ball from invitations from her more general correspondence. "Oh, my goodness. I have a letter from that professor in Cambridge who knew Miss Broomfield."

She opened the seal and unfolded the sheet of paper. Her frown deepened as she read. "He's attempting to suggest that he didn't know Miss Broomfield quite as well as my father thought he did. I wonder why he's changed his mind about the issue."

"Mayhap because Miss Broomfield is no longer alive to coerce him into compliance?"

Lucy lowered the letter. "That is an excellent point. She might have been blackmailing him, as well."

"It seems likely." Robert turned the page. "It seems as if all our hopes of solving this matter now rest on the mysterious Mr. Clapper, who may or may not have come to Kurland St. Mary to see Miss Broomfield. I assume you have written to him, as well?"

"Mr. Stanton agreed to help with that matter. He has set his clerk in London searching for Mr. Clapper's office in Cheapside."

"Then perhaps we will finally learn something useful." He went back to reading his newspaper as Lucy finished her eggs and toast.

"Don't forget that the Christmastide concert is tonight in the church."

Robert groaned. "Ah yes, the yearly torturing of my ears."

"You are being extremely unenthusiastic

this morning, sir." Lucy gave her husband a disapproving look. "It is always wonderful to see the church decorated for the Christmas season and filled to bursting with the villagers."

"Only if you grew up in a rectory," Robert muttered.

"Many of the villagers would disagree with you. They are *especially* looking forward to hearing the children from the school sing."

"Ah, yes. I'd forgotten about that."

"I intend to go down to the school today and listen to their last practice," Lucy said and held her breath.

Robert's newspaper came down. "You know perfectly well that I do not want you anywhere near that schoolhouse."

"But Rebecca will need help," Lucy remonstrated. "What with everything going on at the Greenwell residence, I doubt Josephine will be present. I will take one of the footmen, and he can stay the whole time and escort me home afterward. It will be the last time I need to be there."

Robert sighed. "If you must."

"Thank you." She rewarded him with her sweetest smile. "I've asked some of our friends and the villagers to join us after the church service for hot spiced cider and mince pies."

"I can't wait."

"Robert . . ." Lucy mock frowned at him

and consulted her list. "I've also arranged for Grace to bring some greenery and mistletoe on Christmas Eve, while Mr. Pugh from the home farm will deliver a Yule log of a sufficient size to fit in the large fireplace in the hall."

"You are a marvel of organizational skill, my dear." He smiled at her as he folded his paper.

"I assume the mummers will also call at some point between the villagers' party and the ball."

"I can ask down at the stables about that if you want."

"There's no need," Lucy said quickly. The last thing she wanted was Robert poking around the stables and discovering the two puppies Mr. Hopewell had secreted there for her the previous evening. "I have complete confidence that George Culpepper has the matter well in hand."

"George is involved in that, is he?"

"Only because he has tutored some of the men this year and knows their plans." Lucy looked down at her notes. "I do have *one* more thing to ask you, but with the mood you are in, I am not sure whether I should bother."

He bowed elaborately in his seat. "Ask away, my dear. I can always say no."

"What do you think about installing a Christmas tree in the house?"

"I thought we'd already discussed that. You said Mr. Pugh is dealing with it."

"Mr. Pugh is bringing the Yule log. A Christmas tree is something quite different. It involves bringing a whole tree into the house." Lucy carried on, even though Robert hardly looked impressed. "I read about it in one of the London society columns. Apparently, Queen Charlotte brought the tradition with her from her native land."

"A whole *tree?* Roots and all in a tub?" Robert frowned. "It will die. Why would you want to do that?"

"Because the tree can be decorated with ribbons and baubles. It would look very festive. I saw an illustration of the one Queen Charlotte had in her house, and it was very pretty indeed."

"Why not leave the poor tree outside, where it can continue to grow, and decorate it out there?" Robert asked. "I cannot see such an idea ever becoming popular, can you?"

"Maybe not." Lucy set her notebook aside. "I will not mention it again."

After a short silence, during which Lucy drank more tea and Robert kept reading, he asked in a more conciliatory tone, "I assume we are hosting the Stanfords, the Fletchers, and everyone currently at the rectory on Christmas Day?"

"Yes, and Grace Turner and anyone who cannot get home after the ball."

Robert glanced out of the window at the leaden skies and grimaced. "It does look like it is going to snow. We might end up with a houseful. I am glad Grace is willing to join us."

"So am I. She will not attend the ball or the party but has agreed to spend the day with us—as long as she doesn't have to go to church."

"I always enjoy watching her spar with your father." Robert finished the last of his coffee, wiped his mouth, and dropped his napkin by his plate. "I must be off, my dear. With this bad weather closing in, I have to make sure the cattle and sheep are secure and have access to both food and shelter."

Lucy closed her notebook. "And I must go and speak to Cook."

Lucy clapped as loudly as she could and smiled broadly at the children clustered around her. "That was delightful! I cannot wait to hear you all perform tonight in the church."

"Thank you, Lady Kurland." Rebecca flushed with pride as she surveyed her small choir. "Now, don't forget. You all need to be at the church by six o'clock."

"How will we know when that is?" one of the boys asked.

"Listen for the church bells," Rebecca said. "When you hear them chime five times, that means you've got to start to get ready and then walk to the church."

"It will be dark," one of the little girls

whispered. "I'm not allowed out on my own at that time of night."

"If your parents aren't attending the service, we will arrange for you to be picked up," Lucy said firmly. "Rebecca, if I send Mathias down to you at the smithy, you can give him the names and addresses of anyone who needs a ride to the church."

"Thank you, my lady." Rebecca curtsied. "I'll do that."

Lucy spent a little while longer speaking to Rebecca, who had already heard about the hunting accident and assured her that Josephine would almost certainly be attending the church service. She was just about to lock the school door when a cart pulled up outside and one of the home farmworkers came to greet her.

"Morning, Lady Kurland."

"Good morning, Reg. And what brings you here on this cold grey day?"

"Just before she died, I came by to fix that blocked chimney for Miss Broomfield, and she told me she was otherwise engaged, and to come back another day." Reg scratched under his chin. "I must confess that I forgot about it. We've been that busy up at the farm. Do you still want me to attend to it, my lady?"

"Come in, Reg." Lucy opened the door again and gestured for Reg and James, the footman who had accompanied her that morning, to come back into the school. "It certainly needs to be done before we get a new teacher, or we'll smoke her out on her first day."

Reg cackled with laughter as he carefully wiped his muddy feet on the mat. His equipment seemed to consist of a bucket, a long stick, and a couple of grain sacks. "Aye, it won't take a minute, my lady. Probably a bird's nest or summat stuck in the narrow part of the flue. Happens all the time up at the hall, with those old-fashioned brick chimneys of yours."

"I know all about that," Lucy murmured. In her opinion, Tudor chimneys might *look* very decorative, but they were terribly inefficient.

She stayed down in the schoolroom, listening to the occasional thump or muttered curse word that emanated from above. Within a quarter of an hour, Reg clumped down the stairs, a smile on his face.

"I found what was blocking the chimney, my lady."

"Excellent. What was it?" Lucy tried not to look in the bucket Reg was brandishing in her face.

"This." He handed her a small box. "Someone wedged it up there, and it either shifted from its perch or fell down in the wind, and it got caught up with an old bird's nest that blocked the flow."

"Thank you, Reg."

Reg handed her one of the sacks, and she used it to carefully dust off the sooty metal box, her heart beating rapidly with excitement. Had she finally discovered the box that belonged to the key Miss Broomfield had hidden behind her crucifix?

"It's very good of you both to call." Mr. Greenwell's smile was somewhat distracted. "Please sit down. Would you care for some refreshment? I am sorry that Mrs. Greenwell is unavailable to receive you. She is maintaining a vigil at Margaret's bedside and refuses to leave her."

"Has there been any change in Miss Margaret's condition?" Robert lowered himself onto the nearest seat and propped his cane beside him. "I have a note from my wife, offering any assistance you need. My aunt and I would like to offer you the same support."

"And it is much appreciated." Mr. Greenwell sighed. "I cannot understand how Margaret came off at that bank. She is an accomplished rider, and familiar with the terrain."

"Perhaps her horse was startled by something?" Robert asked. "They aren't the most reliable of creatures at the best of times."

"I was right behind her when she took the jump." Mr. Greenwell shook his head. "She took it perfectly and then just seemed to slide to one side, and she was off. It was one of the worst moments of my life," he said quietly. "Mrs. Greenwell thinks I was negligent in some way, but I have racked my brains, and I cannot think of a single thing that I would've changed as we approached that obstacle."

Rose leaned forward and patted his hand. "Pray do not distress yourself, Mr. Greenwell. Despite the best of intentions, things can go wrong in an instant. All we can do now is pray for a swift return to consciousness and a speedy recovery."

"Thank you, Mrs. Armitage. I appreciate your kindness." Mr. Greenwell looked over at Robert. "I must not take up too much of your time, sir. You must be busy with preparations for the ball and the party." He hesitated. "I don't believe any of our family will be able to attend either event. I'm sure you will forgive us for that, considering the circumstances."

Robert cleared his throat. "As to that, my wife was wondering whether to cancel everything due to the current events. I—"

"Oh, no." Mr. Greenwell looked shocked. "We would *never* deprive the whole community of an event that has been looked forward to for weeks just because of what happened to Margaret."

"Are you quite certain about that, sir?" Robert pressed. "We would not wish to be insensitive."

"And we would not wish our personal tragedy to spoil everyone's Christmastide." Mr. Greenwell met Robert's gaze. "Please rest easy on that score."

"Thank you." Robert stood and helped Rose out of her chair. "I appreciate your candor on the matter, which will relieve my wife's anxiety tremendously."

Deep in thought, Robert allowed Mr. Greenwell to escort them into the hall and out to the carriage. He waited until his host had retreated into the house, and then tapped on the ceiling.

"Mr. Coleman? Will you drive around to the stables before we leave?"

"Yes, sir."

After they completed their half circuit of the house, Robert got out, leaving his aunt comfortably situated in the warmth of the interior. He walked into the stable yard and searched until he found the groom he'd met the previous day.

"Can I help you, sir?"

Robert nodded. "I hope so. Were you the man who took the sidesaddle off Miss Margaret's horse yesterday?"

"Aye, I was."

"Did you notice anything odd about it?"

"I was hoping you'd come by, sir, seeing as you're the local magistrate and all." The man hesitated and dropped his gaze. "I don't want to make no trouble for the family, or lose my place for speaking out or something, but it didn't look right to me."

"What didn't?"

"The girth." The groom grimaced. "Looked to me like someone had deliberately cut through it to try to weaken it."

"Lady Kurland!"

Lucy looked to her right and discovered Mrs. Jarvis waving enthusiastically at her. They were halfway up the High Street, so she ordered the footman to pull the gig over to the side of the road. Seeing as her journey was the shortest, she'd urged Robert to take the closed carriage to Lower Kurland to visit the Greenwells.

"Mrs. Jarvis. How are you?"

"I'm very well, your ladyship." She dragged a tall young boy closer to the gig. "I wanted to introduce you to my son. Do you remember I told you he was coming to live with us and to help out with the inn?"

"I do indeed." Lucy smiled at the sullen youth, who had black hair and a stocky build that bore no relation to his mother's plump fairness. "Welcome to Kurland St. Mary."

He muttered something unintelligible and received a sharp poke in the ribs from his mother.

"Now, you speak up and be respectful to Lady Kurland, who's married to the gentleman you were named after, our Bobby, or you'll be getting a slap."

"Morning, my lady."

"Good morning, Bobby," Lucy replied. "Do you intend to accompany your mother to our village party on Christmas Eve?"

He mumbled what Lucy guessed was an affirmation, and was given a slap on the head from his mother, who had to stand on tiptoes to administer it.

"Speak up! How are you ever going to run an inn if you're too chickenhearted to talk to your betters?" Mrs. Jarvis curtsied to Lucy. "I'm sorry, my lady. He's been brought up better than this, not that you'd know it."

Lucy smiled. "I had better be going, Mrs. Jarvis. I have a lot to accomplish today."

"Well, if you need any extra help, just let me know, and I'll send this young man to work for you. The devil finds work for idle hands, eh?"

"Indeed he does. That's very kind of you." She nodded at the sullen-faced boy, who briefly looked up and then away. "It was a pleasure to meet you."

Fearful that his mother would give him another clout, Lucy didn't wait to see if Bobby replied to her or not, and nodded for James to move on.

Bobby was supposedly the same age as Josephine and Rebecca but had neither their air of competence or their command of language.

Robert had always said that boys were little savages until their twenties, and from the evidence of her own brothers, she tended to agree with him.

She hoped that Robert and Rose were on their way back from Greenwell Manor. She couldn't wait to open the box and find out what she assumed might be Miss Broomfield's most precious secrets. . . .

"Has Lady Kurland returned from the school yet, Foley?"

Robert came down the main staircase and waited for his butler to join him in the center of the hall.

"Yes, indeed, sir. Her ladyship is ensconced in her sitting room. I just took her a fresh pot of tea. Shall I procure a cup for you so that you may join her?"

"Yes, please." Robert watched his old butler's snaillike pace toward the kitchens and paused. "Foley."

"Yes, Sir Robert?"

"Are you ready to retire yet? I can find you a nice cottage in the village or on the estate, and a generous pension."

Foley drew himself up to his full height. "Are you *ordering* me to retire, sir?"

"I wouldn't dare." Robert hesitated. "I just wonder whether there are other things you might wish to fill your days with rather than ordering me around."

"I enjoy working at the hall, sir. If I ever feel that I am becoming a liability rather than an asset, I will be the first to offer my resignation."

"Then let's leave it at that." Robert nodded. "It certainly wouldn't be the same without you."

"Indeed, sir. I suspect the place would quickly fall to rack and ruin." Foley bowed low. "Now, may I get on, sir? I have a lot to accomplish today. The silver needs to be polished, and I'm expecting the musicians for the ball to arrive at any moment."

"My apologies."

Robert continued on his way down the corridor that led to his wife's favored room in the house. He had no wish to force Foley into retirement, but he still made the offer occasionally. He suspected his butler was determined to hang on until he saw an heir to the baronetcy and the estate safely born. Foley had no love or respect for Robert's cousin Paul, who would inherit if Robert died without an heir.

Whether that would occur was somewhat in question. . . . His wife had not responded to his somewhat impulsive offer of a marriage based on companionship rather than physical congress. The fact that he'd made it at all still surprised him, seeing as it was the last thing he really wanted. He had been feeling remarkably useless that day and had found it hard to imagine any woman choosing to put up with his physical frailties. The fact that Lucy hadn't immediately repudiated the idea worried him even more. . . .

He knocked on the door and went in. Lucy was sitting by the fire, wearing a dark reddish dress the color of a horse chestnut that made her eyes look very brown.

"Good afternoon, my dear. I spoke to one of the grooms at the Greenwells'. He reckoned someone had cut into the girth of Miss Margaret's sidesaddle."

She put down her book and gaped at him. *"What?"*

Robert took the seat opposite her. "The trouble is, half the county was there yesterday. *Anyone* could've done it."

"But this makes no sense."

"It suggests to me that either Miss Margaret didn't write those letters or she did, and that the same person who wanted Miss Broomfield to die wanted Miss Margaret dead, as well." He blew out an exasperated breath. "Mayhap Miss Margaret was right. Miss Broomfield *did* have an accomplice, but it wasn't Anna. It was Margaret all along."

"But I don't think Miss Broomfield wrote those letters," Lucy said.

"What?" It was his turn to blink. "Why not?"

302

She handed him a piece of paper. "Read this."

He put on his spectacles, held the scrap of paper closer to the light, and read it out loud. "You are a liar and a cheat, and your false God has forsaken you."

"There is another one." She gave him a second note, this one folded.

"Miss Broomfield received two letters?" Robert unfolded the note and read it aloud. "Norfolk is a cold and unforgiving place. You will burn at the stake with your fellow Catholic martyrs." He lowered his gaze to Lucy. "What's this about Norfolk?"

"I believe that's where Miss Broomfield came from. Do you remember that Dermot told us the diamond and ruby necklace was made for a family called Hillcott? I found an engraving of a Hillcott Hall in a copy of *Ackermann's* Miss Broomfield had on her shelf."

"That certainly seems an unlikely periodical for her to keep and quite a coincidence. I suppose she could have worked there and stolen the jewelry." He handed her back the notes. "Anything else?"

"When I was at the schoolhouse today, Reg came by to check the flow of the kitchen chimney, which Miss Broomfield informed me was blocked just before her death."

"And he found the letters up there?"

"In this box." She showed him the black metal

box on her lap and took out a slim black volume. "There are some other . . . things in there, as well."

"Such as?" Robert asked.

"Her rosary, another prayer book, and her diary." Lucy's lip trembled. "I started to read it, but . . . she was not a nice person, Robert. I fear her mind was unhinged. She revels in hatred and hellfire."

He held out his hand. "Give the book to me. I'll read it. I have a far stronger stomach than you, and it might contain something that helps us work out what the devil is going on."

"Thank you."

She placed the book in his hand, with the letters inside the front cover. He put it in his coat pocket to examine later. She still looked shaken, and that didn't please Robert at all.

"It seems that we are at an impasse," Lucy said quietly. "Margaret is unconscious, Miss Broomfield is dead, and we still have no idea *why*."

He took her hand. "Perhaps this time we will never know exactly what happened."

She nodded and then looked up at him, her chin set at a resolute angle, one he had come to know well. "Tomorrow I am going with Anna, Sophia, and Dermot to purchase the last of the toys for the villagers' party. I will do my best to enjoy my day and to try to forget about the things I cannot solve."

"That's an excellent strategy." He drew her gently to her feet and kissed her brow. "Now come and have dinner with me. Aunt Rose has invited your father, and I need you to defend me against his claims that I am an unintelligent oaf."

Chapter 15

M r. Fletcher?" Lucy called out to her husband's land agent. "Can you wait a moment?"

They were moving through the busy streets of the university town of Cambridge, and Lucy was struggling to keep up with Dermot's longer stride and youthful vigor. It was another gray day, with a biting wind that swept between the stone colleges of the university and the river Cam. The streets were not only narrow but were also packed with people.

"I do apologize, Lady Kurland." Dermot stepped into a low doorway. "I was too busy chatting to Miss Harrington to notice you and Mrs. Stanford had gotten behind me."

"I was going to suggest that you and my sister continue shopping. Mrs. Stanford and I will go back to the inn and deposit all the parcels we are carrying," Lucy said after she caught her breath.

It was not precisely the *thing* for Anna to be out without a chaperone in the city, but Lucy was fairly certain she could rely on Dermot's ability to behave in an appropriate manner.

Sophia touched her arm. "I'll carry on shopping with them, Lucy. I have another gift to buy."

Lucy raised an inquiring eyebrow at her friend

306

but chose not to disagree openly with her. "Then I will return to the inn and meet you there in an hour, before we begin the journey home."

Anna sighed. "I wish we had more time. I've scarcely started on my list."

Dermot bowed to her. "Now that I have completed my commissions for Sir Robert, I am completely at your disposal, Miss Harrington." He offered her his arm. "Where would you like to go next?"

Sophia winked at Lucy as she went to follow the happy pair. "I promise I'll keep an eye on them, not a close eye, but a mindful one, just in case."

"Thank you," Lucy called out as she waited for them all to turn the corner. Not having to explain herself to Sophia was an unforeseen advantage to her next expedition. She consulted the address on the letter and headed toward the Peterhouse College buildings.

"I'll see if Professor Elwood is in his rooms, Lady Kurland."

The porter at the gate didn't seem very willing to help her, which wasn't a surprise. She'd heard many stories of academia from her father and his friends, and none of them had indicated much willingness of the intellectual elite to climb down from their ivory towers and speak to a mere woman.

"Thank you." Lucy sat down on the stone bench in the sheltered gatehouse. "I'll wait."

To her surprise, the man came back relatively quickly. "Professor Elwood is more than willing to receive you in his chamber, my lady. Please follow me."

The college cloisters and grassy quad were deserted as the students had been released for the yuletide season. The ancient architecture was well worth admiring, but Lucy had neither the interest nor the time to contemplate it.

"Lady Kurland, Professor."

"Thank you, Timms. Do come in, my dear."

Lucy entered the book-lined chamber and closely studied the elderly man who rose to greet her. She guessed he was in his seventh decade. He had a long white beard and kind blue eyes.

"Please be seated, Lady Kurland. I have heard much about you from your father. He oft lamented that you weren't born a boy and able to use your intellectual abilities."

"He told me the same thing many times." Lucy maintained her smile as she sat down. "I appreciate your offering me this opportunity to speak to you about Miss Broomfield."

"Ah, yes." He returned to sit behind his desk and dropped his gaze to his folded hands. "I thought that might be your mission. I understand from your letter that she is dead."

"Yes, and in somewhat suspicious circum-

308

stances." Lucy sat forward. "May I ask how you came to write that reference for her?"

"I wrote it as a favor to a member of her family whom I have known since we were both sent away to school at the age of seven. He asked me if I would help him find a secure position for a niece of his who had fallen on hard times."

"This friend of yours is Miss Broomfield's uncle?"

"Yes. A Mr. Richard Hillcott. He is a vicar who inherited the living on the Hillcott estate in Norfolk." He hesitated. "Broomfield is not her real surname. She was born a Hillcott."

Lucy nodded. "I was beginning to suspect she was connected to that family. Did she fall out with them at some point?"

"I fear so. From what I understand, she was brought up under the influence of her Spanish grandmother, who was of a different religious persuasion. At the age of seventeen, when most girls are thinking about their coming-out, she declared she wished to become a nun."

"Good gracious!" Lucy sat up straight.

"As you might imagine, her concerned but loving parents were quick to condemn such foolishness. Their solution was to take her away on a tour of the continent to perhaps change her mind, but she was still determined. While out of the country, she struck up an unfortunate and clandestine friendship with a young student priest she met in Naples.

"Unfortunately, the 'relationship' continued by letter after her return to England. The man eventually dared follow her to Norfolk. While she outwardly conformed to her parents' expectations, in private she was becoming enamored of this young man, who sought to convert her to his religion so that she could fulfill her desire to become a bride of Christ."

"Did he wish to convert her to Roman Catholicism or to himself?" Lucy asked.

"I believe his motives were pure, Lady Kurland. All I can tell you is that when she ran away from home and appeared on his doorstep, saying she loved him, he was the first to insist she return home."

Lucy tried to imagine the stern-faced Miss Broomfield as a young woman willing to risk everything over her misguided infatuation with a man, and shuddered. Even though she had disliked the woman, it must have been particularly humiliating to have her hopes crushed and her so-called lover repudiate her.

"What happened after that?"

Professor Elwood sighed. "I am afraid to say that she became hysterical and, after threatening to take her own life, had to be confined in her bedchamber for almost a year. I believe her parents even considered sending her to a private asylum at one point. It wasn't until she demanded and was given proof that her priest friend had returned to Italy and taken his final vows that she finally collapsed and became . . . acquiescent again."

"Did she ever make her debut to society?"

"No. Her parents decided the excitement and expectation would be too much for her, so she stayed at home."

"Then how did she end up as a teacher?" Lucy asked.

"At some point she answered some applications for teacher and governess positions in the *Lady*, a periodical her mother subscribed to. One day she just left with almost none of her possessions. Her parents were, of course, distraught, thinking she had fled to the continent to follow through on her vow to become a nun, but they could find no trace of her in any of the convents or orders they contacted."

"Because she'd found employment at a school in Cornwall."

"So I understand. Eventually, she wrote to her parents, and she continued to do so once a year."

"I'll wager they had begun to believe she was dead and were probably thrilled to receive any communication from her at all." Lucy shook her head. "What an extraordinary story. I have a letter from the school in Cornwall, which dismissed her for undesirable conduct toward her students."

"That's probably when I became involved in this sorry business." Professor Elwood heaved a sigh. "Richard came to see me and said that his niece had been unfairly dismissed from her previous post, yet she still refused to come home to her parents. He asked if I had any idea where she could seek employment. I had just received your father's letter, and thinking that I could perhaps help two of my oldest friends at the same time, I agreed to write a reference for Miss Broomfield."

"Did you ever meet her?" Lucy asked.

"No, I did not. I wish I had." He held her gaze. "I am truly sorry that my attempt to be helpful caused such a tragic resolution."

"You could not have predicted such an outcome, sir. Who could?" The distress in his eyes moved Lucy considerably. "Do you happen to know whether Miss Broomfield's parents used an intermediary to contact her, or did they do so themselves?"

"She refused to see any of them, so I would assume they used some sort of intermediary from the legal profession."

"Did they offer her any financial assistance?"

"That I do not know." He reached for a piece of paper on his desk. "I have written down the name and address of Mr. Richard Hillcott. I wrote to inform him that you had contacted me. He gave me permission to share his family's personal information with you." He paused. "I assume you will treat this sensitive material with the respect it deserves."

"Naturally." Lucy nodded. "My husband is the local magistrate in Kurland St. Mary and is a man of character and discretion. You can trust him to use what you have told me fairly and only to aid the course of justice."

"I am glad to hear that there are still men with integrity in our land."

Lucy checked the clock hanging on the wall above the fireplace. "Is there anything else you can think of with regards to this matter, sir?"

"No, my dear." He followed her gaze to the clock. "Do you have another appointment? I was going to suggest we share some afternoon tea."

"I wish that were possible, Professor, but I have to return home." Lucy rose and curtsied. "You have been very helpful. Perhaps when you next visit Kurland St. Mary, we can spend a more agreeable afternoon together at the hall."

"I look forward to it." He stood and brought her gloved hand to his lips. "Despite the subject matter, it has been a pleasure meeting you, Lady Kurland, and I do hope to further our acquaintance."

"Are you settled here for the Christmas season, sir?"

"I am expected at my sister's house for the festivities." His blue eyes brightened. "I never married myself, but my sister has a houseful of children and grandchildren for me to spoil and enjoy."

"How lovely." Lucy smiled at him. "Seasons greetings, sir, and all the best wishes for a happy New Year."

Her smile faded as she walked back out onto the street and worked out which direction she needed to take in order to arrive back safely at the correct inn. It seemed Miss Broomfield's life had not been a happy one. But it was extremely unlikely that anyone from her family had wanted her dead. In truth, they had wanted her to stay at home, have a traditional London Season, and get married to a suitable gentleman.

Why had she resisted them? What kind of woman chose to leave her family and become a governess and teacher in a world where those positions were not valued or appreciated? Lucy knew how crushing the weight of familial expectation could be, but she had never developed the courage to flout it completely.

Had Miss Broomfield finally lost her nerve at the thought of venturing onto the war-ravaged continent to find a suitable nunnery? In her debilitated state, had crossing the Channel been too much for her, so she'd chosen to stay as far away from her family as she could manage? Lucy would never know.

She stopped to cross the busy road, which

was crowded with people shopping and others intent on selling their wares. She took a firmer hold on her reticule as a gang of young boys burst through the crowds, fingers outstretched to catch any unsecured purses or dangling treasures. She safely reached the other side of the street just as the town clock struck the hour. If all went well, they would be home in five or six hours.

"Lucy, wake up."

She opened her eyes to see Sophia smiling at her. From the rocking motion, she deduced they were still traveling. It was now dark outside, and it was difficult to see clearly, despite the carriage lamps.

"What is it?"

"Can we stop at the Queen's Head so that I can collect a parcel?"

"Of course. We have to stop at the rectory, anyway."

"Thank you." Sophia nudged her. "Look at Anna."

Lucy peered past her friend to the opposite side of the interior, where her sister had fallen asleep, her head on Dermot's shoulder. He had put his arm around her and was smiling even in his sleep. Thinking about Anna's aversion to marriage made the tableau bittersweet for Lucy.

"We're almost home. We just came off the

Hertford road," Sophia added. "I'll be glad to get out of this cramped space."

Lucy couldn't argue with that. She wasn't quite sure how Robert would react when he heard the news that they'd gone all the way to Cambridge rather than to the much closer town of Hertford. Whatever he thought, she was glad she had gone. They might not be any closer to discovering why Miss Broomfield had died, but Lucy had a much clearer picture of how she had lived.

"I enjoyed the children singing last night immensely," Sophia remarked. "I declare, there was hardly a dry eye in the church. You did an excellent job, my dear."

"I did nothing but supervise Rebecca and Josephine," Lucy said. "They were the ones who put in all the hard work necessary for success. But I think even my father was impressed. He said we should make it an annual tradition."

"If you can find a teacher to keep your school open all year."

"We certainly haven't been very lucky so far." Lucy rubbed the condensation from the small glass window with the tip of her gloved finger. "Let's take Anna to the rectory first and visit the Queen's Head after that."

Lucy kissed Anna good night and watched as she went in the front door of the rectory, accompanied by Dermot, who had insisted on carrying all her parcels. He had also said that the walk back to Kurland Hall would do him good after the restricted hours spent in the carriage and had told them not to bother to return for him.

"Mr. Fletcher is in love with your sister," Sophia remarked.

"I know." Lucy sighed.

"Would you disapprove of such a match?"

"Not at all."

"Would your father?"

"Absolutely. Between his distaste for popish ways and Dermot's social class, the poor man would never stand a chance."

"But what if Anna was in love with him, too?" Sophia persisted.

"She likes him very much, but she certainly hasn't admitted to having any romantical feelings about him to me." Lucy hesitated. "She isn't willing to rush into a marriage just for the sake of it."

"That is very sensible. And she is so beautiful, I doubt she will ever have to worry about finding a gentleman who is worthy of her."

Lucy felt the carriage slow and tried to look out of the window. "We're approaching the Queen's Head."

Sophia put on her bonnet and tied the ribbons. "I suppose I'd better make myself respectable before I descend. I swear, there are more gossips in Kurland St. Mary than in London."

"We both attended a London Season, Sophia, and know better." Lucy smiled at her friend. "But one does have to keep up appearances here, as well."

She took the opportunity to climb down from the carriage to stretch her legs while Sophia hurried into the inn. There was only one other vehicle in the stable yard. It took a few moments of peering through the darkness to establish that it looked like the Kurland gig.

"Thank you so much, Mr. Jarvis."

Lucy turned her attention back to the inn, where Sophia stood illuminated in a square of light from the open door.

She waved at Lucy and came across the yard. "Are you ready to proceed? Mrs. Jarvis was busy, so I had to extricate Mr. Jarvis from serving ale in the tavern. He was very gracious about being disturbed."

Sophia climbed into the carriage, and Lucy followed her.

"I realized I'd left my favorite shawl in London and wrote to ask my housekeeper to send it on to me." Sophia paused and looked over Lucy's shoulder through the still open carriage door. "Is that *Robert* with Mrs. Jarvis?" She chuckled. "I wonder what they were doing in there."

Lucy turned her head and saw her husband emerging from the stables, Mrs. Jarvis clinging to his arm as she chattered away nineteen to the dozen. Lucy slammed the door and rapped on the ceiling to alert the coachman to depart.

"Lucy?" Sophia's puzzled voice came from behind her. "Why didn't you want to stop and speak to Robert?"

Lucy fumbled for her handkerchief as a storm of unforeseen emotions swirled inside her. "Because . . . maybe he wouldn't want to be interrupted."

"Whatever do you mean?" Sophia took her elbow and maneuvered her around. "Are you *crying?* What is wrong? What happened? You can't possibly think that Robert is . . . that Mrs. Jarvis would . . . *could* you?"

"Why not?" Lucy spoke through gulping sobs into her handkerchief. "He hasn't visited my bed for six months." She dissolved into tears and let Sophia sit beside her and pat her shoulders in a most comforting way.

When the carriage stopped, Sophia opened the door and grabbed Lucy's hand. "You are coming in with me. You cannot risk going home in this state."

She led Lucy in through the front door, spoke privately with her mother's butler, and then took Lucy straight up the stairs to her bedchamber.

"I do apologize." Lucy blew her nose, and she sank into a chair by the fire. "I know I am behaving appallingly, but seeing the evidence with my own eyes after all my worrying . . . quite overset me."

Sophia put a glass of brandy into her hand. "Drink up. You have suffered something of a shock." She waited until Lucy took a small sip before continuing. "Now, what is this all about? Do you suspect Robert of being unfaithful to you with Mrs. *Jarvis?*"

"He knew her when he was a young officer in London."

"Robert *told* you this?"

"No, Mrs. Jarvis told me. Robert has seemingly forgotten to mention it. She didn't think it was anything to be embarrassed about. But doesn't it seem odd that she ended up living in Kurland St. Mary?"

"But Robert has eyes for no woman but you," Sophia said gently. "Just because they were acquainted before doesn't mean they are becoming . . . *acquainted* again."

"He suggested we could have a marriage of friendship and mutual respect." Lucy screwed up her handkerchief into a tight ball. "Mayhap he meant that he had already found other methods of physical release."

"Why on earth would he suggest that?"

"We were talking about . . . another person, someone who is afraid of the physical nature of marriage. I asked him if there were men who would marry and not expect the marriage to be consummated. I think he believed I was talking about *our* marriage."

"Do you and Robert still share a bed?"

"We sleep in the same bed, but he makes no effort to . . . seek me out at night."

"And what happens if you seek him out?"

Lucy slowly looked up at Sophia. "I don't."

"Why ever not?"

"Because what if he repudiated me?" Lucy's cheeks heated. She had never before spoken to anyone about the intimate facts of her marriage. "He waits until I am asleep before he comes to bed. He makes no effort to *touch* me."

"Lucy, you did suffer two miscarriages in six months," Sophia said softly and reached out to hold her hand. "Perhaps Robert is afraid, as well."

"So afraid that he chases Mrs. Jarvis into the stables? She had *straw* in her hair, Sophia."

"Then it seems as if you have no choice, Lucy dear." Sophia fixed her with a sympathetic stare. "You need to gather your courage and ask your husband exactly what is going on."

Chapter 16

So Professor Elwood had never even met Miss Broomfield and simply wrote the reference to help his old friend." Robert whistled. "Good Lord."

He glanced over at his wife, who was sitting in the chair in front of his desk, her gaze focused downward on her folded hands. She had gone to bed straight after her return from Cambridge and had risen before him. Persuading her to take the time to speak to him for a few moments had taken some doing.

"I feel sorry for the Hillcott family," Robert added. "I will write them a letter after Christmas and express our condolences."

"As you wish." Lucy's gaze was now fixed on the clock on the mantelpiece. "I have a lot to do today, so is there anything else I can assist you with?"

"Not at this moment." He paused to study her averted face. "Are you feeling all right?"

"Why should I not be?" She rose to her feet. "Pray excuse me."

He stood, as well, and went to open the door for her. "Are you *quite* certain you are well?"

"I have guests arriving in less than an hour and a villagers' party to organize. We are also hosting a ball for the entire county tomorrow night." She didn't even look at him. "I am simply busy."

He caught hold of her elbow. "It's more than that. What's wrong?"

She eased out of his grasp. "I have to go."

"Lucy . . ."

"Please excuse me."

He let her slide past him and returned to his desk, his sense of unease building. It wasn't like his Lucy to be so quiet. He might sometimes be irritated by her forthright nature, but he didn't recollect her ever standing down from a fight. He couldn't discount the fact that she did have a lot to do, but normally, she was in her element on such occasions, not grimly determined and terse. That was normally his modus operandi.

He stared out of the window at the towering black clouds that were advancing across the parkland like massed ranks of infantry. He hoped that all the guests would arrive safely, and that both the ball and the party would take place as planned. From the taste of frost on his tongue, he guessed they were about to welcome winter in all its glory.

"Lady Kurland?"

Lucy broke off from her discussion with her housekeeper and found Foley hovering by her elbow. It was late in the afternoon on an exceedingly long day, and she was beginning to feel somewhat overwhelmed by the tasks still ahead of her. She kept reminding herself that her staff was remarkably competent, and that she had lots of help at hand if she would only remember to call on it.

"Yes?"

"There is a gentleman who wishes to speak to you."

"About the ball or the village party?"

Foley frowned. "He said it was on a matter of business, my lady."

"Did he give you his name?"

"No, my lady, but he did say he had come from London, and it was related to the matter of Miss Broomfield."

"Then I will come at once." She paused. "If you can find Sir Robert, please ask him to join us at his convenience."

She didn't bother to change out of her old gown. She was far too busy to waste half an hour while the poor man kicked his heels in the land agent's office.

When she opened the door, a youngish gentleman jumped to his feet, bowed, and offered her his card.

"My name is Mr. Clapper, Lady Kurland. I received your note through the good offices of Mr. Stanford." He was very much as Bertha had described him, slightly shabby, but handsome enough to get away with it.

"It is very kind of you to come all the way down from London to speak to me." Lucy offered him a seat. "Especially in this awful weather."

"I decided the matter was too important to wait until after Christmastide." He sat down. "I understand that you and Sir Robert Kurland own the school where Miss Broomfield was employed."

"That is correct. It was my husband who discovered Miss Broomfield was dead."

"Her family is desolated to hear that."

"The Hillcott family of Norfolk?"

Mr. Clapper frowned. "With all due respect, how do you know of that connection?"

"I spoke to a Professor Elwood, who wrote a reference for Miss Broomfield, and he revealed the link between our teacher and the Hillcotts." Lucy paused. "I assume that you work for them in some capacity?"

"Not exactly. I deal with issues relating to Miss Broomfield only through a separate law firm. She was quite adamant about that. She didn't trust her parents or their usual solicitors."

"But you acted as some kind of liaison between the parties."

"Exactly." He nodded. "It was my job to transfer Miss Broomfield's allowance to her, and to alert her to any changes in her family circumstances."

"So you did meet with her here a week or so ago?"

"I certainly attempted to do so."

"And are you at liberty to tell me *why* you sought her out?"

"Indeed. I have already communicated with my superiors and the Hillcott family. I've been authorized to deal with any consequences of Miss Broomfield's unexpected death and to answer any of your quite understandable questions." He placed his bag on the table. "I do, however, have a slightly delicate question of my own to ask first."

Lucy assumed her most benign expression. "What would that be?"

He still hesitated. "Did Miss Broomfield take her own life?"

"No, she did not."

He visibly sagged. "Thank God for that small mercy. From what I understand, her mind . . . was not strong, and her emotions sometimes overcame her."

"She certainly had quite a temper."

"Was there a physician present when she died?"

"When my husband realized Miss Broomfield was dead, he fetched our Dr. Fletcher, who confirmed that she had indeed passed away."

"Do you happen to know what the cause of death was?" Mr. Clapper opened his bag, took out a notebook, wrote something, and looked inquiringly at her.

"Someone inserted a twelve-inch hat pin down through the back of her neck."

His mouth opened, and he gaped at her. "*Excuse me?*"

"Some unknown person came up behind her and stabbed her with a hat pin," Lucy repeated patiently.

He visibly swayed in his seat. "Good Lord."

"Do you have any idea *why* someone should have chosen to do that, Mr. Clapper?"

She heard the door open quietly behind her and immediately knew that Robert had joined her. Without turning, she held up her hand. "This is Mr. Clapper, Robert. I was just explaining how Miss Broomfield died."

"So I heard." He limped over to the younger man and shook his hand. "A shame to meet you in such difficult circumstances, Mr. Clapper, but thank you for coming to help us clear up this matter."

"Sir Robert." Mr. Clapper blinked hard. "I had no idea. . . . Are you both suggesting that Miss Broomfield was murdered by persons *unknown?*"

"That depends." Robert took the seat beside Lucy. "Did my wife mention that Miss Broomfield died the day that *you* visited her?"

"I . . ." He looked helplessly from Lucy to Robert. "I had no idea! You cannot think . . . that I had anything to do with the matter. I'm just a glorified clerk!"

"Why did you visit her on that particular day?" Robert asked.

"Because she had a new position and address. I was making sure I knew where she was so that I could safely deliver her yearly allowance to her on the first day of January."

"May I ask how much her family gave her per year?"

"Four hundred pounds, sir."

Robert whistled and turned to look at Lucy. "How much did we pay her to teach?"

"Fifty pounds a year. We also provided her accommodation, coal, wood, and candles."

"I believe Miss Broomfield had certain pieces of valuable family jewelry in her possession." Mr. Clapper cleared his throat. "You *do* have her belongings in a secure place, don't you?"

"In my strong room. Why? Have you been authorized to collect them?" Robert asked.

"I could certainly take everything off your hands and return her effects to her family, sir." Mr. Clapper sat up straight. "In truth, I would consider it my duty to do so."

"Where exactly did you meet with Miss Broomfield when you called on her? Was she in her study, in the schoolroom, or in her own apartment upstairs?" Lucy asked.

"I obviously didn't make myself clear." Mr. Clapper swallowed hard. "I came to see her at the appointed hour and found the schoolhouse locked and seemingly unoccupied. I knocked on both the front and back doors, to no avail."

"At what time did you arrive at the school?"

"I can't quite remember. I was more concerned about finding a blacksmith to ensure I made it back to London that night rather than about noticing the time."

"But you said you had an appointment. What time was Miss Broomfield expecting you?" Lucy persisted.

"Around four o'clock. She said the children would have left for the day by then. She was quite insistent that I didn't make my presence widely known in the village, which is why I didn't stay more than five minutes outside the school." He looked from Lucy to Robert. "Is there something amiss?"

"Not at all. I was just trying to understand the sequence of events," Lucy said soothingly.

"I decided that seeing as I *had* ascertained exactly where Miss Broomfield was living, I would do better off returning in the New Year rather than hanging around and bothering her." He hesitated. "She had quite a sharp tongue."

"But didn't you stay the night at the inn?" Lucy asked. "You could have tried to speak to Miss Broomfield the next morning."

"Alas, I left before dawn." He shrugged. "I had to be back at my desk by midday to deal with another client's affairs."

Robert turned from his contemplation of the window. "I regret that your journey back to

London will not happen today, either. There is a snowstorm coming, and I doubt the roads will be passable." He nodded affably at Mr. Clapper. "I also need to ask my secretary, Mr. Fletcher, to make a comprehensive list of all Miss Broomfield's possessions. When it is completed, you can take it back to the Hillcott family and ask them what they wish to do to retrieve the items."

Mr. Clapper's skin flushed red. "I am quite competent, Sir Robert. I do have the trust of the Hillcott family."

"I'm quite sure you do, but pray consider my position. As the local magistrate, it would not behoove me to be giving away a deceased person's possessions to anyone who just turned up and asked for them, now would it?" His smile held the edge of a challenge. "A simple letter from the Hillcott family acknowledging receipt of our list and authorizing you to collect Miss Broomfield's effects will suffice."

"Yes, Sir Robert. Thank y-you," Mr. Clapper stuttered. "I have no particular *reason* to get back to town. I don't have any family to spend the Christmas season with, anyway."

"As you are being forced to stay overnight and spend Christmas Eve with us, I offer you the hospitality of Kurland Hall and the opportunity to attend our villagers' party tomorrow afternoon and the evening ball."

Mr. Clapper stood up, his expression brightening. "That would be most . . . *gracious* of you, sir."

Robert rang the bell. "Mr. Foley will find you a room, and I'll send Mr. Fletcher to speak to you once you are settled."

"Thank you again, sir."

Robert waited until Mr. Clapper was escorted out before shutting the door and leaning back on it. "I don't think our Mr. Clapper was telling the truth, do you?"

"No," Lucy said decisively. "Why did he come rushing down here at Christmas to sort out a matter of no urgency?"

"And why did he come rushing down to Kurland St. Mary to see Miss Broomfield ahead of his scheduled visit, and run away so quickly afterward in the first place?"

For the first time that day, Lucy directly met her husband's gaze. "I suspect that's because he killed her."

"But he claimed not to know she was dead," Robert objected.

"He certainly did sound surprised when I told him, but he could've been pretending." Lucy paused to reconsider exactly what Mr. Clapper *had* said. "He was also the one who brought up the family jewels. I wonder who told him about those."

"I suppose the Hillcotts might want them back."

"That would be understandable. But would they tell a man who was merely acting as a go-between about them?"

"Perhaps Mr. Clapper was involved in a little bit of skulduggery himself," Robert said.

"That diamond and ruby necklace was separate from everything else." Lucy nodded. "Mayhap Miss Broomfield had it ready to give to him and changed her mind, leaving it hidden on top of the chest of drawers, which ended in an argument, with him killing her."

"We did wonder if Miss Broomfield's killer had been disturbed at some point and had fled the scene before stealing the jewelry. And as Mr. Clapper certainly knew about her secret hoard, he certainly had a motive."

"Then why did he risk staying overnight at the inn?" Lucy wondered aloud.

"Well, as he didn't steal anything, maybe he thought he'd get away with it. Which might explain how *Miss Broomfield* met her end, but not the anonymous letters or what happened to Margaret Greenwell." Robert grimaced. "We can hardly blame Mr. Clapper for those."

"I suppose it is possible that Miss Broomfield wrote all the letters, and that some of them were just discovered or delivered later than intended," Lucy said slowly. "And Margaret's fall could've been because her groom was negligent and didn't notice the saddle girth needed attention."

"You don't sound very convinced of your own argument, my dear."

"That's probably because I'm not." She squeezed her hands together. "And in truth, I do not have time to worry about this particular matter today. There are other far more important things to deal with."

"Which is why I suggested Mr. Clapper stay to enjoy the festivities with us." Robert collected his cane and headed for the door. "We can keep him occupied for a day or so, until we have more time to deal with him."

"That will certainly help. Will you ask Dermot to keep an eye on him? I'd rather he didn't depart with *our* silver tucked in his saddlebags."

"I will make sure that doesn't happen." Robert bowed. "Have you had any news from the Greenwells?"

"Only that Margaret is still unconscious." Lucy sighed and rose to leave, as well. "All we can do is pray and hope for the best at this point."

Chapter 17

The morning of Christmas Eve rolled in with black clouds and rumbling thunder, making the breakfast room gloomy even with all the curtains drawn back. Robert had disappeared to help Dermot and the farmworkers set up for the party, which was being held in the largest barn at the Kurland Hall Home Farm. Barrels of ale, cider and porter were already stacked up by the door, and the trestle tables awaited the sweeping of the floor and the removal of spiderwebs and debris.

All the housemaids were currently over at the barn, cleaning, and were due to return at any moment. Lucy was counting on them to start clearing what had once been the medieval hall of Kurland manor to create enough space for her guests to dance in. The original minstrels' gallery still remained, and the musicians hired from London were due to set up there later in the day.

Already, the house smelled of pine boughs and the holly and rosemary garlands that Grace had already started to drape around the hall when she arrived at dawn. A large bunch of mistletoe had been tacked into place over the fireplace, and the Yule log was ready to be lit.

At two o'clock all the house servants would be released to attend the village party with their friends and families. At six the houseguests would sit down for a festive dinner, and the ball would begin at eight. The Harringtons and the Fletchers were dealing with the majority of the tasks associated with the village party, and Lucy, Sophia, and Aunt Rose were taking care of the ball arrangements.

It was only nine o'clock in the morning, and Lucy was already feeling quite frazzled. She hadn't spoken to Robert about what had occurred between him and Mrs. Jarvis at the inn. To sustain her, she had the excuse that they were both too busy to discuss such an important issue, and she would consider her options after the ball.

She checked the list that was constantly open at her side. She'd ordered a new gown from her dressmaker in Hertford, and it had been delivered the day before. Betty, her maid, had been in raptures about it, but Lucy hadn't even bothered to try it on. She had a horrible suspicion that she had lost weight and that the gown would only emphasize her loss of looks.

Foley came in with the morning mail and deposited it at her side.

"Good morning, my lady. It's quite like old times here today, what with all the comings and goings."

"Indeed it is." Lucy manufactured a smile.

"I'll be visiting the kitchens later to see how everything is coming along."

"Cook was busy steaming plum puddings last time I looked in there," Foley said. "She made an extra dozen for the villagers' tea this year."

"Have the maids come back yet?"

"They just arrived, my lady. They said it's getting very cold out there now, so wrap up warm when you go out to the party later, won't you?"

"Of course. Thank you for everything you do, Foley. I hope you know how much Sir Robert and I appreciate you."

"Thank you for making the major so happy, my lady." Foley's smile was warm. "At one point, I thought no one would ever want to marry him, what with his cantankerous ways and quick temper."

"His bark is definitely worse than his bite," Lucy agreed. "I am glad you consider me a civilizing influence."

Foley chuckled as he turned back to the door. "Meaning no disrespect, my lady, but you certainly keep him on his toes."

Lucy's smile faded as she quickly sorted through the pile of correspondence. There were a couple of replies to the ball that had arrived after the actual responders. That wasn't unusual at this time of the year, when the roads were treacherous and the ability to bring the mail was dependent on someone willing to risk carrying it.

She paused at a small folded sheet with just the

word *Kurland* scrawled on it and slowly turned it over. It was probably meant for Robert, but even after carefully scrutinizing the surface, she couldn't absolutely say it wasn't addressed to them both. There was no seal, so she decided to read it, anyway. If it was for Robert, then she would simply refold it and place it in his study, along with his other correspondence.

Her fingers trembled as she undid the folds and spread out the paper.

> Ask your husband about his child, and consider why his sins mean you will remain barren.

The paper blurred as her eyes filled with tears. With an immense effort, Lucy put the paper down and spent a moment wiping her eyes. The coldness of the room invaded her bones and settled around her heart.

Now you speak up and be respectful to Lady Kurland, who's married to the gentleman you were named after, our Bobby, or you'll be getting a slap.

Mrs. Jarvis's words echoed around Lucy's head like a chant, as clearly as if she were standing there saying them again.

Bobby for Robert. Of course. He was fifteen or so years of age and had black hair and blue eyes. . . .

After picking up the note, she folded it very

carefully into a precise square and put it in her pocket. Without thinking, she headed into the hall and started up the stairs, amazed at some level that she could still function, while inside she wailed and wept and tore at her hair.

Luckily, her bedchamber was empty. She crossed over to the window and curled up on the window seat that overlooked the formal gardens to the rear of the house.

What to do?

She took a deep shuddering breath. She was a practical woman, well known for her good sense and management skills. Firstly, she had to survive the party, the ball, and Christmas Day itself. . . .

But how?

She reminded herself that she had survived her mother's death, had been shot, and had been near death herself. If she feigned illness and spent the next two days in bed, no one would disbelieve her, but their concern and love might be too much to bear. Tears threatened again, and she wrapped her arms around her stomach.

The thought that Robert already had a child bore down on her, making her own efforts to provide him with an heir seem somewhat laughable. Had he always known that Mrs. Jarvis had delivered his child? Had he secretly supported her ever since, or had the recent arrival of the boy been a surprise?

Many of her friends would tell her that whatever happened in the past bore no reflection on either Robert's character or his love for her. In a gentleman's world, there were different classes of females: ladies they married, women who worked for them in their houses or factories, and mistresses who took care of their more basic needs.

Once, long ago, in an exasperated attempt to justify his own conduct, her father had explained that world to her and had expected her simply to accept it.

Even if Robert acknowledged the boy, he could never inherit Kurland Hall or the title. Paul would inherit those. But Bobby still existed. . . .

After lifting her head, Lucy looked out of the diamond-paned window. Marriage was for life. There was no getting around that. She loved Robert, and she was certain that he held her in high regard and would never expose her to the humiliation of accepting his illegitimate child into her home.

Which left her where exactly?

That remained to be seen, but in the meantime, she would simply have to carry on as if her heart wasn't breaking. At least she was busy, and if she really tried, she could probably persuade herself not to think about the matter at all.

"What a wonderful party, Lady Kurland!"

Lucy paused to speak to Rebecca Hall, who was directing one of her younger brothers around the barn in a country-dance. The noise level was high, and it was difficult to hear much beyond the wailing of the pipes and the steady beat of the drums. Everyone appeared to be having a magnificent time. Food was piled high on the trestle tables, there was plenty to drink, and the children were currently being entertained by a Punch-and-Judy show.

"I am glad that you are enjoying yourself, Rebecca."

"I went to Greenwell Manor and asked Mr. Greenwell if Josephine could come to the party, and he gave his permission. She's sitting over there with my mum. She's going to stay the night with me."

"How kind of you." Lucy's cheeks were starting to hurt from all her smiling. At least she didn't have to worry about meeting Mrs. Jarvis. Bobby was there, but the innkeeper's wife had apparently stayed home to care for her Christmas guests. "Did Mr. Greenwell mention how Miss Margaret was faring?"

"He said she was starting to stir, and that Dr. Fletcher is very hopeful she will recover very soon."

"How wonderful." Lucy's voice quavered, and she quickly cleared her throat. "Perhaps you and Josephine might enjoy a glimpse of the guests arriving at the ball tonight. I can arrange with my housekeeper for you to stay at the hall, if your mother agrees."

"Really, my lady?" Rebecca's face glowed, and she grabbed Lucy's hand. "I can show Josephine the library! She will be so excited! Come and ask my mum!"

Lucy allowed herself to be dragged across the barn to where the Hall family was sitting. Mrs. Hall was tapping her feet to the music and enjoying a large slice of Cook's plum pudding.

"Good afternoon, Lady Kurland." She nodded at Josephine, who was looking quite animated for once. "Did Becky tell you we have another guest tonight?"

"Indeed she did," Lucy said. "And I have a favor to ask you. . . ."

After assuring Mrs. Hall that she would take good care of the girls, Lucy threaded her way back through the crowds, stopping at every turn to hear the well wishes of the villagers and their thanks for the party. She bumped into Bertha, the maid from the inn. She was wearing a pink dress that clashed slightly with her red hair, which was already falling out of its haphazard bun from her too-vigorous dancing.

After exchanging pleasantries, Lucy asked, "Do you remember when I asked you about Mr. Clapper?"

"Yes, indeed, my lady."

"Had the rumors that Miss Broomfield was

dead reached the Queen's Head before Mr. Clapper left for London that morning?"

"Oh, yes, my lady. Everyone was talking about it at breakfast time."

"So Mr. Clapper probably heard the news?"

"Unless he was sitting there with his fingers in his ears, which he wasn't, my lady, then he must have heard."

"Thank you." Lucy went to turn away, but Bertha was still speaking.

"Come to think of it, he went a bit green around the gills just before he left. I thought one of the eggs he'd eaten must've been rotten, but you never know. Maybe he didn't care for hearing talk of murder over his breakfast."

"Quite possibly."

Lucy moved on, her gaze occasionally straying to the high table where Robert was entertaining the more upper-class guests who had also joined the party. His normally harsh face looked relaxed, and he was smiling slightly at something her father had just said to him. He would never be the most handsome man in a room, but he certainly had a commanding presence. She quickly looked away, surprised at the visceral throb of pain in her very bosom.

It had been quite easy to avoid him so far. She planned on getting dressed for the ball early and vacating their shared chamber before he came to change. She at least had the excuse of needing to be downstairs to make sure everything was in order for the dinner and the ball.

At some point, she would have to talk to him again, but for some reason, she couldn't even begin to imagine what to say. . . .

"Afternoon, Lady Kurland."

She looked up to see Mathias beaming down at her.

"Good afternoon. I meant to thank you for all your work in delivering the children to the church to sing their Christmas carols."

"It was nothing, my lady." He shrugged. "I knew where most of the little ones lived, because I took a few of them home after the last practice at the school." He chuckled. "I remember young Josephine almost got left behind that day. She had to run and catch us up in the village."

"And she has the farthest journey," Lucy added. "It was kind of you to wait for her."

"Not the first time I've taken her home, and not the first time she's forgotten something." Mathias winked at her. "But she's a polite young thing and always apologizes for keeping me waiting. Sometimes she talked to me about that teacher of yours—not that I needed telling. I take reading and writing lessons with Mr. Culpepper once in a while in the schoolroom. That Miss Broomfield made our lives very difficult if we just breathed too loudly for her liking." He crossed himself. "God rest her soul."

"Indeed. Are you enjoying learning to read?"

"Aye." He hesitated. "When you can open a book and read what's there, you can escape into another world for a while." He looked almost embarrassed. "Not that I ain't happy with my place in life, my lady. I mean no disrespect."

"I am glad that you enjoy reading, Mathias," Lucy said firmly. "What is your favorite book?"

"We're reading *The Pilgrim's Progress* by Mr. John Bunyan. A fine and worthy tale of suffering and godly deliverance."

"Indeed it is."

"The learning to write is much harder." He grimaced and flexed his fingers. "But I'll keep at it. Now I'd better let you go, my lady. I reckon that everyone wants to speak to you and Sir Robert today."

"It seems like it." Lucy nodded. "Merry Christmas, Mathias."

"And to you, my lady."

Perhaps she should reread *The Pilgrim's Progress* herself. She certainly felt like she was mired in the slough of despond . . .

"Are you all right, Lucy?"

She turned to find Anna, flushed and happy, with Dermot at her side.

"Yes. Are you both enjoying yourselves?"

"Indeed we are." Anna looked up at Dermot. "Father is scowling fit to burst, but we're hardly behaving inappropriately by enjoying a dance or two together. This isn't Almack's." She glanced back at the top table and tossed her blond head. "Mrs. Armitage is keeping him company now, and he seems happier. What time are we supposed to be giving out the gifts?"

"Fairly soon, I should think," Dermot said, checking his pocket watch. "It is almost four o'clock, and dinner will be served at six, before the ball. I'll go and consult with Sir Robert."

"Thank you." Lucy said.

Lucy waited until Robert actually called for quiet before making her way slowly toward the front of the barn.

"Thank you all for coming," Robert said. It was interesting to watch him from afar and see how much progress he'd made since returning wounded and bloodied from the battle of Waterloo. "We have had a very successful year at Kurland Hall, and we wanted to share that prosperity with you."

There was a loud cheer, and a few caps were waved in the air.

"I'd like to thank Mr. Dermot Fletcher, Dr. and Mrs. Fletcher, the rector and Miss Harrington for their invaluable support in organizing this party. I'd also like to thank all the Kurland Hall staff, especially Cook, for producing a veritable mountain of food."

People raised their tankards to toast their landlord.

Suddenly, Robert looked straight at her and held out his hand. "I'd particularly like to thank Lady Kurland. Firstly, for her remarkable energy and organizational ability, and secondly, for agreeing to marry an old curmudgeon like me."

Lucy's breath caught in her throat as he beckoned for her to join him. Could she do it? Did she have a choice?

A storm of clapping broke out around her, and a path was cleared leading straight to Robert's side. He was a good man, and he was her husband. She was valued in her community, and that had to count for something. Could she run away from every expectation that had been heaped upon her from birth, as Miss Broomfield had done? She didn't have that kind of strength. She took the first uncertain step and kept going.

Robert swallowed in one go a glass of the brandy he'd asked Foley to bring up to his bedchamber. After three hours of standing around entertaining his tenants and the local villagers, his leg hurt like the devil, and he still had to endure the inanities of the ball. He glanced impatiently around the room, noticing the absence of clutter and the hint of lavender perfume, which indicated that his wife had been there before him.

He limped over to ring the bell for his valet. Lucy had asked him to wear his old dress uniform for the ball, and he'd been more than willing to oblige her. He was far more at home in his blue coat and silver facings than in the ridiculous fashions of his contemporaries. He had no intention of dancing—couldn't perform even if he wanted to—and didn't miss it at all. Although it would be nice to open the ball with his wife, who *did* love to dance and got very few opportunities to do so.

Something was very wrong with her.

He helped himself to more brandy. Was she ill and not telling him, or was it something more fundamental? Getting her to speak to him was proving almost impossible on today of all days, but there was a look in her eyes that tore at his heart. . . .

As if he had conjured her with his concern, the little-used door set in the dividing wall opened and Lucy emerged from it, his aunt Rose at her side. His wife wore a striking crimson gown of soft velvet and gold lace that suited her to perfection. She would never be as beautiful as her sister, Anna, but she was a handsome woman with a dignity and charm that had won his eternal devotion.

Rose smiled at him. "I do apologize, my dear! I didn't realize you were already upstairs. Lucy and I were just considering the logistics of restoring the dressing room and second bedchamber connected to this one."

Robert's gaze snapped to his wife, who was

staring down at the floor. "Will you excuse us, Rose?"

"Of course." His aunt looked worriedly from him to Lucy and backed out of the room. She closed the door, leaving a strained silence behind her.

"Why would we need another bedroom?" Robert said in as level a tone as he could manage.

"It is usual for a husband and wife to have separate chambers, with a dressing room in the middle. In fact, this house was built like that."

"And my parents chose not to follow such an outmoded and ridiculous fashion." He pointed at the large four-poster bed. "This bed was good enough for them, and it's good enough for me."

She walked away from him, presenting him with her back. "You recently offered me a marriage based on mutual respect and loyalty. I am merely acting on the assumption that your offer still stands."

Suddenly, it was hard to breathe as his anger and tiredness coalesced into fury. "*You* wanted that. Not me."

"You agreed." She kept walking. "Perhaps we can discuss the matter more fully after the ball."

Before he could form a coherent reply, she was gone, leaving him furious and afraid and . . .

"Sir Robert?"

"What?"

He swung around to see Silas, his valet,

coming through the door that led to the servants' stairs. He had Robert's pressed uniform over his arm and had already started to retreat, a startled expression on his face.

"Come in, Silas." Robert limped back over to the brandy bottle. "Let's get this damned ball over with."

Chapter 18

It was all proceeding perfectly. The dinner had been spectacular, the service precise, and the conversation civil. The news that Margaret Greenwell appeared to be recovering had lightened the mood considerably, and a toast for her speedy recovery had been drunk at the table.

As she passed on Robert's arm into the former medieval hall at the heart of the manor house, Lucy glanced up at the top of the stairs, where Josephine and Rebecca were watching. Rebecca waved at her, and even Josephine managed a smile. After the ball started, the housekeeper would take the girls down to the kitchens to share the servants' dinner and would send them to bed at the approved hour.

Due to the informal nature of a country ball, Lucy hadn't insisted on strict precedence as to who escorted whom into the temporary ballroom. Rose went by with Lucy's father; Penelope was with her husband and was looking very lovely, her nose in the air. Mr. Clapper had Anna at his side, while Dermot and Nicholas Jenkins looked glumly on.

Since their unfortunate encounter earlier, Robert hadn't directed a single word to Lucy. His arm was rigid under her gloved hand, and his limp more pronounced. She couldn't speak, either, her throat so tight, she feared a single word might unleash a torrent of weeping. How had things come to this? How on earth could they continue their marriage in a state of war?

He stopped at the far end of the space and bowed to her—all military stiffness, precision, and indifference. "Ma'am, with your permission."

He looked up at the minstrels' gallery and gave the signal for the music to begin before turning away from her and making his way toward a group of gentlemen gathered by the roaring fire. They'd decided on a mixture of traditional country-dances and a few formal dances approved by the *ton*.

"Lady Kurland?"

Lucy turned from staring after Robert to find Andrew Stanford smiling at her.

"I have been ordered by my wife to dance the first measure with you. Not that I *needed* to be told. It will indeed be my pleasure."

"Thank you." Lucy gratefully took the hand he offered her. "Robert—"

"Does not like dancing and never has." He drew her slowly out onto the floor, his calm demeanor and smiling competence a balm to the confusion of her spirits. "But I seem to recall from our time together in London that you are an excellent dancer."

The musicians sounded a clashing chord and

started the dance proper. Lucy had to think of her steps, which was a blessing, seeing as everything else seemed far too complicated.

"Robert looks well in his uniform," Andrew remarked.

"Indeed he does."

"Although he seems rather grim this evening." He paused as they executed a pass through the center of their foursome. "Is his leg bothering him?"

"I should imagine so. He was standing for a considerable amount of time at the party."

Lucy wondered if Sophia had confided in her husband about what had happened at the inn, and miserably concluded she probably had.

"He is also rather annoyed at me," she added.

"Ah." Andrew changed partners, and it wasn't until they rejoined each other at the bottom of the set that he was able to speak to her again. "Sophia did mention that you were weathering some marital discord."

Lucy had to smile. It was very obvious why Andrew had become such an excellent lawyer.

"As our relationship has always been 'stormy,' I should imagine we'll survive," Lucy said lightly.

"I do hope so." Andrew hesitated. "You have changed Robert considerably for the better, my lady. I know he would hate to lose you."

Lucy pressed her lips firmly together and concentrated on the music. If she could get through the evening, and deal with Mr. Clapper on the morrow, she would have time to consider the more worrying question of how to proceed with Robert.

At ten, a light supper was served in the dining room, and Lucy made sure she was there to supervise. After doing his duty as host, Robert had escaped into the room set up for cardplayers and had barely emerged since then.

"Lady Kurland?"

"Mr. Culpepper. Are you having a nice time?"

"Yes, my lady." He bowed low, the candlelight making his auburn hair shine like copper. "I have a favor to ask of you." He tugged nervously at his cravat. "I intend to propose to Miss Dorothea Chingford. I wondered if perhaps after supper you could ask the musicians to pause long enough for me to pop the question?"

"What a delightful idea." Lucy smiled encouragingly at the obviously anxious young man. "I will go and ask them immediately."

Robert shooed the last of the cardplayers into the supper room and crossed back across the empty dance floor. Every step was agony. He was tired of seeing the concern on Patrick's face. The doctor had even offered him laudanum earlier, a drug he knew perfectly well Robert never touched. He licked his lips, remembering the seductive sweetness, and for the first time regretted his decision never to allow himself to sink back into its alluring oblivion.

Some of the dancers had returned to the main hall, and the musicians were tuning up in the gallery. His wife came back into the room and went up the stairs, then returned shortly afterward to nod at George Culpepper, who looked as if he was about to cast up his accounts on the flagstone floor.

A clash of cymbals made everyone stop talking as Mr. Culpepper stepped into the middle of the space. His hand was linked with Miss Dorothea's, who looked very pretty in a pale yellow gown that, Robert suspected, had once belonged to Lucy.

Mr. Culpepper cleared his throat. "Miss Dorothea?"

"Yes, Mr. Culpepper?"

He sank down on one knee. "Will you do me the honor of becoming my wife?"

Dorothea gasped and clasped her hands to her bosom. "Oh, yes, please! That would be delightful!"

Everyone around them clapped and cheered as Mr. Culpepper swept his intended into a clumsy embrace. Knowing Dorothea's reduced circumstances, Robert absently reminded himself to offer her a suitable settlement when the marriage contracts were drawn up.

A flash of crimson alerted Robert to the fact that his wife had disappeared in the direction of the kitchens. Fueled by his own disappointment and growing frustration, he followed her, only to find she had stepped outside into the walled garden and was simply standing there, staring into space.

He reached her and grabbed her elbow, then turned her toward him. "Tell me what is wrong. I don't care what it is, but *tell me*."

Her eyes were full of tears.

"Are you ill?" He gently shook her. "Are you *dying?*"

"No, of *course* not. I—"

"Then what in God's name have I done to turn you so thoroughly against me?" She tried to pull out of his grasp, but this time he would not allow it. "What is it? I refuse to go back inside until you tell me."

"I just need time to get *used* to the idea, to accept that—"

"Accept *what?*"

Her eyes flashed. "Mayhap if you stopped bullying and interrupting me, I might be able to put a sentence together!"

"Lucy, it's freezing cold out here, my leg is paining me, and you are avoiding telling me the truth. None of these things are likely to make my mood better!" Robert snarled.

She took a deep shuddering breath. "Firstly,

355

you have no right to be angry at me. *You* are the one creating discord in our marriage!"

"What the *devil* am I supposed to have done now?"

"Only what most gentlemen do when their wives fail to . . . to accommodate them."

"I don't understand you."

"You have made it very clear that you no longer find me desirable."

"What?" He blinked at her. "How in God's name did you conjure up that ridiculous tomfoolery?"

She looked away from him. "You have not sought me out since last summer."

It was his turn to look heavenward. "You almost died last summer."

"Hardly that, but—"

"I was there at your bedside." He gripped her arm more tightly. "You almost *died*. Do you think I am the kind of man who merrily continues to take his pleasure when his wife's health and entire *existence* are in the balance?"

"What are you saying? That you chose to replace me to keep me safe?"

He set his jaw. "I *chose* to abide by my doctor's orders and leave you in peace for six months to recover!"

"Dr. *Fletcher* said that?" For the first time, she searched his face.

"Yes. Are you trying to suggest I have taken a

mistress?" He stepped back, dropping his hold on her arm. He half turned away, his heart sore and sick. "Perhaps it is time to go in, after all."

"I thought I had cause."

He didn't turn completely to face her. "By listening to *gossip?* I thought you knew better than that."

She poked him in the back, and he spun around to find her glaring at him. "I *thought* I had proof."

"Of my philandering ways?" he jeered. "You know damn well that I leave such matters to my cousin, Paul."

"I saw you with Mrs. Jarvis!"

"Doing what?" He blinked at her. "Fornicating in the public bar at the inn?"

"You came out of the stables together. She was holding your arm, and you were laughing and were covered in straw."

"That's it? That's your evidence?" He was shouting now, and he didn't care who heard him. "You said we needed a new kitchen cat. Mrs. Jarvis was showing me a litter of kittens. I was going to surprise you with one on Christmas Day!"

"Oh." Lucy bit her lip.

"*Oh?* Is that all you have to say?" He shook his head. "Your lack of faith in me beggars belief." He inclined his head an uncivil inch. "Perhaps your idea of separate beds has some merit, after all. Good *night,* Lady Kurland."

He'd gone three full steps before Lucy mastered her trembling and found her voice.

"She said she'd known you in London. She suggested that she'd known you intimately."

He stopped walking, his whole body tense in the moonlight.

"I thought maybe you had suggested she come to the village." She shut her eyes and forced herself to continue speaking. "I wondered if you had decided to be practical and were willing to continue our marriage, despite my failures, because you still had some regard for me, and—"

"Lucy . . ." He interrupted her again. "How could you *ever* think I considered you a failure?"

"Because I *have* failed to give you an heir, and I never fail at anything I set my mind to."

His long silence confirmed her worst fears as he turned to look at her.

"Perhaps I value you more highly than you value yourself?" he suggested softly. "Perhaps I would prefer to have *you* in my life rather than some mythical child?"

Hot tears fell down her face. "But *I* want that child. Why don't you?"

"A son who grows up and wants to join the army like his harebrained father?" He shrugged. "A daughter who loses her life while giving birth? Another son who loses his life in a pointless war, as your brother did, as many of my friends did?"

"But the entail, your inheritance, the title . . . ," Lucy whispered.

"Do you value *that* more than your own life?" He swung his arm wide. "More than *mine?* Kurland Hall will still be here when I'm dead regardless of who owns it. One thing war taught me, Lucy, was to live every day as if it were my last."

She nodded, her throat too crowded with tears to speak.

"I'm not like your father." He grimaced. "I have no intention of undermining your authority by installing my mistress in the hall or the local inn."

"I know." She owed him an explanation, but it was so *hard* to continue. "I was very reluctant to believe such a thing of you until today, when I received this."

She'd carried the letter with her all day, too afraid to have it out of her sight. She offered it to Robert, and he hesitated.

"Please read it," she said.

He took the note and unfolded it, then held it close to his nose to read in the dim light. He slowly looked up. "What the *devil* . . . ?"

"Mrs. Jarvis said she named her son Bobby after you. He is of the right age for when she claims she first met you, and he has dark hair and blue eyes." Saying the words out loud made them sound even worse.

"Lucy, I swear on my mother's grave that he is *not* my son."

"How can you say that?"

"Because I never bedded Mrs. Jarvis." He met her gaze head-on. "Would you like my oath on that, as well?"

"She *suggested*—"

"She is something of an attention seeker and is apt to dramatize the more unsavory aspects of her life. I *did* meet her in London, but she was far too free with her favors to appeal to me, and I was far too shy and not aristocratic enough to attract her attention."

"I am *so* glad about that."

He cocked an eyebrow. "That I was insufficiently desirable?"

"Yes." She raised her chin, her whole body trembling. "I owe you an apology."

"For what in particular? Your belief that I had a mistress or an illegitimate child?"

"All of it."

He studied her for a long moment, his head to one side, his blue eyes glinting in the moonlight. "I cannot accept your apology."

"Why not?" Her voice broke.

"Because I am guilty of something far worse." He limped toward her and gently cupped her chin. "Making you cry."

"That is hardly as important as maligning your very character," she countered.

360

"Condemning yourself now?" His voice softened. "I shall have to think of a suitable punishment." He brushed his mouth against hers. "Something . . ."

She stood on tiptoe and kissed him back until his arms locked around her, and nothing else mattered except the essence of him, of his taste and smell, and his willingness to understand and forgive. . . .

"Sir Robert?"

Foley's polite voice floated out over the frosted air. Lucy wrenched her mouth away and buried her face in the lace of Robert's military coat.

"Your guests are beginning to wonder what has befallen you, sir, and in case you hadn't noticed, it is snowing."

Lucy looked up at the silent whiteness falling all around her and then back at Robert.

"Then perhaps we should both go inside." Robert murmured.

Chapter 19

Lucy eased herself out of Robert's arms and got out of bed. Between their obligations as hosts of the ball and their newly resumed nocturnal activities, they had barely slept at all. She was too restless to stay in bed. The house was quiet around her, blanketed in a thick layer of snow, which deadened all sound and made the familiar landmarks of the home park disappear into unending whiteness.

She dressed quickly, without requiring Betty's help, in an informal morning gown. She was eager to make sure that the house had been returned to normal, and that Cook was ready to serve everyone a large meal to break their fast. No one would be leaving the hall today.

If all had gone to plan, Mr. Hopewell would have brought the two collies up to the hall for one of the footmen to watch over until she was ready to give them to Robert. She was fairly certain that Foley and her housekeeper, Mrs. Cooper, would not be thrilled by the addition of two dogs in the house, but Robert would soon have them obeying his every order.

She paused on the landing to view the snow through the large window. He really had been remarkably forgiving of her sins. . . . She truly was blessed. Sometimes he understood her fears better than she did herself. She hadn't acknowledged her secret belief that he was somehow like her father, after all—that all men at their core were like her father. Like Anna, she obviously bore more scars than she had perhaps realized from the abrupt end of their childhood.

Continuing down the stairs, Lucy reviewed the planned activities for the day. Presents would be exchanged when all the guests and family were up and about, which she reckoned would probably stretch toward midday. If they could drive or were prepared to walk, she expected the rectory party for a late dinner, with party games, and cards afterward.

There was still the matter of Mr. Clapper and his presence in Kurland St. Mary to investigate, but that would probably have to wait until St. Stephen's Day. He wasn't likely to be leaving until Robert was satisfied, anyway, and Lucy was fairly certain he was guilty of murder. Picking up her skirts, Lucy set off for the kitchens. She could already smell the greasy scent of cooking goose sliced through with the zest of lemon and orange.

An hour later, after consulting with Cook, viewing the puppies again, and soothing Foley's fears, Lucy saw Robert's valet coming down the back stairs.

"Merry Christmas, my lady. Sir Robert will be joining you for breakfast very shortly."

"Thank you, Silas. I will go to the morning room and await him there."

She was already passing through the main hall before she remembered that Josephine and Rebecca were also still in the house. She doubted the Hall family would be happy for their daughter to miss celebrating Christmas Day with them and turned back to the kitchens, chiding herself for her own lack of thought. She'd completely forgotten about the girls, which was not like her at all.

She found Mrs. Cooper and was assured that her housekeeper would do all that was necessary to ensure that when the girls woke up, they would be returned to the village, even if one of the footmen had to dig a path for them.

By the time she made her third trip to the morning parlor, where breakfast was laid out, Lucy was beginning to flag. There was no sign of Robert in the room, but Foley was placing a pot of coffee on the sideboard.

"Sir Robert has gone to fetch something from his study, my lady. He will probably be back in a moment."

"Thank you, Foley."

She hesitated in the doorway. She wanted to acquaint Robert with Mr. Clapper's early knowledge of Miss Broomfield's death before he met with the young clerk. Why had he lied about it? She also wanted to know if Robert had finished reading Miss Broomfield's diary. . . .

In truth, she just wanted to see him. . . . Lucy smiled at her own silliness and set off for Robert's study. The door was ajar, and she could hear him talking to someone.

"My dear girl, this is ridiculous. Now, put the gun down, and—"

"No."

Lucy went still and pushed the door with the tips of her fingers until it swung noiselessly open. Robert was standing behind his desk, and Josephine Blake was pointing a pistol at his head.

"I am going to kill you. Mr. Greenwell taught me how to fire a pistol properly, so do not assume I will miss," Josephine said, far too calmly for Lucy's liking. "But I also want you to suffer the way my mother suffered for years because of you."

"I hate to be contrary, but I am not aware that I am acquainted with your mother." Robert sounded as reasonable as Josephine and betrayed no awareness of Lucy's presence as she took a small step into the room.

"My mother is *dead*."

"I am sorry to hear that."

"You killed her."

"Are you quite certain?" Robert frowned. "What was her name?"

Josephine's laugh was cutting. "You can't even be bothered to remember the names of the women you have ruined? Her name was April Blake. You met her here when the Greenwells were visiting their house in Lower Kurland."

"I do not recall—"

"You met her, and you seduced her, and when she returned to her family in London and found out she was pregnant, they threw her out. She was a *lady,* and you ruined her. It was only because her brother Grenville took pity on her that she survived at all."

Lucy took another step forward, her gaze fixed on a large brass paperweight sitting on the table that held down a detailed map of the Kurland estate.

Robert let out a slow breath and sat down at his desk. "Are you suggesting that you are my child?"

"Yes." Josephine raised her chin. "I even look like you."

"You certainly share my coloring, but that is hardly unique." Robert met her gaze. "So you are the person who wrote those horrible letters to my wife?"

"I wanted her to be upset. I *wanted* her to know what kind of a man she had married."

"And yet Lady Kurland has always been very kind to you."

"It's easy for her to be kind and condescending

when she has everything that should have belonged to my mother if you had been a man of honor."

"Did you write to Miss Broomfield and Mr. Harrington, as well?" Robert inquired.

"When she realized she was pregnant, my mother came to see Mr. Harrington at the rectory to plead for his help in locating you. He turned her away. He said he would pray for her."

Lucy winced.

"And what about Miss Broomfield?"

"She was deranged," Josephine said coldly. "She was obsessed with the notion of sin."

"So I understand. Did you perhaps write or deliver letters for her? Did that give you the idea for writing your own?"

Josephine shrugged. "Our interests might have crossed paths at some point."

"Until what? She threatened you?"

The heavy pistol in Josephine's grasp started to shake a little.

"She did not approve of me using her school supplies to send out my letters. She apprehended me writing to you and decided that she would rather blackmail you herself."

"And you could not allow that." Robert studied his clasped hands. "When exactly were you born?"

"August the tenth, eighteen hundred and five."

"Which means that by most people's reckoning, you were conceived around November or December of the previous year."

"Yes. What of it?"

"I'm sorry, my dear." Robert sighed. "I wasn't in Kurland St. Mary at that time."

"You lie." The pistol wobbled even more, and both Lucy and Robert tensed.

"I can prove it, if you allow me to. By my general recollection, I had already joined my regiment. Napoleon was threatening to invade England and had built a fleet of barges to bring his troops across the Channel, which meant that I was moved from my barracks in London to the south coast of England. My mother was still alive at the time, and I was bored enough to write to her on many occasions. I believe the letters are in the Kurland archive, along with newspaper clippings of my regimental doings, which my mother liked to collect."

"You are *lying*."

"Why would I lie?" Robert sat forward. "If you were indeed my child, do you think I would repudiate you?"

"Of course you would," Josephine sneered. "Miss Broomfield was right about that. No gentleman likes to acknowledge his bastards."

"Then perhaps I am not much of a gentleman. If I had known of your existence—*if* I had taken advantage of your mother—I would have either married her or made sure she was financially secure for life."

"My mother told me it was you. Why do you continue to lie?"

Lucy reached the table and allowed her shaking hand to close around the heavy brass ornament.

"Why would she lie to me on her deathbed?" Josephine demanded. "She was here in Kurland St. Mary. She was seduced by a scoundrel and left pregnant and alone."

"That might all be true, but that scoundrel wasn't me," Robert said firmly.

With an inarticulate sound, Josephine raised the pistol, and simultaneously, Lucy threw the brass paperweight with all her strength. The gun went off, and the shot went off target, shattering the mirror above the fireplace, sending a shower of glass over them all.

Robert went crashing to the floor, leaving Lucy to tackle Josephine and sit on her until the door burst open to reveal Foley and Dermot.

"Foley, fetch James," Lucy shouted over the ringing in her ears. "Mr. Fletcher, attend to Sir Robert."

Dermot ran over to the desk and went down on one knee.

"I think he knocked his head when he fell, my lady. He wasn't hit. I'll fetch my brother."

Lucy's face stung from the pinpricks of glass

as blood ran down her neck to stain the bodice of her gown. Josephine had fewer cuts, as she had been farther away from the shattered mirror. She wasn't struggling anymore but lay passively on the rug, her face again expressionless.

Despite wanting to go and see if Robert was truly unhurt, Lucy stayed where she was until Foley puffed into the room with James behind him.

"Foley?"

"Yes, my lady?"

"By any chance, was Mr. *Paul* Kurland in residence at Kurland Hall during the winter of eighteen hundred and four?"

"I'd have to check the records, my lady, but I have a feeling that he was here. He'd been sent down from Cambridge again, was in debt and in disgrace. Why do you ask?"

Lucy hauled Josephine to her feet. "James, will you come with me and make sure Josephine doesn't do anything foolish?"

"Of course, my lady."

Holding Josephine tightly by the upper arm, Lucy took her into the portrait gallery of Kurland Hall and marched her down to view the picture of Robert and his untrustworthy scoundrel of a cousin.

"This is a portrait of Robert and his cousin Paul. Do you see how alike they are? I would wager a large sum that if anyone named Kurland *did* seduce your mother, it was more than likely this man."

Josephine stared at the picture for a long moment. "It doesn't matter now, does it?"

"It matters to me," Lucy said fiercely. "It matters that you chose to malign an honorable man and attempted to kill him."

"Why?" Josephine shrugged. "If I'd killed him, you would've been a wealthy widow."

"Like you killed Miss Broomfield?"

A small smile played around Josephine's mouth. "I consider that a service to every child she has ever beaten or attempted to destroy. Did you even know that at her last school, she persecuted one of the girls so badly that the child killed herself? She had no shame for what she did, either."

"Rather like you, then."

"Perhaps," Josephine agreed. "Some of us have to take care of ourselves the best we can."

"Did it not occur to you to simply *ask* Sir Robert if he was your father?"

Josephine looked away, her shoulders slumping. "As I said, it doesn't matter anymore, does it?"

"Well, that was a rather more exciting Christmas morning than I had expected," Lucy said as she removed the bag of ice from Robert's head and checked the swelling. He was lying on the couch in his study, the glass had been cleaned up, and the house had settled back down again. She was immensely glad that the majority of the guests had still been abed when the chaos ensued. "That looks much less swollen now. How is the headache?"

"Better. Thank you. What did you do with Josephine?"

"She's locked in one of the servants' rooms, and James is guarding the door." Lucy sighed. "She's obviously disturbed. She had no remorse about killing Miss Broomfield."

"And to think if I'd arrived at the school ten minutes earlier, I might have caught her in the act. Instead of assuming she was a child running away in fear, I would have known she was a murderer escaping her fate. She seems so *childlike* to have done such a ruthless thing." Robert sighed. "And what if she is Paul's illegitimate daughter? Do I have to send my own niece to the assizes and possibly the gallows?"

"Let's worry about that later," Lucy said soothingly.

Robert sat up and cast the blanket covering him to one side. "I think we should speak to Mr. Clapper, don't you? I'd like to clear up all the loose ends."

"Are you feeling well enough to see him?" Lucy searched Robert's face. There was a severe set to his jaw, which she knew meant he was still in pain.

"I'll survive. Dr. Fletcher says I have a remarkably thick skull."

There was a tap on the door, and Aunt Rose peered in. "Oh good. You're both here. Don't get up, Robert."

Lucy beckoned for Rose to take the seat opposite them. "Is everything all right?"

"Indeed it is." Rose settled her lavender silk skirts around her as she sat down. "I wanted to thank you both for the invitation to come and live permanently at Kurland Hall, but I have decided to decline it."

"That's a shame," Robert said gruffly. "We were rather hoping you'd accept."

"The only reason I am *declining* it is that I have received another offer."

"You have reconciled with your children and are going back to London?" Lucy tried to appear enthusiastic about the idea.

"Ah, not exactly." Rose raised her head, her eyes twinkling. "I have received an offer of marriage from Mr. Harrington, and I plan to accept it."

Concealed in her skirts, Robert's hand clenched around Lucy's.

"That is most unexpected news!" Robert paused. "I apologize for my bluntness, but are you quite sure about this?"

"I am." Rose's smile was glorious. "We are of a similar age, we share many common interests, and best of all, I get to enjoy a second family, including your wonderful wife and her younger brothers and sister."

"Does Anna know?" Lucy squeaked.

"Yes. I spoke to her at the ball, and she gave me her blessing." Rose hesitated. "I should stress that I told Mr. Harrington I would proceed only if you two are both agreeable."

Lucy looked at Robert and took a deep breath. "I wish you both very happy. I cannot think of a single reason why my father will not benefit from your excellent companionship and advice."

"And I second that. Mr. Harrington is a very lucky man." Robert rose to give his aunt a kiss on the cheek. "I wish you all the happiness in the world."

After Rose departed, Lucy shook her head.

"Are you really resigned to this marriage?" Robert asked tentatively.

"The more I think about it, the more I like it," Lucy said decisively. "Aunt Rose will curtail the worst of my father's excesses, and he will offer her the companionship she craves. Also, Anna will be free to make her own choices again."

Robert kissed her hand. "Then shall we deal with Mr. Clapper before we announce this new union to our guests?"

"I suppose we should." Lucy grimaced. "I had convinced myself that he killed Miss Broomfield, but that doesn't appear to be the case. Do we owe him an apology?"

"I'm not so sure about that." Robert nodded at the bell. "Ring for Foley, and ask him to send Mr. Clapper here immediately."

Robert hobbled over to sit behind his desk, and Lucy took a seat to his right. A knock on the door announced the presence of an apprehensive-looking Mr. Clapper. He was wearing a borrowed coat, which Robert thought belonged to Dermot Fletcher.

"You wished to see me, sir?"

"Yes. Please sit down."

Mr. Clapper's sheepish yet defiant demeanor reminded Robert of every young officer he'd had to reprimand and charge during his military career.

"My wife and I don't think you are telling the truth about your dealings with Miss Broomfield. Would you care to change your story?"

"I didn't kill her."

Robert raised an eyebrow. "I don't believe I suggested that you did, but seeing as the subject is obviously on your mind, what else do you have to say about the matter?"

"I told you. I went to the schoolhouse, and Miss Broomfield didn't answer the door."

"And?" Mr. Clapper said nothing, and Robert continued speaking. "You do know that I am the local magistrate? If I believe I have the slightest evidence of your guilt, I can have you sent to Hertford for trial at the local assizes."

"I didn't *kill* her!"

"So what did you do when she didn't answer your knock, Mr. Clapper? Ride tamely away to the inn or attempt to get inside the schoolhouse, because you believed there was something owing to you?"

Mr. Clapper's face blanched. "What are you suggesting, sir?"

"That you didn't just leave but let yourself into the school through the front entrance, which we know was unlocked, intending to claim your reward." Robert sat back. "I would wager that you saw far more than you anticipated and decided to run away *then*. Am I correct?"

"She was sitting at her desk . . . ," Mr. Clapper croaked. "She was *dead,* and someone had stabbed her in the eye with a quill pen. It was . . . *horrible*. I turned and ran, but I swear I didn't touch her."

"You didn't stay and search for the jewelry you were expecting to receive?"

Mr. Clapper went still. "I—"

"You were blackmailing her," Robert said flatly. "You were the only person who knew exactly why she'd left her previous job. You were the *only person* in constant contact with her since she acknowledged her family again, and you knew all about her very checkered past. She was worried that you would reveal that information to the Kurland school board, and she was willing to pay for your silence."

Mr. Clapper shook his head, his mouth opening and closing like that of a hooked salmon.

"Nothing to say, sir?" Robert demanded.

"It was the first time. I swear it." The young man looked from Lucy to Robert. "I needed the money to further my career. *She* didn't need it. She'd chosen her path."

"But the jewelry was not yours. And then there is the other matter that you possibly helped her conceal a terrible miscarriage of justice when she bullied and tormented a child to death." Robert stared the man down. "Neither of these things is admirable, Mr. Clapper, and neither of them will be overlooked."

Robert rose to his feet. "You will remain here until the weather has cleared up, and then I will have you escorted to London, to your employers' office. I believe I will allow them and the Hillcott family to decide *your* fate."

Later that evening, Lucy came to stand behind Robert, who sat in front of the roaring fire in the medieval hall. The smell of pine boughs, nutmeg, and cloves rose and fell with the draughts of cold air swirling through the old building. Anna,

Dermot, Dorothea, George Culpepper, and the twins were playing Snapdragon, which involved snatching burning currants from a bowl of brandy that had been set alight. They all seemed to be enjoying it immensely, while the older couples, such as the Fletchers and the Stanfords, were sitting listening to Aunt Rose play the pianoforte.

Robert had seemed delighted by the two collie puppies and had nominated Joseph Cobbins, who had taken a great liking to the dogs, as their primary keeper. Between the two of them, Lucy was fairly certain the collies would soon settle in. She hadn't received a Christmas kitten. Robert had tactfully suggested she go to the inn and pick out a favorite for herself.

Mr. Clapper had been locked in the room next door to Josephine's so that James could guard him, as well. Andrew had said he was willing to take both of them up to London and consult with the Hillcott family as to their desire for prosecution. Lucy knew that Robert would be relieved not to have to deal with Josephine and might even be inclined to ask for clemency for her.

Robert reached up his hand to grasp hers. "It has certainly been an eventful Christmastide, has it not, my dear?"

"Indeed." She smiled down at him. "I cannot say that I have enjoyed *every* aspect of it. How did you guess that Mr. Clapper was blackmailing Miss Broomfield? That was very clever of you, sir."

He smiled. "I can't take all the credit. I finished reading Miss Broomfield's diary the other night, and she made some mention of being blackmailed. It didn't take much to put two and two together."

"I wonder if Josephine was the one who hid the box containing the diary and the other personal items up the chimney. It certainly would've helped her gain an advantage over Miss Broomfield."

"Seeing as Miss Broomfield was the person who asked to have the chimney cleared, she either suspected something was up there, wanted to get it back, or had no idea." He sighed. "I have no idea *which* is the right answer on that one, but it was a very useful coincidence for us."

"I wonder if the packet I found in the top cupboard contained the letters that were sent out later or if Josephine wrote them?" Lucy wondered aloud. "It would certainly explain why they were taken from me after I fell."

"There are many things, I suspect, we will never fully understand about this matter," Robert mused.

"I went up to see Josephine earlier," Lucy said. "She admitted cutting Margaret Greenwell's saddle girth. Apparently, Margaret had worked out that Josephine was writing the letters, and was threatening to tell her mother. That's how Margaret knew about Miss Broomfield. Josephine was very subdued but showed no guilt or remorse over what she had done. I find that difficult to understand."

"There are people in this world who can kill without emotion. I've met plenty of them in the military. But this is the first time I've seen the signs in someone so young," Robert said.

"I know that Josephine must have had a hard life, but she was never abandoned or left to starve. She had a home, the opportunity to advance herself under our patronage, and, until recently, a mother who loved her." Lucy shook her head. "If she had told you the truth from the start, I know you would've done your utmost to help her."

"But she didn't really want that, either, did she?" Robert pointed out. "She enjoyed dispensing her own particular brand of justice, just as did Miss Broomfield."

Lucy shivered as she pictured Josephine's blank gaze and complete indifference to the havoc she had caused around her.

"I will pray for them," she said.

"That is very generous of you." Robert drew her down to sit on his knee in a very inappropriate manner. "Because I am finding it quite hard to forgive either of them at the moment."

"I will be glad when this year is over."

His grip on her hand tightened, and he leaned in to kiss her mouth. "Perhaps we should look forward to the New Year, agree to put this one behind us, and start afresh," Robert said firmly.

"For once, my very dear Robert," Lucy said, "I am in absolute and complete agreement with you."

Center Point Large Print
600 Brooks Road / PO Box 1
Thorndike, ME 04986-0001 USA

(207) 568-3717

US & Canada:
1 800 929-9108
www.centerpointlargeprint.com